Stolen Hearts

Don't Call Me Hero
Book 6

Eliza Lentzski

Copyright © 2023 Eliza Lentzski
All rights reserved.

This is a work of fiction. All names, characters, places, and incidents are the products of the author's imagination or are used fictitiously. Any resemblance to events, locales, or real persons, living or dead, other than those in the public domain, is entirely coincidental.

No part of this book may be reproduced, re-sold, or transmitted electronically or otherwise, without written permission from the author.

ISBN: 9781687683717
Imprint: Independently published

Other Works by Eliza Lentzski

Don't Call Me Hero Series
Don't Call Me Hero
Damaged Goods
Cold Blooded Lover
One Little Secret
Grave Mistake
Stolen Hearts

∽

Winter Jacket Series
Winter Jacket
Winter Jacket 2: New Beginnings
Winter Jacket 3: Finding Home
Winter Jacket 4: All In
Hunter

http://www.elizalentzski.com

Standalone Novels

Lighthouse Keeper (forthcoming)

Sour Grapes

The Woman in 3B

Sunscreen & Coconuts

The Final Rose

Bittersweet Homecoming

Fragmented

Apophis: Love Story for the End of the World

Second Chances

Date Night

Love, Lust, & Other Mistakes

Diary of a Human

∽

Works as E.L. Blaisdell

Drained: The Lucid (with Nica Curt)

To C

Prologue

Throttle

"I still don't understand the appeal." Julia ran her fingertips along the gunmetal grey handlebars of my Harley Sportster. "It's not a very practical vehicle."

Julia had met me after work at the facility where I stored my motorcycle during the winter months. I was born and raised in Minnesota—with an eight-year detour while being stationed in Afghanistan—but even my hearty upbringing had me admitting defeat to the upper Midwest's brutal winter weather.

"Maybe not," I admitted, "but I look damn good riding it."

I watched Julia's painted mouth part. The tip of her pink tongue poked out from between perfect teeth to flick at the barely visible scar above the right corner of her mouth. "That's not the *only* thing you look good riding, dear."

If her goal was to jumpstart my libido, she'd accomplished her mission—although it had never really taken much effort on her part to get me going.

I swung one long leg over my bike and settled onto the

low seat. The motorcycle was only intended for one rider, but there was just enough room between where I sat and the gas tank for my girlfriend. Julia had never taken me up on my many offers to take her for a ride on my motorcycle, however.

"Come here," I urged.

Her upper lip curled momentarily. "Why?"

I patted the empty space in front of me. "I want to show you something."

"I'm not exactly dressed for a motorcycle ride," she rejected.

Since she'd driven to the storage facility directly after work, she still wore her work clothes from the day—dark grey dress pants and a matching jacket with a dark purple shell underneath. She always looked like she'd stepped off the pages of a glossy magazine, even after a long day of litigation.

I patted the leather seat again and showed her my teeth. "I promise you'll like it."

I spied the quick roll of her caramel-colored eyes, but then had to suppress a victory whoop when Julia stepped closer to me and my bike.

She eyeballed the motorcycle with trepidation. "I've never been on one of these things."

I started up the bike and cranked on the throttle to make the engine roar. "Glad I can be your first time at something," I said cheekily.

Julia pursed her lips. I could see her mentally wrestling between wanting to put up a fight but also her curiosity about what I wanted to show her.

"It's just like riding a regular bicycle," I assured her. "Toss one leg over the seat and sit down."

"You're not planning on driving this thing in here, are you?" she openly worried.

I could have felt insulted that she'd called my beloved motorcycle a *thing*, but I was too focused on getting her on the bike to feign injury about her unfavorable word choice.

"We won't move an inch. I promise."

I kept my feet firmly planted on the concrete floor to make sure the bike wouldn't wobble when Julia finally got into position. Experience with this woman told me she would bolt the moment she believed I had ulterior motives. I *did* have ulterior motives, but it had nothing to do with taking her on a joyride around the storage garage.

Julia sturdied herself with her hands firm on my shoulders before she swung one leg over the leather seat of the Harley. She gingerly lowered herself until she sat in the empty space between my own body and the chrome gas tank.

I leaned forward until my chest pressed against her back. With my leather jacket and her wool blazer sandwiched between us, I couldn't feel much of anything. But this wasn't about me; it was all intended for her.

"Scooch up a little," I coaxed. "And grab onto the handlebars."

Julia slid forward on the seat, but didn't immediately reach for the handlebars.

I kept my boots firm on the ground. I rested my hands on her hips. "I've got you, don't worry." I tightened my hold on her body. "We're not going to move," I reiterated. "I promise I won't let us tip over."

Julia tentatively reached for the handlebars. She lightly rested her manicured hands on either bar. I was impressed by her willingness to trust me and follow my instructions. An earlier version of Julia Desjardin would have been stomping out of the storage facility by now. I was being purposefully vague about my intentions, which she typically didn't have the patience for.

I pressed myself more fully against her back. I leaned forward so she could feel my breath at the back of her neck. "Now open up the throttle."

She turned her head, but with me seated behind her, she couldn't quite address me directly. "The what?"

"Twist the right handle toward you."

I watched the delicate muscles and fine bones of her right wrist shift as she twisted the right handle. The motorcycle's engine growled. Although we didn't budge—like I'd promised—Julia's hand immediately jerked away from the handle with the increased volume. The engine returned to its gentle, idling purr.

"It's okay," I tried to assure her. "It'll get loud, but we're not going to move. Just imagine you're pressing the gas pedal on your Mercedes when it's in neutral."

Julia's hand returned to the right handle. I watched her tapered fingers curl around the bar and twist. When the engine roared again, this time she didn't let go.

I pressed more fully against her back. "Can you feel that?"

Julia didn't immediately respond. I set my right hand on top of hers and cranked harder on the throttle until the engine screamed and whined. I pinned her hand beneath my own and refused to let up. The entire chassis vibrated with pent-up energy.

I grinned when I finally heard her reaction: "For fuckssake."

Multiple layers of wool, cotton, and lace existed between her naked skin and the metal gas tank, but I anticipated the constant vibrations she would be experiencing between her parted thighs. The metal gas tank itself behaved like one oversized vibrator.

I could feel Julia's body wiggle beneath my own. I wasn't sure if she was trying to put more space between herself and the quivering motorcycle or if she was only getting comfortable. Either way, I didn't intend for her to get off so easily.

Correction: that's *exactly* what I wanted to happen.

With my right hand still tightly gripping the respective handlebar, my left hand was free to wander. I sought the bottom hem of her silk shell and slid beneath the front of her shirt. My fingers made contact with naked skin and then the lacy material of her bra. I didn't need sight; I felt my way beneath the bra's underwire until my fingertips brushed across her nipple. I pinched the puckered bud between my middle finger and my thumb, alternating between punishing pressure and a light, tender touch.

"Cassidy." Julia's voice came out like a choking gasp.

I eased up on the throttle, not wanting to overwhelm her senses. Her body collapsed forward, but I kept her steady with an arm around her waist. I didn't let her recover entirely. I revved the engine again and surged my body forward. Pinned between my body and the motorcycle's trembling gas tank, there was no place for her to go. Her hands fell to my upper thighs and she dug her short, polished nails into my rough work pants. Her nails bit through the thick material. I pictured the half-moon welts she would leave behind—battle wounds I could be proud of.

The engine whined, but no louder than my girlfriend.

After a few minutes of constant contact, I felt her entire body spasm. Her head fell forward and she seemed to surrender herself to the quaking between her thighs. I could hear her uncensored cries above the aggressive spewing and sputtering of my Harley.

I gently eased off the throttle for a final time. The bike shuddered, almost as intensely as the woman in my arms. I held her close and breathed her in.

"That wasn't very nice," she murmured.

"No?" I said innocently. I brushed at the dark hair that fell across the nape of her neck. "I thought I was being *extra* nice."

"If I didn't know any better," she remarked, "I would have thought you'd planned this all along."

I leaned back in my seat and grinned. "You know me, babe. I'm more of a pantser than a plotter."

Julia, miraculously, stood from the motorbike. I stared up at her long, lean figure and her elegant pantsuit. If my hands were on her thighs I wondered if I'd feel them shake.

She calmly flicked a lock of glossy, raven-black hair behind one ear. "I think it's time I get you home and get rid of said pants."

I looked around the seemingly empty storage facility. I knew we had the building to ourselves. An acquaintance of my friend Brent owned the warehouse. He generously let me store my bike in the temperature-controlled storage space during the winter months for a nominal fee.

My hands went to my heavy leather belt. I loosened the belt buckle and tugged until the ends fell free. "Why wait?"

A distinct smug feeling washed over me when I realized I'd managed to shock Julia Desjardin. Her look of surprise seamlessly morphed into boredom a split second later. But it was too late. I'd caught her having an emotion.

"How many other women have you dismantled with your traveling vibrator?" she wondered.

I couldn't stifle my sharp laugh. "Have vibrator. Will travel."

Julia continued to stare. I realized her question hadn't been rhetorical.

I shut off my bike and stood up. "I only got the bike when I joined the police academy. It was my first 'adult' purchase after coming back to the States."

Julia folded her arms across her chest. "That's not an answer."

"As soon as I felt that vibration, pretty much the first time I took the bike out for a ride, I wanted to do that with someone. I thought about it," I admitted, "but it never happened with anyone else."

Julia's features softened. "It's nice I can be your first time at something, too."

"You're my first a lot of things," I ventured.

"Such as?" she wanted to know.

"My first real relationship. The first person I've really been in love with. The first person I could see spending the rest of my life with."

I licked my lips. The conversation had become unexpectedly heavy in a short amount of time. I'd half-assedly proposed marriage to her once; I didn't want her to think I was doing it again. She deserved an elaborate proposal with multiple moving parts.

I wiggled my eyebrows. "I think there's enough gas in the tank if you wanna have another go."

"Not here," she decided. "You might be surprised, but motor oil doesn't play a part in my fantasies."

"Fantasies?" An eager smile formed on my lips. "You've been holding out on me?"

Julia grabbed me by the front of my pants, forcing my breath to hitch. "All in good time, darling."

Chapter One

When you're a police officer with a regular beat, you're never late to work. Roll call happens at the same time every day before the start of every shift so your commanding officer can provide updates that could prove to be lifesaving. In the Marines, you were never late either, or if you were, there'd be hell to pay. But I was no longer in the military, and I no longer had my own patrol or a partner to whom I'd been assigned, so maybe that's why I wasn't stressed to be arriving at the Fourth Precinct of the Minneapolis Police Department a few minutes late.

The line at the trendy coffee shop around the corner from Julia's condo had been longer than usual that morning. The baristas seemed to be in no rush as they made patrons' overly complicated coffee orders. Normally the liquid mud they provided at the police station didn't offend my palate—plus, it was free—but I was starting to become more of a regular at the fancy coffee shop. Maybe Julia's high-class living was starting to rub off on me.

I balanced my overpriced coffee and a sweet pastry in one hand so I could open the Cold Case office door. The door to the divisional office was typically unlocked. We rarely got visitors in the basement, plus, you'd have to be pretty ballsy to steal something from a police station—not that there was anything worth stealing in our office.

I was typically the first person, if not the only one, in the office most mornings. Sarah Conrad, our liaison to the Victim's Advocate office across town, only worked part time. My colleague Stanley Harris split his time between the downtown office and the off-site evidence storage facility that he'd nicknamed the Freezer. I had a boss, but Captain Forrester was counting down the minutes until his retirement. He was usually holed up in his private office down the hallway, dusting off his homemade taxidermy statues.

I typically didn't mind being on my own. If I'd still been a beat cop, I would have preferred to patrol on my own instead of being partnered up. Statistics suggested it was actually safer to patrol on one's own versus having a partner. Plus, you never really knew what you might encounter during the day; no shift was like the one before.

In comparison, days with the Cold Case division were pretty monotonous. Sitting at my desk, clicking away at a computer that might have been older than me, that got old pretty quickly. And with the shortened daylight hours as the upper Midwest plunged into winter, I was starting to feel like a bear settling in for a long winter's nap.

I'd been expecting there to be nothing—no one—on the opposite side of the door, but I discovered that I wasn't alone. A woman stood by herself in the shared office space. Her winter jacket, a long grey puffy coat, covered most of her figure. She turned at the sound of my wet boots squeaking against the linoleum floor.

"Not much to look at, huh?" she declared.

I stood in the open doorway, a little like I was the one barging in on her personal space, not the other way around. "I'm sorry—can I help you?"

The woman tugged off her knit cap to reveal bright red hair that fell past her shoulders. She looked young. Pretty in a wholesome girl-next-door way. She couldn't have been much older than my own twenty-eight years.

"Hi. Melody Sternbridge" she introduced herself. "I'm the host of the *Lost Girls* podcast."

She flashed the screen of her cellphone in my direction as if it was a form of identification, like a business card or an official badge. I only caught a brief glimpse of what appeared to be a screenshot of a social media account. "I'd like to speak with you about an unsolved case."

I entered the office more completely and set my things on the desk area I'd claimed as my own a few months back. "Do you have new information you'd like to share with police?" I questioned.

"No. I was thinking more like an interview about how the case is going. Danika Laroque," she identified. "She went missing in the 1980s."

The name was unfamiliar to me, but that didn't mean she wasn't one of our cases. We had hundreds of missing and unidentified individuals in our databases.

I shook my head. "I'm not at liberty to discuss active investigations with the public."

"So it *is* an active case then?" she pressed. "You're looking into this particular missing person?"

"Every case that's been assigned to our division is an active case," I told the woman. "The level of activity depends on new tips or evidence, however."

Her lips flattened. "So you won't talk to me."

"Are you family of the missing girl?"

She shook her head.

"Do you have new information about the case?"

She shook her head again.

I sat down at my desk and popped the top of my coffee so it could start to cool to a drinkable temperature. "Then I guess I'm not going to talk to you."

I heard the quiet, disgruntled noise from the frustrated woman. Maybe I was being a little rude, but we weren't the public library. Civilians couldn't just decide they wanted to flip through police files.

I stared at the woman and anticipated more resistance. But instead of arguing with me about why she should be privy to the details of this specific case, she turned on her heels and stomped out of the office.

I leaned back in my chair and stared through the open office door. The woman hadn't bothered to shut it behind her. "Weird," I murmured to myself.

The open doorway didn't remain empty for long. My colleague Stanley Harris strode into the office a few minutes later. He, too, had opted for a fancy coffee that morning instead of the burnt sludge they served on the first floor.

"Morning," I greeted.

"Morning," he returned.

"Stanley, does the name Danika Laroque ring any bells?"

It was probably unfair to be springing questions on him before he'd even taken off his jacket, but I was curious.

"Check out the playing cards," he said. "I think she's the six of spades."

The division—right before I'd been hired—had created a set of playing cards to distribute to police departments and correctional facilities across the state. Each card was a different unsolved cold case. The military had done the same thing when I'd been a Marine. Our deck of cards were terrorists, however.

I squinted at him. "There's 52 cards. How could you possibly remember that?"

Stanley set his cardboard coffee cup on his desk. "I play Texas Hold'em every Thursday night."

That he used the Cold Case cards for his game night was a little morbid, but Stanley already knew that.

I dug around in the upper right-hand drawer of my desk where I remembered last seeing an extra set of the playing cards. "We've got a lot more than 52 active cases," I observed. "How did you guys decide who got to go on a card?"

"They're all missing persons with virtually no leads," he said. "They're the coldest of the cold cases."

I flicked my eyes to Stanley's face to see if he was smiling at the turn of phrase. He wasn't.

I found the deck of cards and shuffled through the thick cardstock in search of the six of spades. Faces of missing Minnesotans, most of them young women, I couldn't help noticing, passed through my hands. I paused when I reached the card—the missing woman—I'd been seeking.

"Danika Laroque," I read aloud. "Missing since 1984. Date of birth, November 11, 1960."

I did the mental math. Twenty-four. She'd been twenty-four years old when she'd gone missing.

"Remember any other details from her case?" I asked.

I'd only been with the Cold Case division for a few months. I didn't know exactly how long Stanley had been employed in his position, but it had to have been significantly longer than me. Plus, I knew he had a bit of a photographic memory.

Stanley shook his head. "Not more than what's on the card. Whatever we've got in her case file would be in the Freezer."

I stood from my desk and grabbed my leather jacket. "Mind if we take a road trip?"

Stanley looked after me with interest. "Did we get a new tip?"

"A woman was in the office when I showed up today. She said her name was Melody Sternbridge. She hosts a podcast or something," I said with a shake of my head. "She seems to be digging into the Laroque case, and I want to know why."

"What kind of podcast?"

I shrugged. "I don't know. I didn't ask. She acted like I was supposed to know who she was."

Stanley produced his cellphone from the front pocket of his khaki pants. "Melody Sternbridge," he spoke aloud as he presumably typed her name into a search engine. His features broadened into a look of surprise. "Wow. She's got a lot of followers."

"How many?"

"It's not Kardashian-esque, but it's certainly respectable."

"What's her podcast about?"

There was a pause as Stanley continued his internet sleuthing. Then I heard his sigh. "True Crime."

"Great," I deadpanned.

Stanley began to read aloud from his cellphone screen: "*Lost Girls* is a True Crime podcast that highlights the neglected cold cases of the numerous women and girls who go missing each year. Join host, Melody Sternbridge, as she sheds light on each case in the hopes of bringing closure for these lost girls."

He looked away from his cellphone. "She said she's looking into Danika Laroque's case?"

I nodded. "In so many words. She asked what I knew about the case. I told her I wasn't at liberty to discuss it, and then she left. She seemed kind of pissed that I wasn't going to let her dig through our files."

"These online sleuths are the worst," Stanley muttered. There was an uncharacteristic bitterness to his normally jovial tone. "They think they're more clever than the police. They spend all of their free time obsessing over clues on internet discussion boards and Facebook pages."

"What do we do about it?" I couldn't help feeling a little helpless.

While I'd been shooting at sand dunes in Afghanistan, an entire technology—the internet—had passed me by. I wasn't technologically illiterate like somebody's grandparents, but I knew my weaknesses.

"We should probably let Captain Forrester know," Stanley suggested. "There's not much we can do about it, but I know he hates to be blindsided in case this Sternbridge woman shows up at his office next. Did she know your name?"

"No. And I never gave it to her."

"I guess that's one small blessing to our overworked and underfunded IT department," Stanley reflected. "She won't be able to doxx us."

"I want to avoid being doxxed?" I guessed. I had no idea what the word meant or why I should avoid it. Was it a verb? A noun?

"It means posting online who you are and where you live," Stanley explained. "If she gets her listeners all riled up, thinking the police have been negligent with this case, they'll show up at your front door."

I doubted anyone would get past the security at Julia's luxury St. Paul condo, but I wasn't eager to test out that theory.

"*Have* we been negligent?" I pressed.

Stanley's features turned somber. "Let's check out her case files and hope for the best."

∽

I hung back a few feet while Stanley unlocked the padlock that secured the main door of the off-site storage facility. It wasn't much of a formal entrance—more like a manual garage door. I helped him lift the large metal door until it slid along its track. Once inside the building, I deactivated the electronic security system while Stanley walked over to the lone computer station.

The onsite computer provided an index to all of the hundreds, if not thousands, of case files and evidence boxes stored in the Freezer. It was similar to a library's online card catalog. I never claimed to be a great thinker or have natural smarts, but I had done quite a lot of reading when I'd been in the Marines. *Butterfly in the sky* and all that shit. When the world beyond my window was a dull, monochromatic beige, reading had been my escape.

Stanley consulted the online index and jotted a few numbers and letters on to a scrap piece of paper before stepping away from the computer. I followed him down one of the long, narrow walkways that provided just enough space to maneuver between the tall storage shelving units.

I waited while Stanley scanned the shelving unit for the sequence of numbers and letters that matched the online finding aid. He had to stand on his tiptoes to reach a narrow acid-free box. He pulled the archival box from its respective shelf and lifted the lid. His fingers ticked over the multiple file folders inside until he removed one.

He passed me the folder. "Danika Laroque."

"This is it?"

Stanley shrugged. "I guess so."

I looked at the skinny file folder in my hand. It was a drastic contrast to some of the beefier cases that had multiple boxes of evidence collected from the scene. But, I supposed, when someone went missing, there wasn't much to box up.

I opened the folder to inspect the few loose pieces of paper inside. A photograph of a young woman was stapled on top of the thin pile. It was the same picture that had been mass produced for the Cold Case deck of cards. The colorized image was a little grainy and worn at the edges. Danika Laroque didn't smile at the photographer. She was tan with long, black hair that she wore parted down the center.

I flipped through the rest of the documents. Danika hadn't been from the Twin Cities, but some smaller, suburban towns like the one from which she came, kicked their unsolved cases to us. Her parents had been the one to inform Prior Lake police that Danika had gone missing. They'd included a physical description of their daughter along with a report of the clothing she'd last been seen wearing: a polo shirt and blue jeans.

Prior Lake police had conducted a few interviews, largely with other members of her family and a man whom Danika had supposedly been dating. Nothing jumped out as unusual or alarming among the interviews. Danika had gone to work at a gas station convenience store. She hadn't had a car, but she tended to ride her bike from her mom's house to work. Sometimes her boyfriend picked her and her bike up at the end of her shift, but he reportedly hadn't done so on the evening of her disappearance. The police had followed up on his alibi—his whereabouts that night—and it had apparently checked out.

No one had come forward with any additional information, like if they'd seen Danika and her bike on the road that night. The case had quickly gone cold and had passed from Prior Lake police to us in the Twin Cities. No other documents had been added to her file over the years, suggesting that we'd never received any new information or tips that would warrant us re-opening the case. I recalled what Stanley had said about the cases that had made their way on the playing cards—this was one of the coldest of the cold cases.

I handed the case file to Stanley for his own inspection. My lips twisted as I considered the slim case file. When someone went missing there would be no physical evidence to collect unless signs of foul play had been found during the initial investigation. The case file contained no DNA evidence, no scraps of clothing, not even the woman's bicycle had been found. It made me curious why Melody Sternbridge had selected—or even knew about—Danika Laroque's disappearance. The lack of any leads made me more curious about the podcast woman than the missing girl herself.

"Would you have done anything different?" I asked once Stanley had closed the file folder.

"Gas station video footage from 1984?" he proposed.

"Maybe," I thought aloud. "Is that technology even that old though?"

"CCTV has been around since World War II with VHS first introduced in the 1970s," he described. "I don't know how widespread that kind of technology would have been in rural Minnesota though."

That Stanley knew those kind of trivial details was unremarkable. The depth of his knowledge base no longer surprised me.

"So if police didn't have footage of Danika leaving the gas station after work, who else might they have interviewed?" I questioned.

"Co-workers. Whoever had the shift before hers and after hers. They could look at register receipts to see who had been a customer that day. Family, friends, significant other," Stanley ticked off. "But other than that? You just hope that someone who knows something or saw something comes forward. You can't get an alibi for an entire town."

I rubbed my hands over my face. "Why this case? We've got literally nothing to go on."

"Maybe that's exactly why she picked it," Stanley proposed. "More exposure? Maybe someone after thirty years of silence is finally ready to come forward with new information?"

"And if they're not?" I said.

"Then I guess it'll be a really short podcast episode."

Chapter Two

Three framed paintings hung in a tidy row above my therapist, Dr. Susan Warren, in her downtown high-rise office space. My eyes swept back and forth across the horizontal grouping of black ink blobs. A cat chasing a butterfly. A father consoling his child. A tree that had lost all of its leaves.

"Are those new?" I asked.

My therapist turned around to see to what I was referring. "Oh. That," she said, almost dismissively. "Yes, they're new."

"I thought you didn't like distractions in your office."

Dr. Warren picked up a yellow legal pad and clicked her pen awake. "Are they distracting you?"

I couldn't help my chuckle. "Is that a real question, or has our session already begun?"

I hadn't seen Dr. Warren in person for several weeks due to my extended visit to Embarrass—originally for Julia's father's funeral and the settling of his estate, and then because Julia was being investigated for suspected involvement in her father's death. With everything so up in the air, I'd been negligent in writing in my pre-sleep journal, too. The flashbacks had returned with a vengeance.

One minute I was sleeping beside Julia in her rural Embarrass mansion, and the next I was being shot at and dragging my buddy Terrance Pensacola across an Afghanistan desert. Returning to the Twin Cities and settling back into my regular routine had helped me limit my traumatic dreams again. I would never be entirely cured of PTSD —something my therapist routinely reminded me of—but I could hope for longer, more extended, periods between episodes.

Dr. Warren readjusted herself on her chair. "Where would you like to start today?"

My eyes returned to the trio of framed images. The cat chasing a butterfly seemed to be hung a few centimeters lower than the others. It made me wonder if the misalignment was on purpose to flush out anyone with a perfectionism disorder. That seemed unlikely since Dr. Warren specialized in trauma, specifically war trauma. But maybe people with brain injuries sought perfection elsewhere in their lives since they themselves were so broken.

"Cassidy?" Dr. Warren called for my attention.

My gaze lowered to her face. "Sorry, Doc. Your paintings are doing a number on me."

Dr. Warren offered me a placating smile. "How are you sleeping these days?"

I let out a long breath and lightly struck the tops of my thighs with nervous energy. No matter how many times we met, no matter how kind my therapist had been from the start, it was still unnatural for me to voluntarily talk about these things.

"The flashbacks come less and less," I began. "The nightmares are sporadic, but if I do my homework—if I empty my brain in that notebook you gave me—there's nothing left to give me night terrors."

"I'd say that's awfully impressive progress," Dr. Warren approved.

"Yeah," I haltingly agreed. "But once the nightmares are gone, all I'm left with is regret."

Dr. Warren leaned forward in her chair. "Do you regret enlisting?"

I sat with her question for a moment before responding: "I left the Marines with an uncomfortable feeling in my gut. No one met me at the airport to spit on me or call me a baby killer. In fact, I've only ever really experienced praise—most of it performative," I qualified, "about my service to my country. They gave me a parade. They filled my chest with medals. But with the exception of saving Pensacola's life, I didn't do anything really special or important over there. And even saving Pensacola's life came with an asterisks. What kind of quality of life does he even have anymore?"

I paused, realizing I'd strayed from her original question. "Sorry. I don't think I have a point to what I'm saying. I'm just kind of talking it out, if that's okay."

"It's more than okay," Dr. Warren allowed. "It's important that you process all of these emotions and sentiments, no matter how incomplete they may be."

I took a breath and started again. "I'm really happy with my life right now. I like my job. I've got great friends. My girlfriend is the best thing that's ever happened to me," I said in earnest. "My relationship with my parents could be better, but all things considered, it could be much worse."

"I'm not hearing any statements about the military in there," my therapist gently pointed out.

"Can I resent being a Marine and what it did to my body and my brain if the life I've got right now is pretty fucking great?" I winced at the curse word. "Sorry," I immediately apologized, "but, like, if all of that had never happened to me, where would I be now? Would my life even remotely resemble what I've got right now?"

"It is important to you to figure that out?" Dr. Warren questioned.

I leaned back on the couch and exhaled. "It seems like a pretty basic question: do I regret being in the military? Do I resent the things I had to do over there if they all led me to this time and place?"

Dr. Warren's next smile was small, nearly sad. "That's the ten thousand dollar question, isn't it?"

∼

"Not bad, Miller," I murmured to myself. "Maybe there's hope for you after all."

I stood back and admired my work. The dining room table was adorned with two simple place settings and a glass vase of white peonies I'd picked up after my therapy session. Small votive candles waited on the table to be lit. I had dinner prepped in the kitchen—sautéed green beans and salmon fillets that would take only minutes to pan sear once Julia got home from work.

We hadn't eaten at the dining room table since Julia and I

had hosted a few close friends for Thanksgiving dinner. Instead of a place to share an intimate meal, it had transformed into a catch-all workspace for all things related to her mother: health care statements, court documents that had granted Julia guardianship after her father's death, and most recently, printed trifold brochures for assisted living facilities in the Twin Cities.

We'd toured a number of locations already, but Julia had found fault with all of them. Not enough gluten-free options for the residents even though her mother had no special dietary needs. Objectionable wallpaper in the residential rooms. Too much traffic noise polluting otherwise meticulously landscaped gardens. She'd even rejected one of the facilities because she apparently didn't trust doctors with beards. I hadn't known how to broach the sensitive topic without starting a fight, but it was obvious that Julia was unnecessarily delaying relocating her mother from Embarrass to a closer facility.

I looked toward the front door when I heard a key in the lock. Julia entered the apartment moments later. She set her work bag on the floor and silently hung up her wool trench coat in the entryway. I wanted to bound over to her to greet her arrival, but not wanting to resemble an overly eager golden retriever puppy, I remained in the dining room.

"Hey, babe," I called to her.

Julia's high heels struck against marble tile as she left the front foyer. She didn't verbally greet me as I had done, but as she approached, her arms went around my waist and she sagged against me.

"Long day?" I guessed. I pressed an innocent kiss to the side of her exposed throat.

"Mmhmm," she confirmed. I heard her extended sigh. Her fingers twisted around the bottom hem of my button-up flannel, not out of intimate urgency, but like she was clutching on to me like a lifeline.

"Why don't you change into something more comfortable," I suggested, "and I'll make us a drink."

"That sounds divine," came her reply.

"And let me know when you want dinner," I prompted. "I thought we might eat at the table tonight."

At my mentioning of dinner, Julia lifted her head from my shoulder. She looked alarmed rather than pleased by my culinary endeavor. "Where's my mother's paperwork?"

I pointed to a grey plastic bin that sat in a corner of the dining room. I'd anticipated her panic and hadn't wanted the files to be too far away. "Everything is organized in there," I told her. "I made separate hanging files for each category of documentation."

Julia left me and walked directly for the grey bin. She crouched and removed the plastic lid. I had also anticipated her not being satisfied with merely a verbal explanation of what I'd done, so I didn't take offense that she would double-check my work. I watched her fingers rapidly trip over each carefully tabbed label and folder. I wasn't normally so organized—all of my belongings tended to get thrown into a moving box until the next time I needed them again—but I'd taken my time with Olivia Desjardin's documents.

The previously stern look on her features softened. "Everything is in here?"

"Uh huh," I confirmed. "I probably should have done something similar for myself when I got all of those unpaid therapy bills, but better late than never."

Julia swept her hair away from her face. "This is remarkable, Cassidy. Thank you."

"Will you have dinner with me now?" I all but pouted.

Her lipsticked mouth curved up to form a soft, wistful smile. "Yes, of course. Do you have the number for Poison Control on speed dial?"

"Hey!"

I vocalized a protest, but I was secretly thankful for the taunt. She'd been so serious and so stressed out since her father's funeral. I would endure her teasing if it meant having her back—body and soul.

No one needed to call Poison Control that evening. Julia had even asked for seconds. We remained seated at the dining room table at the end of the meal. Plates had yet to be cleared, but neither of us was in a hurry. The votive candles had melted down to liquid wax; tiny yellow flames flickered on the shimmering surface.

Julia swirled the liquid in her wine glass. "I have some news."

I helped myself to more Pinot Grigio—another recent habit that I could only blame on Julia's refined influence. "Good news, I hope?"

"It's a little bit good and bad." Julia bit down on her lower lip. "I'm going to take the job at Grisham & Stein. I've put in my notice at the public defender's office."

Grisham & Stein was one of the top law firms in the Twin Cities. They employed a stable of lawyers with little to no moral compass, able to look beyond their wealthy clients' criminal activity in exchange for a sizable paycheck, luxury vehicles, and paid vacations to exotic locations. Julia had been offered a different role, however—one intended to improve Grisham & Stein's public image. As I understood the position, she would have her choice of *pro bono* cases, largely defending those without means and those who had been unjustly incarcerated.

Her news caught me off guard. I'd thought she'd all but turned down the offer after her father's death.

I sat back in my chair. "Wow. Okay. What made you say yes?"

"The money, honesty," Julia admitted with a small frown. "I wish I had a more honorable reason for leaving the public defender's office for a soul-sucking criminal defense firm, but my mother's care won't be cheap. And since my father got greedy with his life insurance money, I no longer have that to help cover the costs of her assisted living."

"I could help out," I offered. "I don't want you to feel like you have to do this on your own." It was a weak offer without much substance. My compensation through the city of Minneapolis was generous for the area, but it wasn't like I had cash to burn.

Julia inclined her head. "That's kind, dear, but no. I'm being dramatic about the soul sucking. It was only a matter of time before I outgrew the public defender's office, especially after Landon Tauer's case."

It had been her successful defense of Landon Tauer, a young man who'd wrongly been charged with murder, that had put her on Grisham & Stein's radar. The case hadn't technically been assigned to Cold Case—it had been an active homicide investigation at the time—but my colleague Stanley had been a kind of mentor to the deceased girl. Ultimately, we'd uncovered that she'd taken her own life, but the case had been misidentified as a homicide. In the wake of that success, Julia had suspected the public defender's office would want her to start defending more high-profile cases. While she'd found purpose in achieving reduced sentences for those who might otherwise be unduly punished for minimal infractions, she had no interest in defending those who were guilty of more serious crimes.

A number of my law enforcement co-workers gave me a hard time for dating 'the enemy.' But they didn't know Julia the way I did. While I certainly would have felt better about her being an attorney or prosecutor for the city, I also wasn't one of those cops who thought everyone they'd ever arrested was guilty or that they should have the book thrown at them. I anticipated that our careers might again come into conflict down the road, but I wasn't holding my breath until that day came.

"So are we celebrating?" I asked.

I couldn't gauge how she felt about the job. She'd described it as both good and bad news.

"Let's hold off on popping the champagne until I win my first case," she pragmatically suggested.

"Do you know what it will be?"

Julia shook her head. "Nothing has been assigned to me yet. I have two more weeks at the public defender's office just to tie up loose ends. When I officially start at Grisham & Stein, the Partners will want me to get comfortable before tackling anything big. My first priority is bringing on new staff for my team."

"Wow," I openly admired. "You get a whole team?"

"It's not football," she was quick to correct. "But I'll be

able to bring on an assistant, some paralegals, and probably my own independent investigator." She looked purposefully in my direction. "Know of anyone who might fit that job description?"

"You mean me?"

Julia ran a single finger along the top of her wine glass. "I'm sure the pay is much more than what the city can afford."

I shook my head. "It's never been about the money."

As much as the thought of us working side-by-side thrilled me, I was a cop, even if I no longer wore the uniform.

"I thought as much," she nodded. "Well, if you know of any police officers who might be interested in a career change, send them my way."

"Only the old and ugly ones," I decided.

Julia chuckled pleasantly. "And why's that, dear?"

"I'd get jealous," I said with an easy shrug.

"Are you sure I can't convince you to at least *consider* the position?" she proposed.

"You can convince me to take whatever position you want, babe." I leaned forward and wiggled my eyebrows to let her know I was no longer talking about job opportunities. "Just say the word."

Chapter Three

Sarah Conrad, my colleague from the Victim's Advocate office, smiled innocently from her desk.

"Hey, Miller. Truth or Dare."

Her smile was innocent, but that was about the only unassuming thing about her. In our short time of working together, I'd learned that her phone was always buzzing with a message from a potential suitor and that she possessed a particular talent for making me uncomfortable.

"Detective Miller!"

My head swiveled from Sarah to the open office doorway. My direct supervisor, Captain Forrester, strode into the open office area. We typically didn't see much of the man. He had a private, windowless office down the hallway from which he rarely emerged. It was obvious the Captain's countdown-to-retirement clock was his primary concern. That—and his ever-growing taxidermy collection.

I didn't consider the Captain to be an emotive man, but it was clear from his tone and posture that he was annoyed. "I just got off the phone with Prior Lake PD. A woman showed up this morning asking questions about a girl who went missing thirty years ago. Upset the girl's family, too."

"Melody Sternbridge?" I questioned.

Captain Forrester's mouth formed a hard line. "You seem unsurprised."

"Shit. Damn. I mean, I'm sorry, sir." I reflexively winced at my language and scrambled to my feet. While cops tended to be more liberal with their word choice, it was generally not a good idea to swear in front of a superior.

"She came into the office yesterday morning asking questions about the case," I explained. "She's a podcaster or something. I thought Stanley told you."

"No. Stanley did not tell me." Forrester's tone was nearly mocking.

"I'm sorry, sir," I apologized again. "I had no idea she would bother the victim's family."

"Well, she did," Captain Forrester complained. "And now you get to drive all the way to Prior Lake to apologize to them. Congratulations."

"Yes, sir."

"Reassure them we're doing everything and using all of the department's resources to find their daughter and provide them with closure," he instructed me. "And while you're down there, meet with Prior Lake PD, too. Let them know you're taking care of it."

"Are we re-opening the case, sir?" I asked.

Captain Forrester looked sharply in my direction. "Have we gotten any new information?"

I hesitated with my response. "No."

"That's your answer then," Forrester snipped. "Conrad," he barked out.

Sarah flinched in her seat from the volume of his voice. "Yes?"

"Accompany Detective Miller," he ordered. "Make sure she doesn't upset the Laroque family even more."

∽

"Forrester is quite the little ray of sunshine today, eh?"

Sarah accompanied me on our walk to the back lot where the divisional police car was parked. Captain Forrester wasn't a particularly impressive man, but he had the title that compelled my respect. As a civilian and someone not directly employed by Minneapolis PD, Sarah could be a little more open with her criticism.

I shrugged. "I've had worse supervisors. At least he mostly stays out of the way."

"That's true." Sarah nodded in agreement. "Almost has me dreading the day he finally retires. With our luck, they'll promote some micromanager who'll make us fill out self-evaluations and annual reports." She barely repressed a visible shudder.

I unlocked the unmarked Crown Vic that had been assigned to Cold Case and climbed behind the steering wheel. I turned the key in the ignition and let the squad car idle. The colder temperatures dictated I give the engine a little time to wake up. The vehicle was getting on in years—a serious hand-me-down that needed retirement nearly as much as Captain Forrester. But despite the dents in the chassis and the way the engine whined in cold weather, I was starting to feel fondly about our second-hand equipment. It was like we all belonged together. The former Marine with

PTSD. The wannabe coroner who never made it to the morgue. The taxidermist with a police badge.

I turned briefly to Sarah in the passenger seat. Was she an awkward or damaged misfit like the rest of us? At first glance, she seemed beautiful and popular, never short on dates. How had she been banished to the basement of the Fourth Precinct with the rest of us?

"Sorry you had to get dragged along today," I apologized.

Sarah flipped down the passenger-side visor and reapplied her ruby red lipstick. She pursed her lips at her reflection. "S'ok. Did not expect to be headed back to the Res though."

"The what?"

"Indian Reservation?" she clarified. She snapped the visor back to its original position. "I grew up on one. Red Lake band of Chippewa."

I looked at Sarah—really looked at her. "Oh. I didn't realize."

"It's okay," she dismissed. "Most people expect us to be in a museum or something—not working at their grocery store."

It struck me how little I knew of Sarah's background. I hadn't thought to ask. I was so used to avoiding talking about my own past that it hadn't really occurred to me that other people might actually want to tell me those details about themselves.

"Have you ever been on a reservation before?" she asked.

I shook my head. "No. Never."

"Well, after today, you still won't," she said. "The SMSC are rich. Like, you've never seen money like theirs, rich. On a list of federally recognized tribes, they should probably have an asterisks next to their name."

"SMSC. What's that stand for?"

I'd lived all of my life in Minnesota, minus an eight-year detour in Afghanistan, but I'd never heard the acronym before.

"Shakopee Mdewakanton Sioux Community," she recited. "Shakopee is a Dakota word for 'number six.' It comes from an important Dakota leader, Sakpe. *Mdewaknton* means 'dwellers of the spirit lake.'"

"Now you sound like Stanley," I lightly teased.

Sarah snorted at the comparison. "Nah. They're just a big fucking deal around here. They make so much money from their casinos that no one actually has to work. Rumor has it, everyone in the community gets a million dollars a year."

"Geez. *Every* year?" I finally shifted the vehicle into drive and cringed at the sound of grinding gears.

Sarah leaned back in her seat and tried to get more comfortable. "I know, right? I'd probably resent them if they weren't so generous. Red Lake just got a $60 million loan from them to build their own casino."

"That's your, uh, group?" I didn't know the lingo. I knew indigenous people existed, but I'd never consciously met one before.

"Band," she corrected. "Minnesota has eleven tribal nations: seven Ojibwa and four Dakota. The SMSC is one of the four Eastern Dakota Bands. My ancestors were Ojibwa."

"So does that mean you're gonna be rich, too?" I questioned with a quick grin.

Sarah didn't return my smile. "I don't live on the Res anymore, so I'm not entitled to any shared revenue. But Red Lake will never be rich like the SMSC," she prophesied.

"They won the geography lottery being so close to the Twin Cities. You could have the biggest, fanciest casino in the world, but if no one really lives near it, it's just another failing business on the Res."

"I guess I don't understand the appeal," I said. "Casinos, I mean. I'm not much of a gambler."

Sarah looked at me with interest. "Not even Vegas?"

"Never been," I admitted. I'd hardly ever been out of the state, not counting the traveling I'd done in the military.

"You should go. I bet you and your girlfriend would have a great time."

I tried to imagine Julia in a casino. I'd never been inside of one, but if they were anything like in the movies—filled with cigarette smoke, bright lights and loud noises—I could practically see the wrinkled nose and disapproving curled her lip. The more I thought on it, I probably wasn't stable enough for all of that stimuli. A single clap of thunder or a stray firework could trigger one of my episodes.

Sarah turned on the radio once we got on the highway and hummed along with the Top 40 songs. Conversation stalled with the exception of pointing out funny bumper stickers or strange roadside billboards. With the late morning traffic at a minimum it was a relatively quick commute. We eventually reached our exit, and I steered the police car behind a giant purple shuttle affiliated with the Mystic Lake Casino and Hotel.

"You're gonna see those busses everywhere now," Sarah anticipated. "They shuttle people from Minneapolis or the Mall of America directly to their casino. It's quite the tidy little system."

Once we exited the highway, we drove through four miles

of exurbia: gently rolling hills, dotted with trees and lakes and palatial homes. Captain Forrester had indicated that we should speak with Prior Lake police during our visit, plus I needed to get an updated address for the Laroque family, so I stopped at the police station first. I parked our well-used squad car next to a row of brand new police cruisers and SUVs. Their paint seemed to gleam and shimmer under the late morning sun.

Sarah noticed the way my attention lingered on the new equipment even before we exited the car.

"I didn't realize we were poor until my parents moved us to Minneapolis when I was in the fourth grade," she said. "Everyone at my new school seemed to have so much stuff. New stuff, too," she remarked, "not hand-me-downs or things their moms got on deep discount. On the Res we were all poor, but you had no way of knowing it. We all lived in trailer homes, we all wore clothes that didn't quite fit, we all had terrible haircuts that our moms gave us."

I nodded stiffly at her obvious analogy. I had started to feel an affinity for our underfunded department. But seeing Prior Lake's ample resources was making me realize just how much of an afterthought we were in the basement of the Fourth Precinct.

The Prior Lake police department was a freestanding building directly across the street from their city hall. The municipal building was updated with modern architectural features, but the police department was a plain brick building with little frills or embellishments. The modest exterior made me feel a little less out of sorts. After introducing ourselves to the uniformed officer at the front desk area, Sarah and I were led to a cubical that belonged to Prior Lake's tribal liaison officer.

Officer Brendon Azure had been expecting our arrival. He'd preemptively pulled two bottles of water and had commandeered a number of donuts which he offered after we'd exchanged introductions. The first thing that struck me about Officer Brendon Azure was his youth. Brendon Azure was a medium-built man with an eager-to-please face. I'd only been with Minneapolis Police for two years, but after eight years in the Marines, I felt at home in a uniform and gun belt. Officer Azure looked green, like he'd never had the opportunity to use his service weapon. But out in the affluent suburbs, he might never have a reason to draw his firearm, even if he'd been a badge for over forty years.

In addition to his other routine responsibilities, Officer Azure served as a go-between for Prior Lake PD and the SMSC. I knew that some reservations had their own independent tribal police departments, but the SMSC had contracted with Prior Lake to essentially combine resources. I wondered if those new police cruisers I'd seen parked out front were a result of that collaboration.

Azure had a nervous energy about himself. Even seated, he bounced on the balls of his feet. He periodically battled with a stubborn cowlick near the back of his skull. From the way his gaze continually returned to Sarah, I didn't have to ponder very hard from where his anxious energy came.

"So that podcast woman ambushed you, too?" I started.

Azure bobbed his head. "Hadn't even officially started my shift this morning. Showed up to work and she was sitting outside, waiting for me."

His experience sounded comparable to my own first encounter with the woman. It made me wonder if there was a strategic purpose behind Melody Sternbridge's unsolicited approach or if she was simply an early riser.

"Any idea what her connection to the Laroque case might be?" I asked.

We had *hundreds* of unsolved cases, most of which involved missing women—or lost girls—as her podcast was apparently named. Melody Sternbridge's decision to focus on Danika Laroque had puzzled me ever since she'd first introduced herself.

"When I asked her about it, she said she was drawn to the case because of Danika's background," Azure revealed.

Sarah snorted. "You mean because Danika's indigenous? Sounds like this lady has a serious white savior complex."

"I'm not exactly thrilled she's decided she's going to poke around this case," Azure agreed. "The SMSC are very private. The last thing they'll want is attention from the wrong kind of tourists."

"What exactly is the wrong kind of tourist?" I questioned.

"Trauma tourism," Azure answered. "You know—the kind who make pilgrimages to where Jeffrey Dahmer used to live."

The comparison made me sit up. "Is there more than one girl missing?"

I hadn't thought to search the database for additional missing women in the area from around the same time period before that moment.

Azure shook his head. "Not that I know of. But that far back? The, uh, record keeping wasn't too precise."

"Just another missing Indian girl," Sarah said flatly.

Azure's eyes swept from Sarah's unimpressed features back to mine. "I looked through our copy of the original police file after Ms. Sternbridge left. I've never seen such a sparse file before."

"You think police back then missed some things?" I posed. Privately, I'd had the same thought.

Azure lifted his hands. "I'm not suggesting deliberate negligence," he clarified. "Part of the issue is overlapping jurisdictions. We're dealing with federal, tribal, county, and city when it comes to incidents that happen on trust land. No one seems to know who has jurisdiction or which police forces should be doing the investigating. Plus," he continued, "FBI profiling is useless. There's no typical profile for the kind of person who targets indigenous girls and women. They could be a serial killer, someone associated with sex trafficking, or even a family member."

"I bet they're all male," Sarah spoke up.

Officer Azure grimaced at her words. "Okay, so maybe they have *something* in common," he conceded. "But it's really vulnerability that's the common thread. These women are some of the most vulnerable women on the continent. They get targeted because perpetrators believe they'll get away with it."

"And they'd be right," I grimly added.

Officer Azure frowned. "Unfortunately," he agreed. "The SMSC no longer fit that profile because of the casino money, but twenty, thirty years ago was a different scenario."

"We'd like to speak with Danika's family while we're here," I said. "Do you think you could get us an address?"

"Danika's parents are still alive, and they still live on the trust, but they're older," Azure said. "I don't think they really understand this podcast stuff."

"Hell, even I don't understand it," I remarked.

My comment drew a mild smile to Azure's boyish features. "I would recommend speaking to Jenny Laroque. She's the missing girl's sister."

He briefly consulted the laptop on his cubicle desk before scribbling information onto a piece of lined paper. I couldn't help noticing the new computer while we worked on machines from the turn-of-the-century.

Azure handed me the paper. "Do you want me to come with?" he offered.

I took the sheet of paper and looked at the handwritten address. "Do you think we'll need you?"

"I'm sure you're both capable," Azure readily qualified. "I just wanted to extend my services. I wouldn't say that they're necessarily hostile to outsiders, but the SMSC is a private community, just like any other affluent, gated subdivision you'd find in the Twin Cities."

I looked once in Sarah's direction to get her appraisal, but she only shrugged.

We weren't doing much police work that day. Forrester had only tasked us to contact the Laroque family and apologize about the annoying podcaster.

"I think we'll be okay," I decided. "But I appreciate the offer."

Chapter Four

The Shakopee-Mdewakanton Reservation was located entirely within the city limits of Prior Lake, in Scott County, Minnesota. Instead of a settled, established neighborhood with wide streets and mature trees like the St. Cloud community in which I'd grown up, I saw construction everywhere. Houses were being expanded upon, in-ground pools were being dug. The streets themselves were half tore up with giant pipes for wastewater prepped and waiting on the side of the road.

Jenny Laroque lived in a sprawling, French provincial mansion. I normally would have gaped at the home's size, but the neighboring houses were just as large, if not more so. We parked in the half oval driveway in front of the house. The department's cast-off vehicle looked more out of place than usual amongst its settings. I saw no other cars in the driveway, but a detached three-car garage sat adjacent to the main house.

Jenny Laroque answered her own door. I didn't know

why that surprised me. I'd been to fancy neighborhoods before, but the knowledge that the people in this community might earn one million dollars a year had me thrown. If I made that kind of money I'd have robot butlers taking care of mundane tasks like answering the door. Her outfit was a surprise as well. No fancy jewelry, no extensive makeup, no visible designer labels. If she hadn't been standing in the doorway of an uber-sized mansion, I might have mistaken her for any other midwestern mom.

"Tea? Coffee?" she offered in lieu of a proper hello.

We sat at a long glass table in a formal dining room. Sarah and I occupied two stiff, high-backed chairs in the center of the table while Jenny Laroque retrieved cups of coffee from the kitchen. I had a hard time imagining cozy dinners taking place in the room or chaotic holiday meals. I wanted to say as much to Sarah. I wanted to make some kind of comment to maybe lighten the mood, but Ms. Laroque returned before I could come up with anything.

I murmured my thanks when she set the ceramic coffee cup in front of me. In Julia's kitchen, I routinely drank from a law enforcement novelty mug, slightly stained from use with the words "I like big busts and I cannot lie" screen printed on the side. The cup Ms. Laroque placed in front of me was a dark green glazed mug—name brand—something French and unnecessary.

I waited until she took a seat opposite of Sarah and myself before I began.

"Thank you for having us in your home, Ms. Laroque," I started. "I know this probably isn't how you'd like to be spending your day."

The woman nodded curtly, her eyes glued to her hands, which tightly cupped her own coffee mug. It was green, just like the ones she'd given to Sarah and me.

"That woman blindsided us," she said.

"Melody Sternbridge?" I asked for clarification.

"Sure." Jenny Laroque took a small sip from her cup.

"What exactly did she say or ask?" I questioned.

Jenny set her coffee cup back on the glass table. "Only that she was investigating Danika's disappearance. She wasn't a cop though, so I couldn't figure out why'd she want to do that."

"She apparently has a podcast," I remarked.

No recognition registered in Jenny's features.

I cleared my throat. "While we're here, do you mind a few questions?"

The woman shrugged, almost with disinterest. "Shoot."

I shot a furtive glance in Sarah's direction. Captain Forrester had only given us clearance to assure the Laroque family that we were doing everything to resolve this missing persons case. He hadn't expressly given permission to interview the family, but it felt wrong to have come all this way, to leave Prior Lake, without doing *something*.

I couldn't remember if Jenny's name had been among the family members that Prior Lake police had interviewed when Danika first went missing. I wished my recall was half as good as Stanley's.

"What was she like?"

I turned in my chair to appraise my colleague. I hadn't expected Sarah to initiate the questioning; her tone and her word choice humbled me though. I'd been ready to launch into investigation mode—what she remembered about the day in question, for example. The personal, the *human* element, that Sarah conjured was a much better approach.

Jenny released a long breath. "She was wild—didn't follow the rules. She thumbed her nose at convention. No one could tell her what to do." A small, wistful smile crept onto her lips. "And I desperately wanted to be like her."

"She was older than you?" Sarah pressed.

Jenny nodded. "By several years. We didn't get along, but then again, what sisters do? I wanted to hang out with her and her friends, but I was just the annoying little sister to them."

"She went away after high school," Jenny continued. "She wanted to get off the Res like everyone else. None of this was here back then," she described, gesturing to the nice things around her. "Before the casinos came, this was all dirt roads and trailer parks."

"But she came back," I noted. Danika had been working at a local gas station when she'd disappeared.

"She came back," Jenny said with a grimace. "Wasn't able to hack it in the outside world apparently. She moved back in with our family and resented every minute of it. She started to drink a lot. Probably drugs, too. Wasn't able to hold down a job for very long."

"Did the police ever consider that maybe she ran away?" Sarah posed.

"They did," she confirmed. "But there wasn't anything missing from her room. All of her stuff was still there. They watched her savings account, too, and no one ever made deposits or withdrawals. She just ... she disappeared. Her bike was never recovered. Nothing."

"Let me preemptively apologize for this question," I said

with a small wince, "but did your sister have any enemies? Anyone who might want to hurt her?"

Jenny closed her eyes. "No."

I waited, hopeful that she might elaborate, but Jenny Laroque remained silent.

I looked to Sarah to see if she had any additional questions. She shook her head.

"Thank you, Ms. Laroque," I said. "We really appreciate your time. We'll be in touch if anything comes up on our end." I fished out one of my business cards from my wallet and set it on the table between us. "And let us know if Melody Sternbridge tried to contact you and your family again. If she becomes a nuisance, we can file a restraining order to keep her away from your property."

Jenny touched her fingertips to my business card, but she didn't pick it up. "I'll let you know," she promised.

We left our untouched coffee cups on the dining room table and stood to leave. Another set of thank-yous was exchanged before Sarah and I made our way to the front door with Jenny Laroque trailing behind.

I paused on the front stoop when Jenny spoke again: "You know, when we first started to get paid, I couldn't help but think about Danika. Like, if she'd just been here, if she'd just been able to get some of this money, maybe she would have been able to turn things around."

"Or maybe it would have only fueled her destructive behavior," Sarah reasoned.

Jenny nodded grimly. "Yeah. I think about that, too."

. . .

Sarah exhaled loudly when we were both back inside of the squad car. I gave my co-worker a sideways glance as I turned the key in the ignition.

"You okay over there?"

Sarah stared straight ahead. "Yeah. Just working through some things."

I didn't immediately shift the car into drive. "Anything you want to talk about?"

She turned in her seat and flashed me a brief—forced, I thought—smile. "I'm good, Miller. But thanks."

I chewed on my lower lip, not really believing her words, but not really knowing if I should push her for more. I was a professional at assuring the people around me that everything was all right—that I could deal on my own—so as to not be a burden or inconvenience.

I kept the car running, if only to clear the windshield that had become foggy with our warm breath and the early December chill.

Finally, Sarah spoke: "She doesn't seem happy."

"Sorry?"

"Jenny Larocque," she clarified. "Did she seem happy to you?"

"Oh, I ... I guess not?"

I couldn't quite tell what Sarah was really asking or why. In my experience, most people weren't happy if they were in a situation that required speaking to the police.

"Money can't buy you happiness." Sarah picked at the cracking leather of the car's padded dashboard. "When you're poor, you grow to resent that saying. When every meal is white bread and government cheese, you can think of a shit ton of things money can buy."

I stared out the driver's side window at Jenny Larocque's massive mansion. The reflection from the home's front windows made it impossible to determine if she was looking back at us or if she had gone on with her day.

"She's still on the Res," Sarah continued. She spoke aloud, but the words didn't seem to be intended for me. "Bigger house, sure. Lots of fancy toys in the garage. But she's still on the Res."

I couldn't decipher Sarah's tone. Was she smug? Did she resent this woman and her money? Or did she feel sorry for her, despite her extravagant annual income? I felt wildly out of my element, so I finally shifted the police car out of park and began to drive.

∽

We'd only been driving for a few miles when Sarah spoke again: "Pull over, will you?"

I didn't question why; I did as she asked.

Gravel crunched beneath the patrol car's wheels as I pulled onto the unpaved shoulder of the county road. Sarah unfastened her seatbelt and exited the passenger side of the vehicle. Not sure what she was about, I turned off the engine and exited the car as well.

I rounded the front of the unmarked police car and joined Sarah on the other side. She stared out at the uninterrupted landscape. The horizon was remarkably barren. The area was relatively rural, if not exurbia. In Minnesota you'd expect more trees and less open, grassy fields. The horizon seemed to go on forever with the exception of a name-brand gas station positioned on one side of the county road.

"It's totally different," she spoke. "Our crime scene was bulldozed decades ago and covered with blacktop."

I leaned against the hood of the Crown Vic. "Shit. You're right. We couldn't re-stage anything if we tried."

Sarah hollowed out her cheeks. "Danika could be anywhere."

"Or maybe she got out," I offered. "Her sister said she was trying to leave."

"She didn't." Sarah spoke with finality. "The Res dragged her back like lobsters in a barrel."

I knew she was probably right. If you were trying to leave town to start a new life, you'd take more than a bicycle and the clothes on your back.

"What was it like?" I tentatively asked. "For you?"

Sarah rubbed absently at her forearm. "I don't have a lot of memories of that place. I mostly remember sharing a room with my sister and being annoyed when she used my stuff. I got a little melanin out of the deal, but not much else."

I'd grown up feeling solidly middle class in St. Cloud—no more, no less. Our family had shared a cabin up north with my dad's side of the family, and that's where we went on vacation. Some of my friends had gone on vacation to Disney World or Europe, but at least I'd known what a vacation was.

"Forrester doesn't want us spending more time on this," I reminded her.

There was nothing conspiratorial about his refusal. It was just Cold Case policy not to spend resources on re-opening a case without new evidence that might propel it farther than the original investigation.

Sarah began to walk back in the direction of the squad

car. Her words were low and mumbled, but I could still make them out: "Just another missing Indian girl."

Chapter Five

"I feel weird."

It had been an unexpectedly busy morning between the commute to and from Prior Lake, plus our meeting with Prior Lake PD and Jenny Laroque. Upon returning to the basement of the Fourth Precinct, Sarah and I had returned to our respective desks. After an activity-filled morning, my body and brain was ready for more.

We'd put to bed one open cold case in my short time with the division. It had been a sticky thing—not really proving the victim had been murdered or by whom—but we had been able to recover her identity. Jane Doe was now Tracey Green. No other tips had been called in since then, however. We'd assisted on a homicide case that had ended up being a suicide, helping to keep an innocent man from being unjustly incarcerated, but we hadn't reopened any of our own cases. I wasn't certain this drought in tips or new information was unusual, but it was starting to make me itch with inactivity.

"That time of the month?" Sarah asked.

"No, not that," I rejected. "I feel weird about this Danika Laroque case."

"There's not a case, remember?" she returned. "The Boss Man said to leave it be."

"I know what Forrester said," I grumbled. "But doesn't it make you feel weird that someone else is looking into this missing girl and we're not?"

"What do you want to do?" Sarah questioned.

"Talk to Melody Sternbridge."

"Then let's go." Sarah stood from her desk chair, looking determined and ready to launch into action. "Look up her home address."

I stared after my colleague. "Really?"

Sarah looked around the empty office space. The silence of our surroundings was nearly deafening. "You have someplace else to be?"

~

Melody Sternbridge lived in a modest-sized Arts & Crafts house in one of the trendier, up-and-coming neighborhoods in the Twin Cities. A single string of Christmas lights was attached to the triangle-pitched roof. The yards were small and the houses were close together, contributing to the dense suburban feel of the neighborhood. Unlike a cookie-cutter subdivision, however, the homes in this community were diverse in architectural style as well as family dynamics. Pride flags hung from front porches and yard signs proclaimed progressive statements. I would have felt at ease in such a visibly liberal community if not for the gold-plated badge attached to my hip. I was grateful for the unmarked police car, no matter how ancient of a vehicle, so Sarah and I didn't stick out any more obviously in the hipster enslave.

Sarah and I didn't speak as we walked up the narrow concrete walkway to Melody Sternbridge's front door. I rang the doorbell and winced when I heard the loud, aggressive bark of a large-sounding dog coming from inside the house. A sharp, censuring call of the dog's name—Brady, apparently—quieted the animal's protestations. A moment later, the door swung open and a large black snout shoved its way through the open doorway.

I heard a woman call the dog's name again, but the oversized mutt paid no attention. I stumbled backwards a few feet as the dog rushed out of the house. Its excited body crashed into me, sending me tumbling off the raised porch. My backside struck the frozen yard first, followed by the back of my head.

It was only laid out on my back that I got a good look at my assailant—a good-sized black lab with an overly wiggly tail.

"Oh my God," I heard a feminine gasp. "I'm so sorry."

I closed my eyes and winced in pain. I hadn't hit the ground hard enough to break anything or potentially concuss myself, but I suspected I'd have a bruised tailbone later.

"You okay, Miller?" Sarah asked. She remained undisturbed, if not a little amused, on the front porch.

I touched my fingers to the back of my head. Luckily, I had a thick skull. "Just peachy," I grumbled.

Hands grabbed at my arms and armpits, and I found myself being pulled to my feet. My backside felt damp from the dusting of snow that covered the front lawn, but overall, I would survive.

"I'm so sorry," the homeowner—Melody Sternbridge—apologized again. "We don't get a lot of visitors. Brady goes berserk when he hears the doorbell. He wouldn't hurt a fly though," she insisted. "He's just a big, dumb puppy."

I brushed at the back of my pants to dislodge any dirt and snow. "It's okay," I muttered.

Melody held the dog firmly by his collar—something she hadn't been able to do when she'd first opened the door apparently. Her concerned features turned curious. "Wait. You're from Cold Case, right?"

I nodded gruffly. "Detective Cassidy Miller," I introduced myself. "And this is my colleague, Dr. Sarah Conrad, from the Victim Advocate's office."

"Why don't we go inside," Melody offered before I could do much else. "No sense freezing our butts off."

It was significantly warmer inside of Melody Sternbridge's home, almost uncomfortably so. I took off my leather jacket even though I didn't know how long our visit might be. Melody ushered us away from the doorway to the small living room a few feet away. Sarah made herself at home on the couch. My backside still felt wet from being tackled by her dog, so I remained standing.

The front room was small and closed off with no open-floor planning to indicate what the rest of the house might look like. The space was cozy, even without the uncomfortably warm thermostat. Her furniture looked second-hand, yet eclectic enough to look purposefully vintage rather than run-down. Carefully curated knickknacks highlighted the mantle of a faux fireplace and a coffee table probably constructed from reclaimed-wood.

Melody Sternbridge looked at home in the Instagram-ready space. With heavily rimmed eyes and a dusting of pink on her freckled cheeks, she looked as if she'd been expecting company. While I might lounge around in sweatpants and tank tops when not expecting visitors, her cable-knit sweater and high-waisted jeans looked straight out of a retail catalog. I'd only seen a flash of her hair when we'd met the previous day. Her copper-colored locks were long, curled, and parted to one side. The only un-styled thing about the woman might have been her bare feet and unpainted toenails against the hardwood floors.

"Let me just put Brady away and then we can talk," Melody excused herself.

She tugged on the excitable dog's collar, and with little additional coaxing, he laid down inside of a large kennel set up in a corner of the room. Melody fussed over the dog for a few more moments before she returned her attention to us.

"Sorry." Another apology. "He'd be in our hair or our crotches the entire time." She smiled, as if waiting for a reaction. When none came, she cleared her throat. "So what can I do for you?"

I got right to the point: "You went to Prior Lake and tried to speak with Danika Laroque's family."

The smile fell from Melody's lips. "That's not a crime, is it?"

"No, but it can be triggering for the victim's family," Sarah remarked. "Put yourself in their shoes. Your loved one has been missing for thirty years, and then suddenly a stranger shows up at your front door asking questions."

The podcaster's upper lip curled as if smelling something rotten. "I'd be grateful someone was still looking for her—that she hadn't been forgotten."

I asked the question that had been bothering me from the start: "Why this case?"

Melody's blue-green eyes drifted in my direction. "My podcast is called *Lost Girls*."

She spoke as if that justified or explained away everything.

"There are thousands of 'lost girls' in NamUS," Sarah noted, naming the National Missing and Unidentified Persons System.

"Fine," Melody said, tight-lipped. "I got a tip."

I stood a little straighter at the admission. "What?"

"Someone sent me a private message to one of my socials. It happens sometimes," she shrugged it off. "People get into the show, and they start recommending other unsolved cases I should look into next."

I could feel myself becoming agitated. "What was the tip?"

"It wasn't much," Melody allowed. "It described how an indigenous woman named Danika Laroque had gone missing in the early 1980s from this super rich tribe. It reminded me of a news story I read about Native American groups stripping members of their tribal status so their pieces of the financial pie would be larger. The less people in the tribe, the more money for everyone else. I thought maybe something similar, but more sinister, had happened to this girl."

"Danika went missing long before the SMSC had any money," Sarah noted with a shake of her head. "There would be no financial incentive behind her disappearance."

Melody nodded. "I realized that after I did some initial research. But by that point I was in too deep to switch gears. I couldn't just stop looking for her. Did you know that native women are killed and go missing at ten times the national average, yet only two percent of those cases receive federal attention?"

I folded my arms across my chest. "So how does this work? You highlight an unsolved crime and then advertisers give you money to promote their products on air?"

"Well, first of all, there's no 'air' for me to be broadcasting on." She used finger quotes to highlight my mistake. "This isn't some old-timey radio show."

"Whatever," I snorted. "You're making money off of this."

"So are you," she easily returned.

My nostrils flared. "Because it's my job."

"It's my job, too," she cheerily quipped.

"How dare you compare—." I cut my words short rather than tell this woman exactly what I thought about her and her so-called job. I took a deep, calming breath before I said something I would come to regret.

Melody raised her hands in the air. "I'm sorry. We got off on the wrong foot. Let me show you everything I've found so far. You'll see there's nothing nefarious about what I'm doing."

I was more than ready to storm out of Melody Sternbridge's house with little more than an unveiled threat to stay away from our cases, but curiosity overruled my pride. If she'd really found something that could move the stalled investigation forward, or even to justify re-opening the case, it would be worth my current annoyance to discover what she had to share.

. . .

Melody led Sarah and I downstairs into a partially finished basement. The space smelled clean—like fresh paint—unlike the dank Minnesotan basements where I'd underaged drank with my friends in high school.

She flipped a light toggle and the sub-level space filled with soft light. "This is where the magic happens." I could detect a hint of pride in her voice.

The room was uncluttered with only a painted wooden desk and an office chair. A large monitor, keyboard, headphones, and an oversized microphone occupied most of the desk's surface. I passed over the expensive-looking technology for a crowded bulletin board that hung from a far wall.

I scanned over the black and white images and printouts of old newspaper stories pinned to the corkboard display. "This is your research?" I asked.

Melody came to stand beside me. "It's more like an inspiration wall," she identified. "It's like a True Crime Pinterest board." She nodded in the direction of her nearby workstation. "Most of my research is stored on my hard drive."

"So what's your process?" Sarah asked. "How do you make a podcast episode?"

"Lots and lots of research," Melody said, looking away from the bulletin board to address my colleague. "Then I write the script and supplement my narration with a few interviews so it's not just me talking the whole time."

"Who have you interviewed so far?" I questioned.

Melody pursed her lips. "No one. No one will talk to me. It's strange, actually; normally people can't wait for their fifteen minutes of fame."

I found the information unsurprising given the SMSC's

alleged reputation for being private and closed off from outsiders.

She flicked her blue-green eyes in my direction. "Want to be my first interview, Detective?"

I barked out a humorless laugh. "Fat chance of that happening."

Melody's mouth twisted into a smirk. "What's the matter? Afraid of a little 'ol podcast?" She placed an unsolicited hand on my forearm. "Don't worry. I'll be gentle if it's your first time."

I unobtrusively freed myself from the unwanted touch and redirected the conversation. "You said you had information for us?"

"Right. It's all on my computer," Melody confirmed. "I can make a copy of it for you. It's not much right now, but it's probably more than what the initial investigation procured."

The offer was unexpected. "Oh, uh, yeah. That would be great."

Melody sat down at her workstation, and with a few clicks against her laptop's trackpad, she presumably transferred her research. She removed a flash drive from its USB port and held it out for me.

When I reached for the slim device, Melody pulled it back. "*Quid pro quo*, Detective Miller."

I furrowed my brow. "I'm not sharing police files with you."

There wasn't much of a file *to* share, but it would have been inappropriate either way.

Melody briefly considered my statement. "Then I want an interview. With you."

"I'm not doing that," I immediately rejected.

She raised a skeptical eyebrow and waved the thumb drive back and forth like a twisted game of Keep Away.

The action brought a scowl to my face, but I realized I had no leverage. "Fine. You can interview me. But if you ask a question I don't want to answer," I warned, "I'm not going to answer it."

A pleased look passed over the woman's features. "Fantastic. I'm not ready for you right now, but let's do something next week after I've had time to properly prepare."

I held out my hand again and waited for the thumb drive. But instead of handing over the information, she tapped the plastic drive against her pursed lips. "How do I know you're not going to take advantage of my kindness?" she questioned. "That you won't use me to get what you want and then ghost me when I come calling for that interview?"

I shrugged. "You know where to find me. Basement of the Fourth Precinct."

Her lower lip popped out into a deep pout. "You're supposed to threaten to put me in cuffs for withholding information."

My eyes narrowed at the woman. "Is this fun for you? This isn't some glossy Hollywood production. This is someone's sister and daughter and friend."

The playful look on Melody Sternbridge's face shifted to something more serious. "I know that," she said stiffly.

"Then stop acting otherwise." I couldn't help the growl in my tone.

Melody Sternbridge finally extended her hand, and with it, the flash drive. I grabbed the drive from her before she could play more games. I had no idea of the thumb drive's contents, but my cynical side anticipated nothing useful would be on the portable device.

I tucked the flash drive into my pants pocket. "Call the office when you're ready for the interview," I grumbled.

Melody nodded, but had no additional quips for either Sarah or myself. With nothing more to do, we left the basement and the rest of the too hot home.

Sarah didn't wait for the front door to close before asking me her question: "Was she *flirting* with you?"

I pulled on my leather jacket and popped the collar to cover the back of my neck. The outside temperature had dipped since our arrival, and it felt even more brisk after having spent time in Melody Sternbridge's sauna of a house.

"I have no idea what that was," I said in earnest.

Sarah stared at the front door and frowned. "I don't like it," she opined. "I'm the only one who gets to make you squirm."

"I don't *squirm*," I protested. Even though I was wildly in love with my girlfriend, Sarah did have an unwelcomed ability to make me uncomfortable when she wanted to.

"Whatever. You're like a worm on a hook, Miller." Sarah curled her lip and continued to stare up at the silent house. "Why didn't she flirt with *me*? What do you have that I don't?"

I touched my fingers to my pocket to be sure the flash drive was still there and began to stalk down the concrete walkway. I tossed my answer over my shoulder: "Sensible shoes and a girlfriend."

Chapter Six

I was still thinking about Melody Sternbridge and Danika Laroque when I caught the bus to Julia's condo at the end of the work day. As much as I hated to admit it, I'd outgrown public transportation. I needed a vehicle that could handle Minnesota winters; I would have to concede sooner or later and trade in my motorcycle for something with four wheels. I would never say that to Julia though. I would just show up one day with a car to park in her underground lot instead of my Harley.

I heard Julia's voice the moment I let myself into the condo: "Okay. Thank you for the call. Yes, I understand."

I wasn't expecting her home so soon, not that I wasn't over the moon to hear her voice after the day I'd had. Commuting to and from Prior Lake and then negotiating with a self-important social media celebrity had left me physically and mentally drained.

Julia sat at the dining room table with her cellphone in hand. She still wore the clothes she'd worn to work that day, which suggested she'd only recently arrived home.

I kicked off my work boots and left them in the front entry. "Is everything okay?"

I'd only caught the tail end of the conversation, but Julia's displeasure was palpable.

She passed her hand over her face. "Yes. It was just the fertility clinic. They're following up."

"Oh, yeah?" I hoped my voice hadn't cracked. "Did you make an appointment?"

"No." A frown settled onto Julia's beautiful features. "The timing couldn't be worse. I'm still sorting out my father's affairs. My mother isn't settled at a new facility yet. I've just put in my two-week notice at the public defender's office, and then I'll need to establish myself my new firm—."

"Julia." I cut her off before she could completely spiral out. I'd heard all of these excuses before. "Do you want a baby?"

My question effectively silenced her. I watched her work the muscles in her throat and jaw. "Yes," she said thickly. "Terribly so."

"Then the timing is perfect."

Her eyes squeezed shut as if to dam any unwanted emotions. The rest of her body was similarly tense.

I took a few tentative steps closer to where she sat. "It's only the first of many steps," I tried to appease her. "Let's see the doctor about freezing your eggs, and then we'll go from there."

Julia opened her eyes. Warm caramel-colored irises stared back at me. "We?" she echoed. The single word sounded hopeful rather than critical.

"I mean, I guess I shouldn't presume anything." I stumbled over my words. "If you want me to be there. If you want or need my help."

Julia's eyes didn't stray from my face. "You want to have a baby with me?"

When we'd been in Embarrass, I hadn't really had time to properly reflect on her $10,000 down payment for the procedure. The personal check had caused the Embarrass police to believe she'd hired a hitman to kill her father. At the time, I'd been too focused on clearing Julia of any wrongdoings that the end result—a live, human baby—hadn't been on my radar.

I didn't know if I wanted a baby. I had never played with dolls as a child. I hadn't considered what my wedding would be like, or if I even wanted one for that matter—all things I imagined most straight girls had done when they were young. But I wanted to be with Julia. She was the first and only thing I'd ever wanted. So, if she wanted to have a kid, I'd have to be on board with that, too.

I still hadn't answered her question. She stared, silent and waiting for my response.

I wet my lips. "I'd do anything for you."

∽

Julia's lacquered fingernails clicked erratically against the plastic arm of the hard-backed chair in which she sat. Her restless knees perceptively bounced, reminding me of how I'd felt in the moments before we'd first met the woman who would eventually become my therapist. But we weren't in the waiting room of Dr. Susan Warren's office; we sat in the office of a different kind of doctor in a facility in a different part of town.

After signing in with a receptionist, it had only been a short wait—too short, I thought—before the two of us were ushered down a long hallway to wait in the fertility doctor's private office. I'd been fully prepared to bully my way into the doctor's office to support Julia during her consultation, but the receptionist hadn't asked any questions about who I was or why I would be accompanying Julia beyond the waiting room. It was honestly a little disappointing.

I rested my hand on top of Julia's to still and silence the plastic ticking of her fingernails striking the arms of the chair.

She offered me a small, apologetic frown. "I'm sorry."

"It's okay," I reassured her. "Just remember to breathe."

It was a big ask. *Just breathe.*

I kept my hand on top of hers and stroked the pad of my thumb across the top of her hand and the fine bones of her wrist. Her eyes shut and I heard her quiet exhale. I was surprised at how calm I felt. I'd never been in a situation like this before, but maybe seeing how rattled Julia was had unlocked a necessary strength within myself. I could be strong for her. I could be her rock when everything else seemed so unstable.

"You've got this," I murmured. "One bite at a time."

Julia's eyes remained closed, but a small smile appeared on her pursed lips. "We've been eating a lot of elephants lately."

"Are you calling me fat?" I joked.

Her eyes opened at that and they flicked in my direction. "Will you still want me when I'm fat?"

"Babe, you'll be pregnant. Not fat."

I swallowed hard when a lump leapt in my throat. Shit. *Pregnant.* A pregnant Julia. I exhaled loudly as if giving birth myself. *Pregnant.* I cleared my throat and shifted in my chair. The sterile doctor's office seemed to have grown warmer in the past few moments.

The change in my body language didn't go unnoticed. Julia shifted in her own chair and turned toward me. "Are you okay, dear?"

Before I could muster a single syllable, the door to the private office swung open and a man—presumably Julia's fertility doctor—walked in. "Sorry to have kept you waiting," he apologized.

He was younger than I expected, but I was confident that Julia had thoroughly vetted whomever was in charge of her being able to have a baby. I involuntarily swallowed. *Baby.* Infant. Child. *Fuck.* A heaviness settled on my chest like a Kevlar vest.

The man sat in the high-backed leather office chair; a large wooden desk divided the space between us. He flipped through several folders on his desk before settling on the one he desired. He seemed to consult some notes before finally acknowledging that there were two women, not one, in the room.

The doctor's grey-blue eyes trained on me. "Hello."

"Hey," I tightly returned.

Julia took it upon herself to introduce me: "Dr. Bryant, this is my partner, Cassidy. I hope it's okay that she sits in on our meeting today."

"Of course," the doctor readily approved. "It's good for both of you to be on the same page and have an opportunity to ask any questions or vocalize any concerns before moving forward." He looked purposefully in my direction. "Do you have any questions right now?"

I had about a billion questions, but I doubted the doctor could answer any of them. Was I ready to co-parent? Would I be any good at it? Would the kid even consider me their parent if I wasn't biologically involved? The heaviness on my chest intensified.

"What, uh, how does this work?" I stumbled on my question.

"Harvesting the eggs?" he asked.

I nodded. I knew, in theory, how babies were made, but this was new territory.

"Well, after today's meeting, we'll schedule a baseline ultrasound just to make sure everything looks okay. Then we'll start stimulation hormones. We can start that as soon as your next menstruation cycle," he noted. "The medications will stimulate the ovaries into producing multiple eggs, not just one. You'll come back for frequent monitoring between that initial ultrasound and the actual procedure."

I hadn't realized the preparation would be so intricate. I hadn't given much thought to it; I hadn't considered the procedure ever. But if pressed, I'd probably believed a doctor could just dig around in there whenever to extract eggs. The more I thought on it though, the more it made sense. It wasn't like women just bebopped around with a pile of unfertilized eggs in their bodies like an Easter basket or something.

"Would you like to schedule the surgery now?" Dr. Bryant asked.

I sucked in a sharp, audible breath without intending to. Julia glanced in my direction. I forced a smile to my lips, but showed no teeth. I continued to focus on breathing through my nose as an unexpected wave of nausea wracked my seated form.

"We use the word 'surgery,' but egg retrieval is minimally invasive," the doctor insisted, as if sensing my mildly veiled panic. "The procedure itself lasts only ten to fifteen minutes, and that includes administration of anesthetic. No scars, no stitches, and a short recovery time," he assured. "Some of our patients are even able to go back to work the day after the procedure."

"How convenient," I managed to mutter.

"Following retrieval, the eggs will be taken to an embryology lab to be frozen," the doctor described. "They'll stay in our in-house long-term storage tanks until you're ready for them."

The doctor's features began to soften and blur at their edges. The invisible weight on my chest had become unbearable. I worried I might pass out where I sat if not for Julia's palm resting on my knee.

"I'm not ready to make an appointment just yet," Julia decided. "I'll have to consult my calendar to see when I'm available."

The doctor bobbed his head. "Of course. The decision is totally up to you and your deposit won't expire. I only caution you not to wait until you think it's convenient or when the timing's right. In my experience, if you're waiting for that to happen, you might never go through with the pregnancy."

Julia rose from her chair and I followed suit. After thanking and shaking hands with the doctor, we removed ourselves from his private office.

We didn't speak on the way out. Julia remained silent until we were alone in the elevator. Even without looking in her direction, I could tell she was observing me. I could feel her eyes appraising me, looking for something.

Julia pressed the button for the lobby floor. "This isn't freaking you out?"

"I'm terrified," I admitted. "I have absolutely no experience with any of this. I'm a fish out of water here." There was no use pretending otherwise. "But I love you. And I know how much love you have to give. I can't be selfish and hog all of it for myself."

Julia regarded me with an acute intensity. "Are you getting everything you need from me? And I don't just mean orgasms," she noted before I could make a snarky comment. "I don't want you to feel neglected or like a check box that needs to be ticked."

"You're awfully good at ticking my box."

Julia frowned. "Cassidy. Be serious, please."

Julia's daily schedule was already compromised. She worked long days at the public defender's office and had suggested that her new position at Grisham & Stein would be even more taxing. Oftentimes she had more paperwork to consult after dinner while I watched mindless television before she shut everything down, exhausted, to go to bed. I didn't reasonably see how she would be able to add a newborn to that schedule, plus regularly visit her mother once she was re-homed closer to us, but this wasn't the time for me to bring that up.

"A date," I proposed. "Saturday. Let me plan everything."

I saw her small frown of hesitation. My girlfriend was terrible about letting go of control.

"What are you hoping that will achieve?" she questioned.

"I don't have an agenda, and it's not a test," I promised. "I only want to spend time with you. Have *fun* with you. Think you can handle that?"

The elevator lurched when we reached the ground floor.

"I suppose I've earned a little down time," she seemed to reason with herself.

I couldn't help my juvenile smirk. "I wouldn't mind a little down time, if you know what I mean."

Julia surprised me by cupping me hard over my jeans. I sucked in a sharp breath for an entirely different reason than when my breathing had become labored in the doctor's office.

She lowered her voice even though we were the only ones in the elevator: "Play your cards right, Marine, and you'll get all the *down time* you can handle."

Chapter Seven

Going on a date with Julia was a little less dramatic these days now that we lived together. I could still leave and pretend to be picking her up with a bouquet of flowers, but Julia was too practical for those kinds of chivalrous gestures. She'd always been the one to drive since she refused to ride on the back of my Harley, so anything that might mimic a more traditional date with accepted roles had never really been reality for us.

At the start of our relationship, I'd been so fixated on getting her to go on dates with me that I hadn't been able to enjoy the organic, unforced way in which our partnership had evolved and grown. We hadn't even had a proper second date before exchanging the L-word. I knew we didn't require antiquated gestures and rituals, but it was the only way I knew how to get Julia to loosen the stranglehold she typically held over the power dynamics in our relationship. Only when she agreed to go on a *date* was I allowed to surprise and treat her.

I waited in the living room while Julia finished getting

ready. I hadn't revealed my plans to her despite her repeated efforts to cajole those details from me, but I had given her instructions on what to wear. While the typical Midwesterner was probably most comfortable in jeans and a sweatshirt, Julia favored dresses and fitted skirts. While I had no complaints about the leg-baring outfits, it wouldn't quite work for my plans for us that day.

I hopped to my feet when Julia entered the room. She flashed an indulgent smile as she finished fastening small, silver hoop earrings. "Thank you for your patience, darling," she approved. "I know you said nothing fancy, but I just couldn't decide what to wear."

Her sweater and jeans combination was sensible, but somehow she'd managed to make the normally relaxed outfit choice look expensive. Her dark blue jeans hugged every modest curve as though they'd been tailor-made for her. The sweater was probably cashmere, and more expensive than any single clothing item I owned, but it was about as casual as Julia could manage if we were actually leaving the condo.

"Good things come to those who wait, right?" I returned.

She balanced on one foot and then the next as she slipped into ankle-high leather boots. "That depends," she remarked. "Am I going to *like* whatever we're doing or wherever we're going on this date?"

"I have absolutely no idea," I said in earnest.

Julia arched an eyebrow. "You're not sure?"

I shrugged. "If you're the kind of woman I think you are, you'll be into it."

She smirked at my response and started to head for the door. "That's clever."

"Is it?" I questioned.

She nodded. "Now I have no choice but to like it."

I took her hand in mine and kissed her knuckles. "You'll like it."

∽

"Figure or hockey skates?"

If Julia was surprised that our date was to take place at a local indoor ice rink, her features didn't give her away. When we'd been packing up her childhood home in the previous weeks, I'd lamented how many typical Minnesotan activities we hadn't yet done together. I wanted to be greedy with her time and blast through my To Do list, but she'd reassured me at the time that we had all of our lives to tackle that list. It was exactly the kind of thing I'd wanted to hear from her, but I still couldn't wait to start checking off activities.

"Guess," she seemed to dare me.

I didn't take long with my decision. "Hockey."

One might have expected, based on her refined, polished exterior, that Julia herself was delicate like a figure skater. But from what I knew of her childhood, she'd been a tomboy: climbing trees, fishing in ponds, skinning her knees. Julia wouldn't have learned how to skate with figure skates and their befuddling toe pick. She would have skated on frozen northern Minnesotan ponds with the same kind of skates as her younger brother, Jonathan.

I hooked pinkie fingers with Julia while we waited in line to rent our skates. The indoor rink was warm enough that we didn't need heavy jackets, hats, or gloves.

Julia looked down at our lightly locked hands. "Enjoying yourself, dear?"

Her tone was bright and slightly teasing.

"I'm totally geeked," I wasn't ashamed to admit. "I feel like I missed out on so much being in the military—like ten years of my life was stolen. I missed out on being young and having fun. *This* is what I should have been doing in my early twenties," I said emphatically, "taking my girlfriend ice skating."

Julia smiled, no longer teasing me or my exuberance. "I'm happy you finally get to do these things. And I'm even happier that I'm the person you get to do them with."

"You don't think it's corny?" I worried. "Ice skating and holding hands and hot chocolate? Like we're starring in our very own Hallmark Christmas movie?"

"None of us has a maple syrup company or a Christmas tree farm that needs saving, so I think we'll be alright."

My mouth fell open a little at her statement. "Wait. Do you *actually* watch those?"

Julia curled her upper lip, but otherwise looked unaffected by my accusation. "Not everything I do has to be highbrow. I'm allowed to eat ice cream from the container and watch mindless TV, aren't I?"

"Of course!" I hastily agreed. "In fact, you've just added something new to our bucket list."

Julia smirked as my excitement returned, but she allowed me the indulgence of just having fun. But in many ways, she was giving that grace to herself as well. Between my PTSD, her chronic stubbornness, and the drama of her father—first his criminal case, then the guardianship trial over her mother, and finally the suspicious nature of his sudden death—so much of our relationship had been interrupted by unfortunate circumstances. Maybe we were finally getting a reprieve from all of that drama. I thought we deserved a break, at least.

We brought our rented ice skates to a freestanding bench adjacent to the community rink. Beyond the high plexiglass walls, couples and families with small children skated in a slow, wide loop along the boards. A pop version of a classic Christmas song blared over the PA system.

Julia sat down on the metal bench and removed her boots. She shoved her feet into the hard-shelled skates and began to tighten the long laces. When I didn't immediately sit beside her to do the same, she looked up at me.

"Is something wrong, dear?"

I chewed on the inside of my lip. "This is going to sound crazy, but can I do that for you?"

"Tie my shoes?" she questioned.

"Lace up your skates so they're tight enough around your ankles," I said. The air inside of the indoor rink was relatively refrigerated, but I still felt my face grow hot. "My dad used to tighten my laces for me when I was little. I ... I've always wanted to do that for someone else."

The critical look on Julia's features softened. "Of course, darling. You can tighten my skates for me."

I didn't doubt that Julia's fingers were strong enough to wedge beneath the nylon laces to pull them tight so her skating would be better stabilized. But I liked the idea of being able to do something for her. She was fiercely independent and rarely asked for help, even from me. She hardly let me pay for things, and she was the one to chauffeur me around. It felt good to do this.

I stood before Julia and grabbed her right foot. I trapped the blade of her skate between my knees so I had better leverage to tighten her laces. My request wasn't the result of a foot fetish—although Julia did have beautiful feet. It was actually very practical. If your laces were too loose, your ankles would rock back and forth when you tried to skate. Floppy ankles were not compatible with ice skating.

Julia was quiet while I worked, cramming my stiff fingers beneath the laces and pulling so hard that either the laces or my fingers might break. I looped the long laces around her ankle twice and then proceeded to tie off her right skate with a double knot.

"I think—." Julia cut her statement short.

I paused long enough to glance up at her.

"I didn't mean to speak aloud," she revealed.

I arched a quizzical eyebrow with the toe of her skate's blade still wedged securely between my knees. "What's up?"

Julia looked hesitant; her mouth couldn't quite settle on either a smile or a frown. "I think," she cautiously continued, "that you'd make a wonderful parent."

My fingers shook a little as I moved to her left skate. "Y-You do?"

"I can imagine you tying our children's skates tight," she said quietly. "Helping so they wouldn't fall on the ice."

I began to feel lightheaded—probably from having my head tilted down for so long while I tightened Julia's skates, I reasoned. I was too caught up with the new word to appreciate the compliment. Somehow we'd gone from *baby* to *children*.

I finished lacing Julia's left skate. I set her blade firm on the spongy-rubber flooring that surrounded the indoor rink. "Tight enough?" I asked. I was grateful that my voice still sounded like me.

I could tell Julia was carefully observing me and my reaction. *Was I going to freak out?* Did I want the same things as her in the future?

Julia dropped her scrutinizing gaze from my face down to her feet. She seemed to flex her feet inside of the ice skates. "My circulation has been sufficiently cut off," she quipped, "so I think we're good."

I sat down on the cool metal bench to exchange my own boots for skates. Julia waited for me. She stretched out her legs in front of her, stabbing the back of the rounded blades into the black padded floor.

"You've got to let them fall," I finally spoke.

"Sorry?"

"Kids. When they skate," I grunted. I shoved my right foot deep into my rented skate. "You can't always keep them from falling. They've got to be able to pick themselves back up, you know?"

I glanced in Julia's direction. Her caramel-colored eyes looked a little watery. She rapidly blinked, but a few tears seemed to get caught in her long eyelashes.

"Are you okay?"

She smiled wetly and wiped away the moisture from her cheeks. "Yes, dear. Thank you."

"Oh. Okay. Good?" I struggled.

Julia stood from the bench and took a few unsteady steps in her skates. "Come on, Miss Miller. Time to impress me with your skating skills."

I stepped out onto the ice rink and took an initial, tentative stride. I hadn't been skating in a number of years—close to a decade—but I knew that it wouldn't be long until muscle memory kicked in. Julia shuffled onto the ice behind me. I wondered about the last time she'd been skating. I had a hard time picturing her going ice skating in Embarrass by herself, but maybe she'd gone all the time.

I flipped my hips and spun on the ice to face her. She stayed close to the ice rink's plexiglass boards with a leather-gloved hand hovering over the waist-high wall.

"How are your skates?" I asked.

She didn't look in my direction. "They're fine."

I dug the front of my blades into the ice and pushed off to skate backwards next to her. Julia's own steps were small, shaky, and unsure.

"Don't pick up your feet," I instructed. "Let the skates do the work."

I heard Julia's sigh. "Cassidy, you look like a race horse at the starting gate." She waved at me with the gloved hand not ghosting over the hockey boards. "Go skate a few laps and get it out of your system."

"But, I—."

"*Go*," she told me. "Then come back and skate with me like a regular person."

I assumed Julia wanted to acclimate herself to the new environment without me hovering next to her, so I did as I was told. Despite my better judgment, I left her by the hockey boards to skate a few independent laps. I crossed my right foot over my left to make a sharp, crisp turn around the first corner. The sound of sharp blades cutting into the ice was familiar and comforting, transporting me back to simpler days. Gaining confidence, I skated faster in a wide loop around the oval rink. I bypassed slower, less skilled skaters, but left enough room to not startle them into falling.

I quickened my pace so that my long, wavy hair flew loose behind me. We were inside, but my speed had created a brisk wind that bit at my exposed skin. I breathed in deeply, enjoying the familiar smell of the cold ice. The distinct scent took me back to my childhood of skating on frozen ponds that my dad had cleared for my cousins and me. We would spend hours on the makeshift rinks until our cheeks were red and our toes and fingers were frozen.

I maintained the elevated speed until my upper thigh muscles and ankles began to burn. Ice skating used decidedly different muscles than running on the indoor track at the police academy or swimming in the pool. I slowed down without fully stopping and looked around the rink in search of Julia. The skating complex was busy, but not so crowded that I might lose her among the other skaters. She continued to skate close to the wall of the rink, but her erect figure appeared more confident than when I'd left her. I crossed the center of the rink with even, elongated strides to return to her side.

I pulled up beside her and skated with my hands behind my back. "Hey, pretty lady."

"Hey, yourself," she returned.

"Thanks for letting me get in a few laps. I didn't realize I needed to do that," I admitted.

"You were practically vibrating," Julia noted. "Jonathan would get the same look when we went skating as a family," she described. "All he wanted to do was go fast."

Julia held out her hand to me. When our fingers loosely

intertwined, she let me guide her away from the safety of the plexiglass boards and their brightly colored advertisements.

"You're doing good," I praised. "You look more confident."

"I might have to come back by myself and practice," she wryly observed. "I had no idea you were such a professional."

"You can let me be better than you at something," I said, only half teasing. "It's allowed."

I heard her scoff. "Not a chance."

I abruptly stopped before a small boy could crash into our legs and take us down like bowling pins. He and a few other children were apparently playing tag, with little regard for the other skaters on the ice.

I saw Julia wobble. Her hands flailed at her sides as she struggled to stay upright. I hooked my arm around her waist to keep her from falling.

"Goodness!" she breathed out in annoyance. "Where are their parents?"

"Sure you want one of those?" I lightly joked.

"Not one of those specific children, no."

I let go of Julia's waist when I was confident she'd regained her footing. We continued to skate after our close encounter. Each lap around the rink became a little faster than the one before. Predictably, Julia had pretty much mastered the whole ice skating thing in record time.

"So what's next after this?" she posed.

I twisted my features in mock offense. "What? Ice skating isn't enough?"

I heard her dark chuckle. "You know it takes much more to satisfy me, Miss Miller."

Julia twisted to skate backwards in front of me. She'd

started to get a little cocky, a little reckless on the ice. Earlier she'd been clutching the edge of the rink like a lifeboat lost at sea, but now she was literally skating circles around me. When she wobbled for a second time, I wasn't quick enough to catch her. Her arms flailed for only a second before she fell onto her backside.

I bit back a laugh. Julia looked stunned as if she couldn't believe her body had betrayed her. "Ouch. Are you okay?"

Julia wiped her right palm across the top of her jeans, leaving a snowy residue behind. "I guess that's my punishment for bad mouthing your date," she mumbled.

I reached down to help lift her off the ice, but when I grabbed her outstretched hands and pulled, Julia recoiled and cried out in pain.

"Shit. What's wrong? Are you hurt?" I panicked.

Julia's gloved fingers curled around her left wrist. "Something's not right."

I dropped down to my knees, not caring that the icy surface would seep through my jeans. "Here. Let me see," I urged.

Julia's body seemed to fold in on itself. Her shoulders hunched forward and she tucked her hands into her waist. "It hurts," came her quiet complaint.

"I know, baby," I said gently. "Which is why you should let me see it."

I was no doctor, but between my time in the military and on the police force, I did have some basic first responder training.

Julia's painted lips flattened into a pained grimace. She raised her left hand and extended her arm toward me. Others continued to skate around us, providing us a wide berth, but no one actually stopped to help or see if we were both okay. So much for Midwest Nice.

I started at her elbow and worked my way toward her fingers, feeling the solid bones between my probing fingers. When I reached her wrist, Julia hissed and yanked her hand away.

"That's not good," I observed with a frown. "I'm guessing a sprain. Maybe even broken bones."

"Don't be ridiculous," Julia clipped. "I've never broken a bone in my life."

"I'm taking you to the hospital."

"I'm fine," she continued to stubbornly resist.

"You have no choice."

I'd dragged my buddy Terrance Pensacola halfway across an Afghani desert, but I didn't possess the strength or skating skills to scoop Julia off the ice. I knew she couldn't sit in the middle of the ice rink forever though. I popped back up on my skates and circled behind her. Dropping to one knee, I ducked my head and shoulders beneath her right arm. When I stood back up, I lifted Julia to her feet.

Thankfully, Julia didn't continue to put up a fight. I wondered if the shock or the adrenaline from her fall was starting to fade, only to be replaced with pain. Under ordinary circumstances, she would have been unnerved to be making a scene. She must have really been hurt.

We slowly shuffled from the center of the rink to one of the side exits. This time I didn't ask for permission to take off her skates. After I removed my own, I all but threw our rented skates at the person working at the skate return booth.

Julia looked unsteady trying to put on her ankle-high

boots. Again, I didn't give her the opportunity to reject my assistance. I stooped down and helped her step into the shoes.

I heard her heavy sigh above me.

I looked up to her beautiful face. "What is it? What's wrong?"

"You own me a hot chocolate."

"Let me take you to the hospital, and I will *bathe* you in hot chocolate," I bargained. "Mini marshmallows and everything."

Julia's eyes closed and her head tilted forward. "Okay."

Chapter Eight

Afghanistan, 2012

We've been driving for several hours. Pensacola periodically slips in and out of consciousness. When he wakes up, he tells me about the time his little cousin hit him in the head with a golf club when he was six. It had been an accident, but it had left him with a visible scar on his forehead. I've heard the same story about his childhood so many times, it's starting to feel like it's mine.

I haven't seen any other vehicles on the road since we commandeered the Jeep. It's a small blessing. If I'd been in a different state of mind, I would have thought to steal the dead men's outfits along with their vehicle. If I had been thinking more clearly, I would have at least dragged their bodies farther away from the road. It would have been a waste of energy to dig them shallow graves, but I worry now that someone will see their bodies and come looking for us.

But hindsight is 20/20 and all that.

We're going to get caught. There's no reason why we

shouldn't. A blonde girl from Minnesota and a Black kid from Detroit aren't exactly camouflaged in a place like this. It makes me think of the ending to the film *Night of the Living Dead*. The protagonist survives a zombie outbreak only to be on the wrong end of a military sniper rifle at the film's end.

But we've made it so far. We survived the dirty bomb that killed the rest of our friends. We endured innumerable days baking under the unforgiving Afghani sun in the bombed out safe house. We've humped across who knows how many miles of barren wasteland.

I wipe at my stinging, tired eyes. My face feels gritty from dirt, sand, blood, and salt. It can't be much more. It can't take much longer. I don't think either of us has much more to give.

∽

Julia was disconcertingly quiet. She held onto her injured wrist, slightly slumped over at the waist. Sitting in the passenger seat of her Mercedes, the color seemed to have drained from her normally light olive complexion.

"We're almost there," I spoke aloud. The words were intended to assure her, but probably myself as well.

I had graduated top of my class at the police academy not that long ago. My precision driving had been one of the skills my instructors had found most impressive. But I was no longer trying to stand out from my mostly-male peers. I needed to get Julia to the emergency room.

"Come on, come on," I muttered at a particularly long red light. I tapped my fingers against the leather steering wheel with impatience.

My palm struck the car horn the moment the light turned

green and the car in front of me didn't move. "Get the fuck off your phone!"

There was no way the other driver could hear me, but I couldn't help myself.

A light touch to my forearm had me curbing my road rage. "I'm not going to die, darling."

"I know. But it's all my fault. We could have done anything, but I'm the one who insisted we go ice skating."

"It's not like you suggested we go sky diving, dear."

We arrived at the hospital a few minutes later. I illegally parked Julia's Mercedes in front of the emergency room entrance and rushed to the passenger side door. Julia swatted me away when I tried to unbuckle her seatbelt.

"Cassidy. Take a breath."

I stood back rather than trying to carry her through the automatic doors. Nervous energy buzzed through my body. It was of the side effects of my PTSD. For other people, once the danger or surprise was over, their body and brain reset. Their hearts no longer raced. They no longer felt panicked. I, however, continued to struggle with my fight or flight reflex.

Julia resumed holding her left wrist close to her body. We walked through the automatic doors together, but once we entered the building, I bolted towards the reception desk.

"My girlfriend hurt her wrist," I said in a rush. "We were ice skating and she fell. I think it could be broken, but there could be tendon damage, too."

The receptionist handed me a thin stack of forms attached to a clipboard. "Fill these out."

I stared dumbly. "But she's hurt. She needs your help."

"Fill these out," the woman told me, "and we'll get to her in time."

"In time?" I squeaked.

"Cassidy." Julia's voice called to me. I whipped around to see her standing a few feet behind me. "Would you be a dear and park the car?"

Julia Desjardin was the most formidable person I'd ever met. She stomped around court rooms in pencil skirts and skyscraper heels that would have me spraining both ankles. She was fierce. Powerful. Both in public and in private. She'd dominated me in the bedroom more times than I could count. But the woman who stood in the lobby of the Minneapolis emergency room didn't resemble that person. This version of Julia needed me to get my shit together.

My pulse throbbed in my neck. "Yeah. I can do that."

∽

I'd had to circle the hospital's parking structure a few times before I finally found an empty spot. Apparently a Saturday in the weeks leading up to Christmas was prime time for accidents and doctor appointments. Julia had been admitted while I'd driven around, so I'd had nothing to do but sit and wait. Her injury obviously wasn't life threatening, but that thought didn't put me at ease. Time passed slowly in the hospital waiting room. I could have gone for a walk—done a few laps around the hospital complex—but I didn't want to miss the moment Julia was released.

It was late by the time the double doors swung open and

Julia reappeared. I immediately stood up on legs made stiff from inactivity. I held two cardboard coffee cups in slightly clammy hands.

Julia walked in my direction. As she approached, my eyes fell to the canvas sling that held her left arm immobile.

I licked my lips. "So?"

"It's not broken," she told me. "Just a bad sprain. I'll be healed up in a few weeks." She looked at the two cups I continued to hold. "What's that?"

"Hot chocolate. I got it from a vending machine," I said. "It's terrible."

It had seemed like a cute and funny thing to do at the time, but as it had cooled, the dark liquid had coagulated into a thick, murky mess.

"Will you be terribly offended if I take a raincheck?" Julia posed.

I dumped the untouched cups of hot chocolate into the nearest garbage can.

～

We didn't speak on the ride back to Julia's condo. She let me drive the Mercedes without much fanfare, but I wondered how amenable she would be to me helping her with other things. Grocery shopping? Cleaning? Making meals? Showering? Getting dressed? If she didn't take it easy, if she pushed herself too hard, she would only end up re-injuring herself. Accepting that one's body had limitations was hard enough for the average person. How would Julia fare?

When I'd been healing up in the VA hospital once

Terrance and I had returned to the States, I'd felt invincible compared to my good friend. The nurses had had a hell of a time keeping me in my bed. I could imagine Julia would be a similarly stubborn patient. Her wrist wasn't broken—her streak of not having a broken bone was still intact—why in the world would she slow down?

I parked the black sedan in Julia's designated parking spot in the condo's underground garage. I waited patiently for her to unbuckle her seatbelt and exit the passenger side of the car. I continually examined her face for signs of discomfort or struggle, but Julia had always had a better poker face than myself.

I didn't hustle to open doors I knew she could handle or push elevator buttons that she could do herself. She stared straight ahead, stone faced, as we rode the elevator to the upper level condo. I unlocked the front door, but only because I retained her key ring from driving her car. Julia wore her purse slung over her right shoulder. With her left arm secured in a sling, I privately wondered how she would have planned on getting to her keys.

Julia stood in the front foyer and slid out of one ankle boot and then the other. We'd missed dinner, but I no longer had much of an appetite. I watched Julia disappear in the direction of the bedroom. I remained in the entryway, full of indecision. Was I supposed to follow, or was I being too clingy?

I took my time with my own boots and my leather jacket. Julia had uncharacteristically left her shoes in the middle of the entryway; I moved them and lined them up with the other shoes in the foyer.

I'd just hung up my jacket in the front closet when I heard Julia call my name: "Cassidy?"

"Coming!"

The lights were off in the back bedroom. The sun had set hours ago, leaving Julia in the dark. No street lights, not even the moon or the stars, lit up the room. I found her standing in the center of the room, with her head tilted down.

"I'm here," I announced.

"I need your help." Her request was small, but important.

"Of course," I agreed in a rush. "What can I do?"

I heard her quiet sigh. "Undress me."

I knew she hadn't intended for the request to be sexy or intimate, but my breath still caught in my throat. I couldn't help it; she still gave me massive butterflies.

"I can do that."

I stood before her in the darkened bedroom. Her sweater was going to be a problem, or at least removing it without jostling her injured wrist, so I started with the top button of her jeans. I unfastened it and slid the front zipper down. I dropped to my knees and gently lifted her right leg so I could remove her sock. I did the same to her left foot. I grabbed the waistline of her jeans and shimmied them down her hips, thighs, and knees. Together, we repeated the same routine to remove her jeans as I'd done with her socks.

I sat up on my knees so I was at her bellybutton level. I lifted the bottom hem of her cashmere sweater. I couldn't help myself; I leaned forward and softly pressed my lips against the bare skin just above the waistline of her underwear.

Julia dropped her right hand to my hair. Her fingers

curled around the chaotic tendrils. I looked up to gauge how she was feeling, but the shadows in the room were too dark.

I peeled the front of her underwear down about an inch and placed another soft kiss against the newly exposed skin. I inhaled and took in the scent of her lotion, her fabric softener, and her womanhood. It was quite possibly my favorite combination.

I pulled down the front panel of her underwear a little more. I placed a soft kiss against her fragrant skin. "Is this okay?"

She breathed out a single word: "Please."

I slipped her underwear down the rest of her hips and thighs until they fell silently to the floor.

I held Julia by the back of her thighs and pressed my face against her. My eyes shut of their own volition as I held her. I felt the warmth of her body, the solidness of her form. I hadn't been able to get my emotions in check in the hospital, but now my heartbeat lowered and my mind became quiet.

Strong, needy fingers in my hair reminded me of my mission.

I nuzzled my nose along the thin strip of closely manicured hair until I reached her slightly protruding clit. I placed a gentle kiss against the tender nub before parting her lips. I swirled the tip of my tongue around the sensitive flesh. Fingers tightened in my hair, and I heard her sharp exhale.

Normally this was the moment where I'd dig my fingernails into her thighs or lift her off the ground and tumble into bed so I could properly fuck her. Instead, I shut my eyes. I slowed my breathing and my heart rate. I alternated between suckling her clit into my mouth and drawing slow, lazy circles with my tongue.

We'd had sex on practically every surface in her one-bedroom condo. We'd fucked in her law office and her parents' closet, in public parks and police cars. But had we ever done this before? Had it ever been soft and gentle and tender?

I left her sex momentarily to place soft, lingering kisses on her quivering thighs. I gently sucked on the sensitive flesh, but not hard enough to leave a mark.

I pressed the tip of my middle finger against her clit and looked up to her beautiful face. Her dark eyes fluttered shut and her lips slightly parted. I could feel her pulse throb through the sensitive nub. I pressed harder until her hips bucked forward and her thigh muscles twitched.

I placed another digit at the entrance of her weeping sex and slowly worked my finger inside. She was wet and ready for me. I took my time and slowly drew the single digit in and out. I slowly penetrated her as deep as my finger could reach before unhurriedly withdrawing.

"Cassidy." She sighed my name like a prayer. The fingers on her uninjured hand curled around the top of my shoulder. "That's perfect. Fuck me. Just. Like. That."

I could never deny her.

Her pussy muscles tightened around my finger. I resisted the selfish impulse to quicken my pace or intensify the force behind each penetration. I continued the slow but steady tempo between her thighs.

"Rub your clit," she commanded. "I want to see you cum."

I couldn't bite back my needy whine.

Obediently, my hand slipped past the waistband of my jeans and wiggled beneath my underwear. My fingers instinctively sought out my clit, which I began to rub with vigor.

I heard Julia's soft cry and the fingers around my shoulder tightened. "Oh, God."

I'd never been adept at multitasking. I tried to focus on my patient, measured tempo to bring Julia closer to orgasm, but her breathy cries, her sex clamped tight around my finger, combined with the frantic movement of my free hand against my clit, were making it next to impossible.

"I'm close," I inelegantly grunted.

"Me, too."

I didn't trust I would be able to get her there if I was preoccupied with my own orgasm. I yanked my hand out of my jeans and fell face forward into Julia's naked sex. I twirled the tip of my tongue around her clit before sucking it firmly into my mouth. I buried my finger deep in her pussy and curled my finger inside her. I pressed the flat of my tongue solidly against her clit and licked her hard, over and over again.

Fingernails pierced the thin material of my top. "Jesus," I heard Julia's groan.

I continued to undulate the flat of my tongue against her engorged clit. I drank greedily from her sex as my saliva combined with her arousal.

Julia's knees buckled as if she was still on ice skates, but this time I successfully kept her upright. I could feel the vibrations of her lower body like a miniature earthquake was rattling her foundation. Her mouth fell open, but no fully-formed words appeared.

The fingers around my shoulder eventually relaxed, but

Julia seemed to slump against me in exhaustion. Her breath came in uneven gasps. "You weren't supposed to do that."

"Make you cum that hard?"

She shook her head. "You didn't get to. You stopped."

"It's okay. I'll survive." I wiped at my cheeks with the back of my hand. "Better than hot chocolate?"

Julia's eyes seemed to narrow at the question. "You're not getting off that easily, Miss Miller."

I couldn't help my cocky grin. "Funny. I thought *you* were the one getting off easily."

The bedroom was dark with the exception of the pale moon outside. I'd successfully helped Julia exchange her clothes from the day for pajamas. Her nakedness had resulted in a minor delay, but neither of us had minded. I'd put my own pajamas on and had joined Julia in bed. Even though I would never describe Julia as clingy, she never slept completely on her side of the bed, especially after we'd been intimate. She rested with the length of her body tight against my own. Her bare feet pressed against my calf muscles.

I curled my body to press more solidly against hers. "I know it's just your wrist, but I kind of wish your doctor had put you on bed rest."

Julia's laughter filled my ears. Her arms tightened around me, but I heard a discernible hiss like she'd unintentionally tweaked her injured wrist.

"You've got to take it easy," I scolded her. "Doctor's orders."

Julia sighed deeply. "The one thing I'm terrible at."

I set my teeth into my lower lip before vocalizing my apprehension. "I'm sorry I freaked out earlier."

"You did no such thing," Julia denied.

"I wasn't exactly calm," I countered. I continued chewing on the inside of my cheek. "I normally perform much better under pressure."

"I'm sure you're a cool customer on the job," she said, simultaneously stroking my ego and my hair. "It's different when the person injured is someone you know though, someone you love."

I nodded beneath her loving touch. Idle, lazy fingers twisted my already wild curls. Typically Julia need only play with my hair for a few minutes before I passed out from the soothing, rhythmic touch. It was late, and my brain was exhausted from the day's unexpected events. And yet, a single thought bounced around in my head, refusing to let me fall asleep.

"You really think I'd be a good parent?"

"You don't see it?"

I shook my head. "I'm not very grown up myself."

"I think we'd make a good team."

"Good Cop, Bad Cop?" I guessed.

I could practically hear her roll her eyes. "I refuse to be Bad Cop."

I turned onto my side to face her. "We can take turns," I offered.

Julia toyed with collar of my t-shirt. "That's my one big fear," she admitted. "I'm not very fun."

"What? You're fun!"

Even in the darkened room I could see her look of disbelief.

"Remember that time with the kitchen faucet?" I offered. "Or skinny dipping at your family's cabin? That was fun."

"Those were all prompted by you, darling," she protested.

"How about when we carved those pumpkins?" I said. "That was all your idea."

Julia chewed on her lower lip, looking unmoved by my examples.

"When are you going to make an appointment for the initial ultrasound?" I asked.

Julia turned her gaze from me. I watched her flex her recently bandaged wrist. "I'm not sure now is the right time."

"You don't need two good wrists for that," I challenged.

"Maybe I was too hasty, too impulsive about the baby thing," she said. "My mother's care is only going to become more labor intensive as her dementia worsens. I had a busy schedule as a public defender, and I imagine it will only become more hectic when I start my new job."

I could hear in her words the myriad of reasons why the timing wasn't right. She was trying to convince herself that postponing was the smart thing to do. But this wasn't a decision for the brain; it was a decision for the heart.

I ran a single, careful finger along the ace bandage that wrapped around her wrist. "It's not selfish to want it all."

"No?" Her single-worded question was barely a whisper.

"Julia, I love you. And I want you to have it all. I want you to have whatever your heart wants."

"I want ... I want a baby." I heard her audible swallow, like she was working hard to keep her emotions in check. "I never thought I would feel this way. I've never had a maternal urge before. But now ... it's practically all I can think about."

I was still terrified about what this would mean for us.

And, selfishly, I worried I would take a backseat to all of her other commitments. But it wasn't like a baby would appear on our doorstep the next day. There would be time. We would make time.

I searched for her uninjured hand beneath the blankets and intertwined our fingers. "Then let's make a baby."

Chapter Nine

Stanley Harris hovered over my shoulder. "I think I know how we can recreate the crime scene—or at least the last place anyone saw Danika Laroque."

I swiveled around in my office chair. "The floor is all yours, Stanley."

"Okay. So we don't have any video footage, and our probable crime scene has been bulldozed," Stanley prompted as introduction. "We may not be able to reconstruct what that area looked like in the 1980s, but we can go back even earlier."

He set a silver laptop on my desk and opened the lid. Sarah left her own desk area to join us. It was a rare day where all three of us were in the office at the same time.

"I went to a workshop recently on geospatial information systems," Stanley explained. "We layered two-dimensional historic maps on top of contemporary maps. I figured I could probably apply the same principles to photography."

"I saw an artist do this," Sarah noted. "She hyper imposes historic photographs on top of what the area looks like today."

"That's art?" I naively stated.

"Fuck if I know. I went for the free wine and cheese," Sarah admitted with a shrug.

"So *anyway*," Stanley said loudly before we could get too off topic. "I was able to locate some old digitized photos of Prior Lake from their public library's website. I layered them over contemporary Google street views, and ..." He moved his fingers over his laptop's trackpad and clicked a few keys. "*Voilà*."

I leaned forward in my chair to better see the laptop's screen. Stanley had layered a sepia-colored photograph of an old storefront on top of what I assumed was what downtown Prior Lake currently looked like. The white men in the photograph wore vests and trousers and pageboy hats. Another man sat in a horse-drawn carriage.

"That's a pretty neat trick," I approved.

"This is much earlier in Prior Lake's history than what would be useful for us," Stanley described, "but I wanted to run it by you first to see if I should continue."

Captain Forrester still hadn't given us the go-ahead to move forward with the case, but I saw no harm in Stanley doing a little computer work while he babysat evidence at the Freezer.

"Knock yourself out," I approved. "By the way, was there anything interesting on that flash drive we got from Melody Sternbridge?"

Being relatively technologically inept, I'd immediately handed over the podcaster's research to Stanley.

He shook his head. "Nothing we didn't already know. It's mostly background information on the SMSC. Tribal history. A timeline of when the casinos started making money. A master list of the groups the SMSC have donated money to."

I frowned at Stanley's discovery. I should have insisted on seeing what was on the flash drive before agreeing to be interviewed for the woman's podcast. "Okay. Thanks."

The aging landline phone on my office desk jangled with an incoming call.

"Cold Case," I answered.

"Hi. Is Detective Miller there?" a male voice asked.

"Speaking."

"Detective, this is Brendon Azure with Prior Lake PD. I wanted to give you the heads up that Danika Laroque's bicycle was recently recovered."

I sat up straighter in my chair. I felt a little breathless. "*What?* Where?"

"In someone's yard on trust land. Folks were breaking ground to build the foundation for a new garage when their excavator dug it up."

"How do you know it belonged to Danika?" I asked.

Both Stanley and Sarah looked on with interest at the mentioning of the missing woman's name.

"Her family identified the bike," he said. "It's a bright yellow frame bicycle with a banana seat. Pretty distinctive."

"Any signs of human remains?" I asked. "Or the possibility of DNA on the bike?"

"Nothing but the bike was recovered. But they stopped digging as soon as the bike appeared," he noted. "We sent it to the lab for DNA, but that could take a while."

"No offense, but why did you get called about a bicycle?" I thought it peculiar that anyone would think to call the police over finding a bicycle buried in their yard.

"People around here are pretty sensitive about what they find in the ground," Azure gravely noted.

I bobbed my head in thought as I took in the new information. Captain Forrester would have no choice now. He'd have to let us fully investigate the missing persons case after this discovery.

"Do you need extra resources to look for more evidence?" I asked. "Cadaver dogs? Forensic teams? How can we help?"

There was a pregnant pause on the other end of the phone call before Azure spoke again. "Chairman Strong hasn't given us permission."

"Chairman Strong?" I echoed.

"He's the elected leader of the SMSC. They don't use words like sachem or chief anymore," Azure explained.

"And he's refusing to let Prior Lake PD investigate the disappearance and possible murder of one of his own people?" I instantly became suspicious.

"I told you. They've very private."

"Not good enough," I decided. "Can you get me in touch with Strong? I'd like to speak with him. Face-to-face if possible."

"I'll do my best," Office Azure said. "I'll be in touch."

I hung up with Azure feeling encouraged, but also perplexed. What were the chances that a cold case someone else had been digging into had randomly produced new evidence? Danika Laroque had been missing for close to thirty years with no new leads. Why was this happening now? And now that it was, I couldn't understand why the leader of the SMSC might refuse law enforcement access to this new, potential crime scene.

Her recovered bicycle might hold important DNA

evidence, especially since it had been buried rather than being tossed in a wooded area where it would have been exposed to the elements for thirty years. The fact that it had been buried, and not randomly found on the side of the road or ditched in a field somewhere, also confirmed foul play rather than Danika simply running away.

"What happened?" Sarah asked. "Did they find something?"

The office phone rang again, interrupting my thoughts with its shrill jangle. I assumed it was Azure getting back to me about a meeting with the Chairman. I held up a finger, bookmarking our conversation.

"Cold Case," I answered. "Miller speaking."

"Detective Miller?" A new voice—this one female—echoed through the receiver. "It's Melody Sternbridge."

"Shit." I swore without meaning to.

I heard her chuckle. "It's nice to talk to you again, too."

"Sorry," I uselessly apologized. "What can I do for you?"

"*Quid pro quo.* You still owe me an interview."

I wanted to swear again, but I knew it would have been unprofessional. "There was nothing on that flash drive," I told her. "Nothing that we didn't already know, at least."

"That wasn't the deal, Detective."

"I'm waiting for an important call," I excused myself.

Sarah or Stanley could easily field a return call from Officer Azure, but more than that, I really didn't want to go to this woman's house.

"You can't forward calls to your cellphone?" she challenged.

I doubted it was appropriate to record a podcast interview during work hours, but I didn't want to pass my limited free time—time that should be spent with Julia—at this woman's house. But, I suspected that Melody Sternbridge wasn't going to forget that I apparently owed her a favor. She would only continue to hassle me about an interview until I satisfied my part of the bargain.

I sighed deeply. "Fine. I'm leaving the office right now."

The front door of Melody Sternbridge's house opened before I had the chance to knock or ring the doorbell.

"They found Danika's bike."

Her statement caught me off guard. I was too surprised to deny the discovery or to give her a vague response about ongoing investigations.

"How did you—."

"Come in," she said gravely.

I thought she looked a little wild, standing on the other side of the threshold. Her copper-colored hair had worked itself free from the confines of a French braid. Her eyeliner was a little too pronounced. The cream colored sweater she wore was several sizes too big. She seemed to be drowning in the material.

I removed my leather jacket once I stepped inside her house. Like my previous visit, the temperature was uncomfortably warm. At least there was no evidence of her overly excitable dog.

"Where's your dog?" I asked.

"In the basement. I figured you'd appreciate not being tackled again."

I nodded, but I had more important questions that needed answers. "How did you hear about the bicycle?"

Melody's blue-green eyes shifted back and forth. "I didn't tell you the whole truth before," she disassembled. "I led you to believe that the person who first told me about Danika's disappearance was anonymous, but that's not really true. They *thought* they were being anonymous—they set up a fake social media account and everything—but I had a friend who's good with computers find their IP address. The call was coming from inside the house."

"Say that again?"

She arched an eyebrow. "You know ... the classic horror film trope? *Black Christmas*? *When a Stranger Calls*?" she supplied.

I shook my head. "Sorry."

"Not important," Melody readily dismissed. "My friend was able to track the IP address of the person who DM'd me. It came from a computer in Prior Lake. Specifically the SMSC's tribal land."

"That's not so suspicious," I observed. "If someone in your community went missing, wouldn't you want to find out what had happened to them? Reach out to every news media on the planet, even a podcaster?"

"But the fake account," Melody pointed out. "Why not just contact me as yourself instead of hiding?"

"How did you know it was fake?" I questioned.

"The account had been created the same day they contacted me. No followers. No profile picture," she listed.

Social media was like an alien planet to me, so I would have to take her word for it.

"Did this person tell you about Danika's bike being found?"

Melody nodded. "Same fake profile. They messaged me a few minutes ago. Who told you?"

"Brendon Azure. He's the tribal liaison officer for Prior Lake PD."

"Do you think he could be our fake profile user?" Melody posed.

I didn't particularly enjoy her word choice. There wasn't an *our* in this scenario. As much as she wanted to insert herself, she wasn't part of this investigation.

I shook my head. "Not likely. He'd be risking his job leaking information like that to an outsider."

"There can't be too many people who know about the bike," Melody speculated.

"Probably more than you think. They're a small, tight-knit community," I observed. "I don't know if you've ever lived in a small town before, but gossip travels pretty fast. I *do* find it suspicious that they discovered the bike in the first place, however," I observed. "No new leads for thirty years. *You* come along and suddenly someone digs up her bike? That's quite the coincidence."

Melody looked taken aback, wounded really, rather than offended. "What are you suggesting? That I planted a bicycle on the reservation?"

I held up my hands. "Hey, I'm not making any accusations here. I just think the timing of this is interesting."

Melody hollowed out her cheeks. "How would I know what kind of bicycle she had?"

"Again, not making any accusations," I clarified. "It was only an observation."

"Are you going to arrest me?"

"Geez." I rolled my eyes. "Forget I said anything, okay?"

"Are you going to Prior Lake to see the bike?" she demanded.

"It's not there anymore. Prior Lake PD sent it for DNA testing."

Melody folded her arms across her chest. "*Quid pro quo*, Detective."

"Every time you say that, I can't help but think of Hannibal Lecter."

An impressed look crossed Melody's features. "So you're not completely pop culture illiterate."

I wanted to defend myself that I'd been holed up at a military base for eight years where we only got second-run movies, but I had no reason to share those kinds of details with this woman.

"New proposal," Melody announced. "Let me tag along on your next trip to Prior Lake, and I won't make you do the interview."

My knee-jerk reaction was to automatically reject her. But at the same time, I was loathe to sit in front of a microphone where my recorded voice could be cut and edited into misleading sound bites.

I didn't know when next I might be in Prior Lake, especially if Chairman Strong refused our help. I hesitated before giving her a response.

"*Don't* get in the way," I warned her. "You're an observer. Nothing else."

Her ear-to-ear grin made me wonder if I'd chosen the lesser of two evils.

Stolen Hearts

∼

Officer Azure had called the Cold Case office again while I'd been taken hostage by the pesky podcast woman. I was annoyed that I'd had to take time out of my day to visit her at her home, but at least Azure had been able to secure a meeting for me to plead our case with Chairman Strong. I could understand the innate desire for privacy, and even the SMSC leader's hesitancy to allow law enforcement onto trust land. Police in 1984 had clearly done the bare minimum when it came to trying to find the missing woman. But this wasn't 1984. And I wasn't the kind of cop who would be satisfied with the bare minimum.

At the end of the workday, I took the bus from the police station to Julia's public defender office in St. Paul. Julia's office space was typically hyper organized, but over the past few days she'd been boxing up her belongings in preparation of the move to her new law office. Everything was almost packed, with the exception of her leather-bound law books. They were heavy and unwieldy, so she'd left them for me to finish packing up. They had also been a present from her father when she'd graduated from law school. I half suspected that leaving the packing to me wasn't the result of her injured left wrist. Handling the giant leather-bound tomes might irritate wounds that were only just beginning to heal.

"Last day," I observed. I ripped off a particularly long piece of packing tape and sealed up one of the final boxes. "How does it feel?"

Julia was perched on the edge of her office desk, overseeing my work. "Overwhelming. And a little like a traitor."

I paused my task long enough to lift an eyebrow in her direction. "Traitor?"

Julia shrugged delicately beneath her tailored suit jacket. "This was never supposed to be my forever job, but I can't help feeling like I'm abandoning a sinking ship."

"You're not the captain, babe," I tried to appease her. "It's not your job to go down with the ship."

I was tempted to remind her she could always *go down* on me, but I was trying not to behave like a teenaged boy.

"I know," she sighed, "but between leaving the job in Embarrass and now this, I'm feeling a little rootless."

I swallowed down a complicated emotion. "You're making a home with me though, right? That seems pretty, uh, root-y?"

Julia's mouth curved into a wonderfully warm and adoring smile—the kind of smile that made me feel safe and loved, like homemade chocolate chip cookies. "You're right," she agreed. "I think for so long my worth was bound up with my career. I didn't have a life beyond the courtroom or my office. It's a bit of an adjustment to realize that being a lawyer isn't my entire personality."

I responded to the rare vulnerability with a small, encouraging smile. "Sometimes when you talk it's like listening to my own inner thoughts."

Julia hummed. "I suppose you're right. After being a Marine for so long, it must have been challenging returning to civilian life. To image a life where you're not singularly focused on one mission."

"And it wasn't even like I had an individual identity over there," I added. "With all of that gear—after all of that training—I wasn't Cassidy Miller from St. Cloud, Minnesota anymore. She was gone, and all that was left was a Marine. It was easy to feel like a replaceable part within a larger machine," I remarked. "And when I got injured, when I no longer worked, I got tossed in the trash. I could no longer serve my intended purpose, so they replaced me with another dumb eighteen-year-old kid."

Another wave of emotion had me choking up. I self-consciously wiped at my eyes, sure they were leaking.

"Geez." I barked out a rough, embarrassed laugh. "You might be a better therapist than Dr. Warren."

Julia smirked. "My fees are far higher, I'm afraid."

"That's right!" I said with forced brightness. I was eager for a subject change; I hadn't intended the verbal vomit. "I'm gonna have a Sugar Mama soon. How much is Grisham & Stein paying you?"

"You don't strike me as the kept woman type," Julia wryly observed.

I flashed a brilliant smile, one that was sure to show off my dimples. "Give me a chance. I've never been in this position before."

Julia unexpectedly groaned. Her features turned sour and she rubbed at her temples.

"What's wrong?"

"You said 'position.' You in new positions. *God*, I feel like a prepubescent boy." She waggled a scolding finger at me. "You realize this is your doing, right?"

A proud smile found its way to my lips. I abandoned my moving boxes and approached Julia who had remained leaning against her office desk. I widened my stance so I was somewhat straddling her skirted legs, crossed at the ankles. My lucky hands fell to her cinched waist.

"I love every version of you," I stated. "Buttoned up, polished and professional. Dressed down in a ratty, stained t-shirt."

Julia wrinkled her nose and curled her upper lip. "My clothes are not stained."

"Okay. Wearing one of *my* t-shirts, then," I corrected. "And if you devolve even further to meet me at my level, I'm going to love that version of you, too."

"You're very sweet, Cassidy."

I shrugged, not wanting to make a big deal out of it. She was easy to love. I was still in awe that a beautiful, successful, and driven woman like Julia might love all of my versions. The damaged ex-Marine. The Cold Case detective who routinely felt out of her element. The self-conscious teenaged girl in a twenty-eight-year-old body.

I brushed my fingertips against her left wrist. She no longer wore a sling to hold the wrist immobile, but the heavy brace and wrap that remained limited her mobility. "I'm glad you're still taking it easy with your wrist and asked me to help pack you up," I approved.

"Alice offered to stay late and help," she noted, naming the pretty office assistant, "but I didn't want to take advantage."

"None of that," I censured. I dipped my head lower to brush my lips against her welcoming mouth. "I'm the only one you get to take advantage of."

Chapter Ten

Afghanistan, 2012

We're running out of gas. I've tried to be smart about our stolen vehicle's fuel efficiency, but we didn't start with a full tank. It's not uncommon to see an abandoned vehicle on the side of the road, but it's too much of a gamble to stop and check if the other car has gas. All I can do is pray that we make it back to Camp Leatherneck before the Jeep gives up on us. I'm not religious though. Neither of my parents are either unless you count my dad bargaining with some higher power to make sure the Viking's kicker doesn't miss the next field goal.

I jostle Pensacola, who's slumped forward in the passenger seat. His eyes don't open but he groans, letting me know he hasn't given up on us either.

"Hey, Pense," I say, my eyes never leaving the stretch of unpaved road ahead of us, "did I ever tell you about the time my cousin hit me in the head with a golf club?"

I woke up alone. The bedroom was dark, but I no longer saw Julia's silhouette. The space beside me where she had been sleeping was empty. I grabbed my phone off the end table to check on the time. I squinted at the early hour. Where had Julia gone at 4:00 a.m.?

I sat up in bed and swung my feet to the floor. An involuntary noise got caught in my throat. My lower back was sore, maybe residual muscle ache from hauling heavy boxes of leather-bound books from Julia's office or from the unfavorable commute to and from Prior Lake in the stiff-riding Crown Vic.

When I stood up, I noticed the door to the *en suite* bathroom was closed. A sliver of light illuminated the narrow gap beneath the floor and the bathroom door. My feet were silent on the plush carpet. I raised my hand to knock and make sure Julia was okay, but I paused when I heard the sound of running water.

I bent my head toward the closed door and listened harder. In addition to the sound of the shower, I thought I heard a breathy sigh. Followed by ... a groan? In recent days, Julia had been able to shower on her own, but I still worried she was trying to do too much with her sprained wrist. The ligaments would heal in time without needing surgery, but only if she took it easy.

I twisted the door handle and silently let myself into the master bathroom. It was hot inside; the air was thick and muggy from the shower. Julia's bathroom was equipped with both a soaking bathtub and a standalone shower. The glass-encased shower featured a rainfall shower head and a river rock accent wall. Neither high-end feature managed to capture my attention, however.

Julia stood directly beneath the shower head's gentle rainfall spray. Her head was tilted back and her eyes were closed. Water streamed down her face. Julia's lips parted and another breathy sigh followed. Her light Mediterranean skin tone appeared more flushed than usual; her cheeks were red and a healthy blush had spread across her collarbone.

My own eyes greedily drank in her firm, naked body. I silently admired the lean, feminine figure that seemed to defy age. Her upturned breasts rejected gravity. Unblemished skin. Her narrow torso gently flared at the hip.

I frowned when I realized she'd removed the protective wrap and brace from her left wrist. My frown was short-lived, however, when I saw her injured hand clutching the shower's adjustable handheld attachment. Julia typically used the second shower head to clean the interior walls of the shower. She was decidedly *not* using that function at the moment.

She'd braced herself with her uninjured palm pressed flat against the shower's floor-to-ceiling glass partitioning. She stood with her legs spread slightly apart. The second, smaller shower head was strategically placed in front of her lower torso. The mechanism partially blocked my view, but I had a pretty good idea where the spray of water was aimed.

I wanted to stay and watch—and maybe even join in—but something about the moment felt too private, too vulnerable. I took a step backwards, fully intending to go back to the bedroom, although definitely not back to sleep, until I heard Julia's voice: "Don't go."

Her eyes opened and immediately trained on me.

I froze in place. "How did you—."

"You wanted to watch?" she challenged. "So watch."

I opened my mouth, but the words died in my throat when Julia shifted her legs even farther apart. Her abdomen visibly tensed, and I heard her breath hitch.

I took a tentative step closer if only to afford myself a better view. I lifted my hand to the shower's glass wall and pressed my palm against its cool exterior so our hands lined up.

Her dark eyes bore into mine; she didn't look away from my face. I could hardly allow myself to blink. I wanted to touch myself while I watched her, but I somehow resisted the carnal desire to shove my hand down the front of my sweatpants.

Her top teeth dug into her bottom lip. "Cassidy," came her strangled cry.

I dropped my gaze to her lower body where the second shower head continued to do its magic. I could see the struggle in her upper thighs; the fine muscles tensed and twitched beneath the unblemished skin. I imagined her battling to stay upright despite the concentrated water spray relentlessly pummeling her clit.

Her needy, almost frustrated whine filled the shower. I could have helped her along, could have tweaked her dusty pink nipples or slid my fingers through her swollen folds, but I remained on the other side of the glass. I'd been invited to watch—nothing more, nothing less.

More throaty groans and stifled cries tumbled past her parted lips. Her breath became labored, and I watched how her exhalations fogged up the glass partition. The hand—her injured one—that held the shower extension looked unsteady. I worried the device might slip out of her hand, until I realized she was moving the shower head not to regain her grip, but to manipulate where the water struck her.

"Fuck," came my barely audible whisper.

I lifted up on my toes with an urge to bust through the glass partition that separated us. I wanted to fall to my knees on the unforgiving shower floor. I wanted to suck on her clit and drink directly from her source. But somehow, I remained a witness rather than a participant.

Her legs shifted a second time. Julia's head fell back and her eyes closed. Her breath came in ragged bursts. She moaned my name again: "Cassidy."

My ego swelled with the thought that she might masturbate with me on her lips. I licked my own lips as I continued to watch her. It was overwhelming, really. I didn't know where to look. Her strained, beautiful face. Her tightened nipples. Her flexing abdomen. The frenetic movement at the apex of her parted thighs.

"Oh God," she choked out. "I'm there. It's-it's … right there."

I shuddered when a fresh wave of arousal crested over me. I'd never before witnessed something so intimate, so erotic.

More stifled cries caught in her throat. "Cassidy," she breathed.

I leaned closer to the shower wall. "That's it, baby," I quietly coaxed. "Get yourself off. You look so fucking hot."

Her breathing had become loud, staccato bursts. "I'm close," she gasped.

"Do it, baby," I continued to urge.

"Fuck!" The expletive tore up her throat and echoed off the bathroom walls.

Julia's shoulders slumped forward. She let the still-pulsing shower extension fall to her side. Eventually, she reached a shaky hand toward the faucet and turned off the water. Her chest visibly heaved as she returned the handheld shower extension to its original position.

"Goodness," she breathed out.

I didn't know if it would be appropriate to clap; she'd put on quite the show. It was still before dawn, yet I had the energy to run through a wall.

I knew she didn't need my assistance, but I still helped her step out of the shower. She landed safely on the bath mat and waited for me to hand her a new towel.

"You're amazing," I praised.

Julia inclined her head. "Thank you, dear. I wasn't really expecting an audience."

I watched her pat down her sleek, agile figure before slipping into a short, silky robe that had been hanging on the back of the bathroom door. The robes were my favorite. If I had my way, she'd never wear clothes in the condo. But the way the short robe hit across her upper thighs created just the right amount of erotic mystery.

"I wasn't sure where you'd gone," I said. "I wanted to make sure you were okay."

"I couldn't sleep," she revealed. "My brain was racing, so I decided to just get up and get ready for the day."

I leaned against the double vanity. "What a way to start the day," I smirked.

Julia laughed softly, almost sounding embarrassed. "I thought it might help take the edge off."

"You should have woken me up," I urged. "I'm feeling a little jealous of that shower head now."

"I wanted you to sleep." Julia shook her head. "You've had long days. I can see it on your face."

"That's just my face," I resisted.

Julia sat on the edge of the soaking tub and began to towel dry her raven hair. I retrieved a fresh ace bandage for her wrist from the bathroom's linen closet and sat in the empty space beside her. Julia paused drying her hair long enough for me to rewrap her left wrist. I loosely wrapped the stretchy bandage around the injured area.

"It's been a lot lately," Julia observed. "My wrist. My mother still being in Embarrass. Your Cold Case re-opening. My new job." She paused to lick her lips. "Baby things."

"Grownups have complicated, layered lives," I deflected. "I can't freak out every time something new happens or when life gets busy."

"You can freak out," Julia allowed. "In fact, I wish you would."

I stopped short of fastening the metal clips that held her beige bandage in place. "Huh?"

"You're so good at hiding your emotions, even from me. I don't know if that's your military training or from being a cop, or even just stubborn Scandinavian heritage."

"Y-You're the one with the poker face," I insisted. "You're so damn cool and collected. You take everything in stride. If I let myself slip, I'd be like a damn hysterical woman."

"Okay," Julia allowed, "we *both* could be more emotive. That sounds like a reasonable goal."

I leaned into her so my shoulder pressed more solidly against hers. "Want to come back to bed with me? I'm feeling a little emotional."

"Horny is not an emotion, darling."

. . .

Julia did come back to bed, but it was only to lay with me for a few more hours until her alarm clock officially went off. She'd planned on having an early morning anyway to get to her new office space before everyone else and start to set things up. I would have called in sick so I could help her with the heavy lifting, but I was supposed to be meeting with Chairman Strong, the elected leader of the SMSC, later that day. Julia assured me she would take it easy and let the movers that Grisham & Stein had hired do most of the work.

From my place in bed, I watched her assemble her battle armor. I didn't need to be at the police station for a few more hours, so I enjoyed this second performance of the early morning. Julia carefully selected a serious grey suit and paired the outfit with red bottomed heels. Delicate lingerie went on first, followed by the professionally pressed shirt, pants, and jacket. She stood before her dresser in the impeccably tailored suit and fastened a double string of pearls around her elegant neck. The necklace hung in the hollow of her throat.

She looked good. Confident. In control. It was a pretty effective way to win an argument. As a lawyer, Julia was supposed to be able to persuade with her words, but this worked, too. I allowed myself a long, indulgent stare. *Uh huh.* It definitely worked.

I knew it was all a mask, though. She was feeling the pressure of the new position. Her job at the public defender's office was never intended to be her forever job. It had served its purpose to bridge the gap after she'd resigned as Embarrass' city attorney. This new opportunity—

if it worked out for both sides—it could take her through retirement. It was the kind of lofty job that someone might work their entire life for and never quite achieve it.

"I love you."

The words unintentionally came out, but that didn't mean I wanted to take them back.

Julia paused her morning routine to return to the bed. She sat close to me on a corner of the mattress. "I love you, too, dear."

"You're going to be so great today," I enthused. "I'm really proud of you."

Julia turned her face away from me. "No one has said that to me in a very long time."

I paused to consider the truth behind her words. Her mother had never been quite herself after Jonathan's death, even before the dementia had set in. Her father had always seemed like a bit of a cool customer, aloof and hard to impress. I was sure he'd been proud of all that she'd accomplished—basically following in his footsteps—and yet I had a hard time picturing him being effusive with praise.

I grabbed her hand. "I'm your biggest cheerleader."

She finally turned back to me. The lighting in the bedroom was minimal, but I could tell that her eyes were wet.

"Dinner? Tonight?" I proposed. "I know you're not ready for champagne yet, but I want to celebrate you."

She gave me a curt nod. "I'd like that."

"I'll be in Prior Lake this morning, but I should be done at my usual time."

I watched her hesitate. "I'm not sure when I'll be done."

"That's okay," I assured her. "We'll play it by ear. I could always bring something to your office if you're running late."

She seemed to sag where she sat. "Why are you so wonderful?"

This time it was my turn to grow uncomfortable with the praise. I deflected rather than lean into the compliment. "I'm not sure I can take a shower later. That shower extension is gonna be all braggy about where it was this morning."

Julia rested her hand on mine. "You're wonderful, Cassidy. You're the best thing in my life."

I started the feel a little leaky around the eyes. "Oh, yeah?" I croaked.

She smiled, perhaps pleased that her words had such an impact on me. "I'm looking forward to dinner tonight. I'll text you if I think I'll be late."

I took her hand and brought it to my lips. "Go be great."

Chapter Eleven

It was only a half an hour drive from the Twin Cities to Prior Lake, but it felt much longer that morning. Officer Azure had arranged for a meeting with Chairman Strong and Sarah had insisted on coming along. The backseat of the department-issued Crown Vic was also occupied with Melody Sternbridge and her recording equipment.

I had initially balked at the idea of Melody recording anything, but she'd assured me she would be discrete, respectful, and would obtain permission before ever hitting the record button. It made for a cozy ride between the three of us and Melody's gear. Thankfully Stanley hadn't also wanted to come along. He'd stayed behind and continued to work on a digital reconstruction of what the trust land might have looked like thirty years ago.

Our meeting with Chairman Strong was scheduled at Hocokati Ti, the SMSC's cultural center and museum. Hocokati Ti was located three miles from Mystic Lake Casino and Hotel, but it might as well have been another world. Mystic Lake, which opened in May 1992, was a sprawling fantasyland anchored by a 150,000 square foot casino and a hotel tower with 586 rooms. The complex boasted a 70,000-square foot conference and events space, an 18-hole golf course, and a 2,000-seat concert venue that regularly hosted performances. It wasn't surprising that the casino was the largest employer in the county.

Across a vast parking lot was the smaller, quieter Little Six Casino, which had first opened in 1982. Growth and prosperity had eventually followed. A lot of it. Mystic Lake reportedly earned $1 billion in revenue every year, which was then split among the tribal community's 500 members.

The parking lot for Hocokati Ti, the cultural epicenter for the SMSC, was significantly less crowded than that for the casinos. The property and the complex were beautiful though; the landscape was almost like a work of art. Seven large teepee structures sat along a small, but pristine frozen lake. Set behind the seven teepees was Hocokati Ti itself which housed a 3,800 square foot museum space that educated visitors on the history of the SMSC.

A receptionist met our group at the front entrance and led the three of us to an impressive atrium where Chairman Strong awaited our arrival. Bruce Strong was a handsome man. He was tall and broad shouldered with a head of jet black hair that gave no indication of his age. His black suit looked expensive and his serious features mirrored the nature of our visit. Dark eyes silently regarded us as we approached.

Sarah, as usual, greeted the community leader before I could: "*Háu kola*, Chairman."

The man gave my partner a curious look. "You speak Dakota?"

Sarah bent her head in reverence. "My grandmother taught me a little. I grew up on the Red Lake reservation, so I'm more fluent in Anishinaabemowin."

"*Mino gigizheb,*" he said.

A small smile appeared on Sarah's ruby red lips. "*Enh, gaawiin niiskaadasinoon.*"

I looked back and forth between my colleague and Chairman Strong, not understanding a single syllable.

"Sorry," the Chairman apologized after a moment. His broad grin told me Sarah had effectively broken the ice and perhaps even his hesitance to let us assist. "We should probably speak English for the pale faces in the room."

"Appreciated," I mumbled.

"This building is beautiful, Chairman," Sarah approved.

"This was all prairie not so long ago if you can believe it," Chairman Strong remarked. "We've come a long way since termination."

"Termination?" I asked. The term sounded like something from an apocalyptic film.

"Just after World War II ended, the federal government decided to end its relationship with sovereign Indian Nations," Sarah supplied. "They wanted us to assimilate. Leave the reservations and live in the cities."

"My family stayed," Chairman Strong said. "We've been here since the late 19th century when the U.S. government purchased property for the Mdewakanton, including the land in Prior Lake where we're located today."

"My grandparents stayed, too," Sarah reflected. "I haven't been to Red Lake since middle school, when my parents moved us to the Twin Cities."

"You should go back," Chairman Strong urged. "If only

for a visit. We need young people to help keep the old ways alive. The elders won't be around forever."

"How did all of this growth happen?" I questioned. I glanced briefly in Sarah's direction. She looked lost to her thoughts. "From what I understand, the SMSC are unique in their, uh, prosperity."

"The money's relatively new," Chairman Strong conceded. "Things started to change in '69 when the federal government granted us official recognition as a Native American tribe. But there was no money with that recognition. You don't have to look too far to find elder who remember the rundown trailers, no running water, and sharing outhouses with their neighbors," he observed. "Around that time, the City of Prior Lake annexed the trust—claimed the reservation as its own."

"They can do that?" I marveled.

"Wouldn't have been the first time," Sarah muttered darkly.

"In 1983, the Courts decided that annexation was illegal," Chairman Strong noted. "Once we reestablished our sovereignty, we invested in the casino. The rest, as they say, is history."

"Did you know Danika Laroque, Chairman?" I asked. I couldn't pinpoint Chairman Strong's exact age, but he couldn't have been too much older than Jenny Laroque.

"Not personally, no. We're a small, close-knit community," he said, "but she was several years ahead of me in school."

"Because you're so close-knit," I tried to leverage, "certainly you would want to provide closure for the family."

Chairman Strong held up his hands as if anticipating the trajectory of our conversation. "Listen, Detective. I'm sorry you drove all this way. But I'm going to have to respectfully refuse your help. I can't permit your people to start randomly digging on trust land. I want that girl found as much as the next person," he insisted, "but you've got to give me something more—some evidence that she's actually there."

"More evidence than her bicycle being found?" I challenged.

"It could have been stolen and dumped after she disappeared," Chairman Strong noted. "Bikes get stolen all the time. Besides, how do we know for sure that it belonged to her? It could be wishful thinking on her family's behalf and they misidentified the bike."

"Ground penetrating radar," Melody announced. The words came out like an explosion. She had kept her word about being seen and not heard so far, but apparently she couldn't handle the extended silence any longer. "They don't have to dig up anything; they zip the radar machine over the ground and can figure out what's underground."

I looked from Melody back to Chairman Strong. "Ground penetrating radar," I repeated.

Despite what I thought was a solid compromise, Chairman Strong still looked unconvinced. "What do I tell the community members?" he questioned. "That you're looking for a dead girl in their backyards?"

I stood a little taller. "Tell them whatever you want—we're land surveyors, we're looking for gold—it doesn't matter to me as long as we can do our work uninterrupted."

Chairman Strong eventually relented to our request. If we could identify someone with expertise in ground penetrating radar, Strong wouldn't get in the way of our investigation. I considered his blessing to be a small miracle and, privately, I no longer considered him a person of interest. I'd thought it suspicious when he'd initially refused law enforcement help in finding Danika Laroque, but learning a little more about the SMSC's history had helped me better appreciate his community's complicated relationship with outsiders. We left Chairman Strong with assurances that we'd be in touch soon.

The sun sat a little higher in the sky when Sarah, Melody, and I left Hocokati Ti not long after our arrival.

"Ground penetrating radar—where'd that come from?" Sarah inquired. I couldn't tell if she was annoyed or impressed.

"I listened to a podcast the other day about historians using it to find the execution site for the Salem witch trials," Melody explained. "They used ground penetrating radar to discover if there were any buried bodies at the suspected execution site or if the remnants of gallows were still beneath the earth. You were smart back there, too," she complimented. "Your little Rosetta Stone show-and-tell totally charmed the Chairman."

"That wasn't an act," Sarah fired off. "I actually do speak multiple indigenous languages."

I held up my hands to keep the peace. "You were both great back there."

"We make a pretty great team, ladies." Melody hummed and seemed to have a new bounce to her step. She skipped ahead of us in the direction of the parked police car. "*Sisters are doing it for themselves,*" she sang off-key.

Sarah stayed a few steps behind with me. "Is she for

real?" she quietly scowled. "It's like she's starring in a movie and she's the star."

"She won't be tagging along anymore; it was a one-time thing," I assured her. "But you have to admit, that ground penetrating radar suggestion was pretty genius."

Sarah wrinkled her nose and sniffed. "I don't have to admit anything, Miller."

∽

I met up with Julia for dinner downtown at the end of our respective work days. I felt a little guilty that I hadn't thought much about her that day. Driving to and from Prior Lake to meet with Chairman Strong had monopolized all of my brain bandwidth. It might have been a blessing though. With nothing else to occupy my thoughts, I probably would have fretted about her first day at Grisham & Stein. How were her meetings going? Did she feel like she belonged? Had she taken time to have lunch? Was she making friends?

Julia had been the one to pick out where we'd be eating that night. I'd never been, so she'd texted me the information at the end of the day. I was the first to arrive. I took in the large, open floor plan of the high-rise restaurant. Dark wood accents and low, intimate lighting. High-top tables for two or four. Larger padded booths closer to the floor. A large bar where restaurant patrons drank wine in long-stem glasses and ate from small plates. It was nice I decided. It wasn't the fancy French eatery we went to sometimes, but it also wasn't an animal-themed restaurant in the Mall of America.

The hostess guided me to a high-top table close to the floor-to-ceiling windows. I glanced over the drink menu, but waited for Julia's arrival to actually order anything. I didn't have to wait very long to see her confident stride across the span of the restaurant floor. I noticed the appreciative stare from a number of the other patrons as she passed their tables. Instead of insecure or jealous, however, I only felt proud.

I hopped down from my elevated chair to greet her arrival. Her right hand, the one without the brace, lightly touched my hip. She pressed her lips to my cheek. The red stain had largely worn off after a long day of work, so she didn't need to wipe away any residue.

Julia slid onto her high top chair and released a sigh that sounded like she'd held her breath all day. The drink menu in the center of the table went untouched.

"How was it?" I asked.

"A whirlwind. I was whisked from one meeting to the next all day. It felt like the Partners wanted everyone in the building to meet me."

"That doesn't surprise me," I observed with a smile. "You're a super star."

"It's encouraging," she agreed. "I was worried the position was a PR stunt, but the firm is allocating a lot of resources to this pet project of theirs."

"That's awesome, babe," I approved.

"Tomorrow I'll work with HR to send out job ads for an assistant and some paralegals. Normally I'd select from the pool the firm already has working for them," she noted, "but I have no interest in being a stepping stone to something else. I only want to work with a team that's truly committed to this cause." A fierce looked flashed across her refined features. "No more snot-nosed law students biding their time until they can become an ambulance chaser."

Her words pulled a smirk to my lips. I'd heard this particular rant several times before when she'd been a public defender.

"But enough about me," she said with a dismissive hand. "How was your day? You met with the SMSC's leader?"

I nodded. "The meeting could have gone better, but he's letting us move forward with the investigation."

"That's a positive development."

"Uh huh. But it was really all Sarah's doing. She's indigenous herself, so I'm piggybacking off her insider status."

"I'm sure you're pulling your weight, darling," she appeased. "You always do."

Our conversation momentarily paused when a server came by to get our drink and food order. My stomach rumbled, reminding me that lunch had happened without me that day. Drinks were swiftly delivered—a lager in a tall glass for me and a martini with three olives for Julia. Full plates of food followed. Julia had ordered something with salmon and couscous while I'd gone for a reliable New York strip with green beans and potatoes.

I sliced into the medium rare piece of meat with enthusiasm. "I'm still hung up on them finding Danika's bike. What are the chances we start working this thirty-year-old case and suddenly a giant piece of evidence gets recovered?"

"It does seem like a remarkable coincidence," Julia validated. "How did they end up finding it?"

"The trust is one big construction zone," I explained between bites. "A family was breaking ground for a new garage and they found the bike wrapped in a tarp."

Julia tilted her head to the side. "Breaking new ground in December?"

I stabbed a single green bean with my fork and awkwardly angled it into my mouth. "Yeah. I thought that was weird, too."

"Have you spoken to the people who dug it up?"

I shook my head. "No."

"You should," she encouraged. "It would be worth a phone call at least. When you've got nothing to go on, even the most minuscule anomalies could lead to something more."

I sat forward in my chair, feeling a little animated. "I love this. I love talking through cases with you. It reminds me of when we first met."

"If you came on as my private investigator," Julia mused, "we could do this all the time."

I frowned at the thinly veiled proposition. Julia immediately held up a hand when she saw my reaction. "I'm sorry. I won't nag you about it anymore. I know your allegiance is to law enforcement."

My frown deepened. It wasn't like I was really enforcing any laws these days.

A loud noise erupted at an adjacent table. A little boy who couldn't have been more than three years old had knocked something onto the floor. The man and woman at the table, presumably his parents, scrambled to retrieve it. The restaurant wasn't necessarily an adults-only venue, but the new family looked more out of place than me in the refined surroundings; Julia typically selected restaurants you wouldn't bring a kid to. I tried to picture her in the ball pit at a fast food joint, but immediately dismissed the ridiculous imagery.

I saw Julia's attention stray to the table and the family of three. I wondered what she might be thinking, but I wasn't brave enough to ask.

I cleared my throat and asked a different question instead: "Have you made the appointment for the ultrasound yet?"

Her gaze left the small family and her eyes dropped to her plate. I saw the perceptible shake of her head. "I'll do it after New Years. I'll feel better about the timing then."

I doubted either of our lives would be less hectic in January, but ultimately this was her decision. "Okay. After New Years."

Chapter Twelve

Afghanistan, 2012

The Jeep had run out of gas several miles ago. It had served us well, saving my body from more wear and tear and getting us closer—hopefully—to safety. Typically it was men who were notorious for not asking directions, but I can't very well flag down someone to make sure we're actually heading toward Camp Leatherneck. I can only hope my crude understanding of Helmand geography is getting us closer to friendlies and not deeper into opium territory.

"Can you turn on the radio?"

Pensacola's voice nearly startles me. He's been silent for the past hour, at least, and I've been lulled almost into a trance, focusing solely on putting one foot in front of the other. Without the Jeep, I've had to resume dragging his body behind me on the makeshift sled. I wonder where he thinks he is to be asking about the radio.

"Got any requests?" I toss over my shoulder. I don't stop moving my feet. If I stop, I might not be able to start again.

"Surprise me," he croaks. The gravel in his voice reminds me of our surrounding landscape.

We shouldn't speak. We shouldn't do anything that might draw unnecessarily attention to ourselves. But a part of me imagines that being captured can't be any worse than this.

I clear my throat. *"My loneliness is killing me, and I, I must confess, I still believe ... still believe..."*

My voice is terribly off-key, but I'm struggling under Pensacola's weight. Singing and dragging a full-grown man do not go together.

"When I'm not with you, I lose my mind. Give me a siiiiign..."

Behind me, I hear Pense's voice. It's quiet, almost dream-like: *"Hit me baby, one more time."*

∽

"It looks like a lawnmower." Sarah's tone was decidedly unimpressed.

"A very *expensive* lawnmower," the man defended.

It had taken a few days, but we'd contacted an archaeology professor at the local university to travel to Prior Lake with his ground penetrating radar equipment. We stood on the same plot of land where Danika Laroque's bicycle had been retrieved. Sentient excavators that had been hired to clear land for the foundation of a three-car garage loomed in the background, their work momentarily shelved.

"So how exactly does this work?" I asked.

Professor Carson Washington stooped and tapped the

plastic body of the machine, the area where the blade would have been on an actual lawn mower. "There's an antenna in here that sends energy waves into the ground. A mechanism in the wheels counts the exact distance you're moving. And then the final element is this tablet." He stood and motioned to the digital screen affixed to the top of the GPR machine. "The table talks to the antenna and collects the data."

"What kind of data?" Sarah posed. Her voice sounded suspicious.

If Stanley had been the one to suggest we use ground penetrating radar to investigate the site, Sarah might not have insisted on accompanying me that day to Prior Lake. But because Melody Sternbridge had come up with the idea, Sarah had been the first one to volunteer coming along with me. I hadn't extended the invitation to Melody, but Sarah still seemed to be in a bad mood.

"We're not necessarily looking for things under the ground, like water pipes or bones or building foundations," Professor Washington said. "The machine can only detect old holes—disturbances in the soil—like an old hole that was filled back in."

"Like a grave," I remarked.

"Right," the professor concurred. "But just because we find a hole, that doesn't mean there's anything inside of it. You'll need to follow up. We'll know more once I bring the data back to the lab."

Professor Washington began to push the GPR machine in a tidy line in someone's backyard. We hadn't known how wide and how long of a plot of land we should search, but Stanley had consulted his GIS layered maps to suggest which square footage wouldn't have been covered by trailer homes in the 1980s. A winter wind continued to whip around us, disturbing the ground cover of fallen leaves and small, dead twigs. The ground was going to freeze soon. Even if we did find evidence of something underneath the topsoil, we'd probably have to wait until spring to be able to do any digging if it got much later in the season.

I thought about Julia's father's death. His murder had occurred just in time for a burial to be possible. If it had happened later in the winter season his body would have remained in frozen storage until the ground at the Embarrass cemetery thawed. I was thankful for the small bit of luck. I doubted Julia's sanity would have survived that loose end until spring.

My lips twisted in contemplation. "Do you think evidence of underground holes will be enough to convince the Chairman to let us dig up trust land?"

Sarah hugged herself when a particularly brutal gust of wind whipped around us. "We've got to at least try."

∽

Melody Sternbridge didn't knock. The unlocked office door swung open and she marched inside. We'd been keeping the door to the Cold Case office closed to maintain a livable heat level while the outside temperatures continued to drop. The basement stayed cool in the warm, summer months, but it apparently remained an ice box in the winter as well.

Melody lifted her nose in the air. "Is something burning?"

Sarah had brought in a small space heater to fight the chill in the basement. It also created a suspicious smell like it was going to burn down the building. She'd gone off to get lunch after we'd returned from Prior Lake. I'd decided to stay in the office, not that it required much babysitting.

"It's fine," I appeased.

She didn't wait for an invitation to sit down. She grabbed a spare office chair and dragged it closer to the desk where I sat. I winced at the awful sound the metal chair legs made as they scratched across the cheaply tiled floor.

"Make yourself at home," I deadpanned.

Melody removed her knit winter hat and fluffed at her loose locks. Her long winter jacket remained, which I hoped was an indication that she didn't plan on staying very long. "Did my invitation get lost?"

I arched an eyebrow. "What?"

"I'm sure there must have been a delay at the post office or your email went to my SPAM folder," she continued, "because there's no way you *wouldn't* not invite me for the ground penetrating radar."

I took a breath to avoid snapping at her. "We agreed that you could tag along for *one* visit to Prior Lake. I held up my part of the deal."

"But it was *my* idea!" she protested. "You never would have considered GPR if I hadn't been there."

"This is a police investigation," I said flatly. "And you're not police."

"If the police are actually investigating, how come no one has spoken to Jim Knutson?" she challenged.

"Who's Jim Knutson?"

I heard the displeased intake of air. "Danika's boyfriend. Why haven't you spoken to him?"

"We're waiting on evidence—either DNA recovered

from the yellow bike or evidence of something beneath the ground."

Both leads would probably take at least a week, with the DNA recovery potentially taking much longer. Professor Washington had final exams to contend with, but I'd expressed to him how time sensitive his data was. The case was cold, but we couldn't afford the ground getting too much colder, too.

"I thought you were re-opening the case," Melody all but pouted.

"We are—we *have*," I insisted. "But it does no good to start re-interviewing people until those other things happen first."

Melody lifted her arms at her sides and flopped them back down like a small child annoyed with a cumbersome snowsuit. "Well, when will that happen?"

"These things take time." I thought about Sarah's observation from when we'd visited Chairman Strong a few days earlier—how Melody seemed to think she was starring in a movie. "This isn't a Hollywood film with a tidy conclusion after 90 minutes," I remarked.

"I know that," she said, rolling her eyes. "Do you want to know what he told me, or not? The boyfriend?"

"That depends," I posed. "Am I going to owe you?"

Melody scoffed. 'Don't worry. I'm not going to bug you for an interview anymore. I doubt my listeners would find you all that interesting."

"Well, that's a relief."

Melody retrieved a spiral-bound notebook from her messenger bag. "I take notes while I record an interview, just in case the audio fails," she explained without me asking.

She flipped a few pages into the notebook and peered at the page upon which she'd stopped. "Jim Knutson. Sixty-three years old," she read aloud. "Retired machinist. Never married."

"Hold up." I interrupted before she could say more. "Did you tell him who you were and what this was for?"

"Of course!"

"And he agreed to be recorded for your podcast?" My voice was filled with skepticism. "Do sixty-three-year-old men even know what podcasts are?"

Melody snorted. "Ageist much, Detective? Not everyone is a neophyte like yourself."

"Whatever," I breathed. "What did Jim Knutson tell you?" I saw no harm in humoring her.

"I'm getting there. Don't rush me," she chastised. "Okay. Jim Knutson. Sixty-three. Retired machinist. Never married," she stated again as if setting the scene. "He met Danika Laroque after she returned to the Prior Lake area. When she came back after her brief time off the trust land after graduation. He's not Native American, but they met through a mutual friend. He'd just returned from military involvement in Grenada. Didn't really know what was next. The way he spins it, Danika was his first—and last—real love."

"Last?" I questioned. "He hasn't dated anyone in the past thirty years?"

"You don't have to love someone to date them, Detective," Melody all but snorted.

I was tempted to ask about her own dating record, but I imagined that was a can of worms best left unopened.

"Where was he the night of Danika's disappearance?" I asked instead.

"He claims he was at a bar with some friends. Arkansas beat Michael Jordan's Tar Heels. I looked online and the game checks out."

I sat back in my chair, but didn't immediately respond. It was surprising that police at the time had cleared Knutson from being a person of interest. His wasn't a completely rock-solid alibi. People binge-drinking and watching sports weren't necessarily the most reliable eye witnesses. They could have been mistaken about the time frame in which they'd seen the suspect. Someone might also claim they were going to the bathroom or outside for a cigarette and use that window to commit a crime. Regardless of what I believed, however, law enforcement in 1984 had been satisfied with the boyfriend's alleged whereabouts.

"Anything else?" I probed.

"No. But he did it." Melody snapped her notebook shut. "It's always the husband or the boyfriend," she proclaimed. "Those are the rules."

"The rules?" I echoed. "In the playbook for murder?"

"It might not make sense, but that's reality. A relationship comes to an end. A husband wants to be with someone else, but chooses violence over divorce."

"So you think—what? Jim Knutson wants to break up with Danika so he killed her to avoid an uncomfortable conversation?"

"It's murder, not logic," she explained away.

I shook my head. "Don't you think it more likely that someone saw her walking home from work, they offered to give her a ride home, and then they attacked her? In my experience, the simplest explanation is usually the correct one. Occam's razor."

"You lack imagination, Detective," the woman complained.

That's not what my girlfriend says.

I wasn't there to start a fight. "I guess that's why I'm the cop and you're the podcaster."

"I keep thinking about *Oliphant v. Suquamish*," she mused.

"What's that?"

Melody wrinkled her nose. "It was on the flash drive I gave you. Didn't you look?"

In truth, I'd given that task to Stanley, but I didn't need to share that information with this woman. She already thought I wasn't going above and beyond for this case.

"Doesn't mean I have everything memorized," I deflected.

"*Oliphant v. Suquamish*," Melody recited. Annoyance crept into her voice like a teacher frustrated with unruly students. "It's a Supreme Court decision from 1978. Tribal nations cannot prosecute non-native people in tribal courts for any crime. White people can literally get away with murder."

I'd never heard of the case before, but that didn't mean much. Julia was the lawyer, not me.

"So you think police didn't bother following up at the time because there wasn't much they could do?" I proposed.

"The SMSC didn't have tribal courts," Melody clarified, "but the sentiment would have still been there. If you were white and you did bad things to native girls on the reservation ..." She shrugged. "Oh well."

An uneasy feeling settled in the pit of my stomach.

"We need more than hunches in police work, you know," I reminded her.

"Why are you always here when I show up?" Melody asked.

I furrowed my brow. "Because this is my office? This is where I work?" I wasn't sure what she was really asking.

"Shouldn't you be out there pounding the sidewalks?" she demanded. "Harassing suspects and chasing down witnesses?"

I bristled at her suggestion that I was being too casual about my work. "Police work takes time. We're collecting evidence. We're building a case and following leads when those leads are fact-based."

What I'd expressed earlier was true. We needed to wait until we received lab results from the recovered bicycle or the findings from Professor Washington's ground penetrating radar. Waiting behind a desk was never easy though, and it certainly didn't feel productive.

"Just say the word, and I'll have my listeners solve the case." Her tone was decidedly smug.

I shook my finger in her direction. "You are *not* to harass the Laroque family," I said sternly. "You've already caused them enough of a heartache."

"At least I was looking for her," she said hotly. "You wouldn't have even known the name Danika Laroque if it wasn't for me."

My mouth reflexively opened to defend myself and the department, but I knew that she was right. Until she had shown up in our office weeks ago, Danika hadn't been on my radar.

"Leave the police work to the actual police," I told her instead.

She snorted with distain. "Typical cop."

～

My cellphone rang with an incoming call from Julia a few hours later. I typically didn't answer personal calls during work hours, but it was close enough to the end of the work day that I didn't let it go to voicemail.

"Hey, babe," I greeted. "Are you done for the day?"

"I'm afraid it's just the opposite," came her bad news. "I'm held up at work. HR is being stubborn about the language in my job ad, so I need to revise it before I can come home. Will you be okay for dinner on your own?"

I frowned at the question. It was the second night in a row she'd had to work late. I hoped it was only this first week at her new job and not our new normal.

"Yeah. I'll survive."

"Thank goodness for small miracles," I heard her chuckle.

"How has your day been?" I asked.

"More routine than the day before," she noted. "I'm starting to feel more comfortable, like I don't need a map to find the bathroom or write down the key code to the photocopier."

"You need to hire an assistant, ASAP," I opined. "I can't imagine you doing something so mundane as making photocopies."

"I'm not above a little collating," she defended with a laugh. "How did your archaeology adventure go today?"

"Fine," I decided. "We won't know anything until the professor has time to read and interpret the data though."

"And the people who found Danika's bike?" she pressed. "Did you speak with them?"

"Uh huh," I confirmed. "Nothing suspicious there. They've got so much construction on the trust land that the family hadn't been able to schedule an excavator until now. Apparently there's a waitlist for that kind of work."

"I suppose that makes sense," Julia allowed. "I'm curious though why her body wasn't discovered with the bike."

"I know," I agreed. "That's been bothering me, too. Why go through all the trouble of wrapping the bike in a tarp but not bury the body as well?"

"You're assuming the bike was disposed of at the same time as the body."

I let Julia's statement sit with me. "You'd get rid of the body first. But why hold on to the bike?"

"A trophy?" Julia suggested.

"We're not dealing with a serial killer," I rejected. "No other area girls went missing around the same time. Plus, if it had been a trophy, they'd still have it, not randomly bury it later."

Julia made a thoughtful noise in agreement. "There's got to be a practical reason why the body and bike weren't found together."

"Separate them to make identification harder?" I posed.

I heard her skeptical hum. "You might separate body parts if that was your goal—not a bike and a body."

I pressed my palm into my forehead. "I'm not smart enough for this. I'm a bludgeoning tool who's supposed to stop people from speeding."

"Hey." Julia's stern word delayed my downward spiral. "Do not doubt your abilities, Cassidy. If I thought you were unfit for this kind of work, I never would have offered you an investigative job."

"And here I thought you just wanted eye candy around the office," I deflected with a joke.

"Well, the thought *did* cross my mind," she admitted.

"Does the court case *Oliphant versus Squamish* ring any bells?" I asked.

"*Suquamish*," Julia corrected. "Sure. It was pretty controversial in its day. The Supreme Court basically ruled that despite Native American sovereignty that tribal courts had no power. They couldn't prosecute non-natives or even indigenous people who didn't belong to their community. And even for someone within their Band," she continued, "they could only penalize that person with a maximum sentence of one year in jail for any crime and a maximum fine of $5,000."

"How do you know this stuff?" I marveled.

I could hear the smile in Julia's tone. "Because I'm very good at what I do. Is this about your missing girl?"

"Uh huh," I confirmed. "The podcaster lady thinks police gave up on Danika in 1984."

"She's probably right," Julia agreed.

I chewed on my lower lip. "Does *Oliphant* still exist? Like, is it still the way things are?"

"In parts. It was partially nullified when Congress reauthorized the federal Violence Against Women Act in 2013. The Act gave Indian Nations jurisdiction to prosecute felony domestic violence offenses involving non-Native offenders."

"So if a white guy beats up his indigenous girlfriend on

the reservation, now it's actually a crime?" I marveled. "How did that only get changed less than ten years ago?"

"I think you know, darling."

The sick feeling from before intensified. "I'm going to figure this out," I announced. "Police failed Danika Laroque in 1984. I'm not going to fail her again."

Chapter Thirteen

I was fully dedicated to resolving Danika Laroque's missing person case. But that didn't mean tips and new evidence would magically make themselves known. We received our first piece of bad news early that morning when Dr. Carson Washington, the local professor who specialized in digital archaeology, called with the results of the ground penetrating radar.

"Nothing," the man on the phone told me.

My heart sank. "Nothing?" I repeated.

"I'm sorry, Detective," Professor Washington apologized. "There's nothing—no one—down there. We could expand the search and look at a bigger piece of land, but we should probably wait until spring when the ground thaws."

I nodded in agreement even though he couldn't see me on the phone. It probably would be a waste of his time and departmental money to keep searching, trying to find a needle in the haystack. I had been hoping Stanley's GIS work would identify an anomaly, something that suggested where we should look for Danika, but so far his project hadn't produced any results either.

I thanked the professor for his time before hanging up.

"Another dead end," I announced to the room. It was a rare day when Stanley, Sarah, and I were all in the office at the same time. "Dr. Washington didn't find anything with his radar."

"At least that terrible woman won't have extra ammunition to gloat over," Sarah mumbled. "Can you imagine the smug look on her face if Dr. Washington had actually found something?"

I would have endured all of the smack talk in the world if it meant getting us one step closer to resolving this case, but I could understand Sarah's misgivings about Melody Sternbridge. I had the same misgivings myself.

"Stanley, no pressure," I remarked, "but until we get lab results back on Danika's bike, you may be our last hope for a break in the case."

"I can show you what I've got. It's not much," he admitted, "but maybe you'll see something I missed."

The three of us gathered around Stanley's open laptop.

"Here's what I've got so far. The area where Danika's bike was recovered is densely-settled suburbia." He pulled up an arial photo of what the subdivision looked like in present day. "But in 1984, this was all unsettled prairie."

With another click of the trackpad, the tiny houses and manicured lawns disappeared. A sepia-toned arial shot of undeveloped land took it place.

"This property wasn't originally trust land though," Stanley continued. "Over the years, the SMSC leveraged for more land to be added to the boundaries of the trust."

"So this was just a big field when someone buried Danika's bike," I followed. "But why wouldn't they bury her body in the same area?"

My thoughts continually returned to my conversation with Julia from the previous night. Why wasn't Danika's body discovered along with the yellow bicycle?

"The land where they discovered the bicycle," I continued to think aloud, "it used to be prairie. But what came after that? Was it always single-family homes?"

Stanley shook his head. "Single family, but different houses than what's there now. It was a trailer park in the mid- to-late 1980s."

"Probably wouldn't make sense to look up property maps," I decided. "No one's going to bury a missing girl's bicycle outside of their front door."

"Probably not," Stanley agreed.

"So now what?" Sarah questioned. "We wait until someone digs a hole for an in-ground pool to find her?"

I chewed on my lower lip. "What if she was already dug up?"

"What are you thinking?" Stanley asked.

"The entire reservation has been one big construction area since the 1990s. What if Danika was dug up back then but no one thought to, or didn't have the resources to, identify the body?"

"CODIS wasn't established until 1998," he observed, naming the Combined DNA Index System.

"And the Mystic Lake Casino opened in 1992," Sarah supplied. "That's what sparked the economic growth on the trust."

"So we've got a six-year gap where Danika's body could

have been recovered with no way to identify it," I said, thinking aloud.

"What about dental records?" Stanley suggested. "Forensic dentistry has been around forever."

"The SMSC lived well below the poverty line in the 1980s," Sarah reminded us. "It's likely Danika wouldn't have had a regular dentist who might have stored her dental records. Plus, when she left the reservation after high school, if those records did exist, they could have been transferred to wherever she moved to or destroyed."

"She could be a Jane Doe," I said, still thinking aloud. "We could ask a family member for a DNA sample. We could send it to the Doe Network and hope for a match."

The Doe Network was a non-profit organization that worked with law enforcement agencies across the country to connect missing person cases like ours to the physical remains of John or Jane Does. Sometimes people weren't actually missing; they'd been found but no one could verify their identity.

"Shit," Sarah suddenly swore.

"What?" I asked.

She shook her head and looked almost amused. "The timing of this is crazy."

"How so?" I questioned.

"In the early 1990s, the federal government passed laws to return Native American remains and artifacts to their respective tribal governments. It necessitated the return of tens of thousands of skeletons that previously had been on display in museums," she described. "If a body has been found on tribal lands during that time, there's a very good possibility that the SMSC was given permission to immediately re-bury it."

"And it never would have been entered into the Doe Network." I echoed Sarah's earlier assessment: "Shit. So now what?"

My brain hurt from all of these details and the muddied lines of law enforcement jurisdictions.

Sarah grimaced. "I don't suppose we can ask Chairman Strong if they found any bodies during that time period and where they reburied their dead?"

"There's no way in hell he's going to let us exhume bodies from a tribal graveyard," I prophesied. Not even Sarah's linguistic talents could finagle that. I pressed my fingertips to my temples. "This is feeling impossible."

Sarah offered me a sympathetic smile. "If it was easy, Danika would have already been found."

I knew Sarah had intended her words to reassure me, but it was going to take a lot more than gentle words to make me feel better about this case. Every possible lead had only led to one dead end after another.

∽

I let myself into Julia's condo after a disappointing day of work, fully expecting to come home to an empty space. Julia had been working longer hours, deeper into the evenings, in an effort to get acclimated to her new work environment at Grisham & Stein. But instead of silence and darkness, soft piano music played in the background and a fire flickered in the gas fireplace in the living room.

I stood in the front foyer and took in the altered

surroundings. In addition to the music and ambiance, someone had set up a small evergreen tree in the corner of the living room. The furniture had been slightly rearranged to make room for the new addition.

"Julia?" I called out as I removed my leather jacket.

I hadn't expected her home for several hours, yet I doubted we were being robbed by a thief with a penchant for Christmas and romance.

My girlfriend walked into the living room from the back of the condo. The tailored suit I'd helped her into earlier that morning had been exchanged for a wide-necked sweater and yoga pants.

"You're home," I said, stating the obvious. "And you decorated."

Julia joined me in the foyer and pressed a small kiss to the corner of my mouth. "It's just a little tree," she dismissed. "Plus, it's fake. Apparently the condo association doesn't allow real trees. Some nonsense about it being a fire hazard."

"How did you manage all of this with your wrist?" I questioned. My tone was a little accusatory.

"The doorman helped."

"Did he help you change clothes, too?"

"Funny girl," Julia smirked. "No, I was able to do that on my own."

She looked dynamic in the oversized sweater. She'd probably chosen it so her bandaged wrist could fit more easily through the wide sleeves, but I had to admire how the scooped neck accentuated her chiseled collarbone. If we had any barbecue sauce in the house I might have been tempted to nibble at that particularly delicious-looking bone.

"Come. I have something for you," she announced.

I had no choice but to leave the foyer and follow her into kitchen, where the sweet scent of chocolate perfumed the air. A single sauce pan sat on the gas range, quietly simmering on its burner. Julia grabbed an oversized ceramic cup from the granite counter top. She dipped a soup ladle into the sauce pan and transferred some of the chocolate liquid to the waiting mug.

"Homemade hot chocolate?" I guessed. "I thought I was the one who owed you."

Julia hummed in the affirmative. She handed me the warm mug, but held up a manicured finger. "Just a second."

She went to the refrigerator and retrieved a can of pressurized whipped cream. After a vigorous shake of the can with her good hand, she pressed the plastic nozzle and filled the empty space in the hot chocolate mug with white, frothy foam. The store-bought confection seemed a little working class for Julia Desjardin, but I supposed it was challenging to make fresh whipped cream with only one good wrist.

"Open," she commanded.

My mouth obediently popped open as if my jaw was on a hinge. My eyes opened wider when Julia proceeded to fill my mouth with whipped cream, straight from the pressurized can.

"Good girl," she murmured her approval.

I swallowed down the mouthful of cream, still a little dazed. I licked at the corners of my mouth to collect the leftover sweet stuff. "What's all this about?"

"A surprise."

"I *am* surprised," I confirmed with a short laugh.

"I decided to take a half day," she said. "And when I got home, I realized it didn't feel very Christmas-y in here."

"So you took off work and then did more work," I couldn't help pointing out.

"This is different," Julia rejected.

"It's amazing babe, it really is. But I'm serious about you taking it easy."

"I know, I know," she sighed. She flicked an annoyed hand through her dark locks. "I'll let you do the rest of the decorating."

All I wanted to do was take a hot shower and then veg out on the couch with her, but I knew Julia would never rest until her master Christmas design was complete.

"Okay," I agreed. "Let me change out of these clothes first."

"I put an outfit on the bed for you," Julia told me.

My features scrunched. "You picked out my clothes?"

"You'll see."

Curious, I set my hot chocolate on the kitchen counter and retreated to the rear bedroom. I didn't know what to expect. Julia was full of surprises these days. I doubted I'd find some kind of lingerie or revealing outfit—that wasn't really my style—but I certainly didn't expect the ugly Christmas sweater and equally obnoxious printed boxer shorts laid out on the bed.

"Are you serious?" I called out.

"Like a heart attack." Julia's voice was unexpectedly close. I turned on my heel to find her standing in the bedroom doorway. I hadn't realized she'd followed me.

I gestured wildly to the green and red sweater carefully laid out on the down comforter. "You really want me to wear that?"

She nodded. "And you should hurry, dear. Your hot chocolate is getting cold."

Julia left me and the bedroom without another word. I turned back to the garish outfit spread across the bed. My upper lip curled, and I picked at the cotton-blend material. "The things I do for love."

I changed out of my work clothes and into the curious outfit Julia had selected for me. The boxers were alright—forest green with oversized reindeer faces—but the sweater was something else altogether. For one, it was almost comically large. I pulled up the sleeves to my elbows where it bunched in an orgy of fabric. Secondly, the red top was designed to look like Santa's suit, complete with three-dimensional cotton puffs for the trim on his classic outfit. I couldn't imagine what had possessed Julia to buy the sweater or her expectation that I wear it. Maybe the pain killers prescribed for her injured wrist had impacted her decision making.

I walked from the back bedroom to the living room where Julia was sitting on the couch. I stood beneath the arch that separated the dining room from the living room.

I stared down at my ridiculous ensemble. "I'm being punked, right?"

Julia couldn't hide her smile, even behind the oversized cocoa mug in her hands. "It's a good look."

"Where's *your* ugly sweater?" I posed.

"Nothing I own is ugly," she sniffed.

"Well, now you do," I countered, "because there's no way in hell I'm claiming this outfit as mine."

Julia smiled more broadly while she sipped from her mug of hot chocolate. "You're sweet to humor me."

A retort about coming down her chimney or stuffing her

stocking came to mind, but I kept my comments to myself. "So I'm decorating this tree?"

Julia flicked her fingers in the direction of a storage container that sat on the coffee table. "The ornaments are in there."

I popped the top of the plastic bin, expecting to find handmade ornaments from Julia's childhood. Only generic glass bulbs were inside.

"Where's all the popsicle sticks?" I frowned.

"Sorry?"

I gestured to the red, white, and silver bulbs in the box. "Where's all the Christmas ornaments from when you were little?"

Julia shrugged. "In my parents' attic, I suppose. Where are yours?"

"The same," I admitted.

Julia stood from the couch as only she could. Long, lean legs uncrossed before she rose from the couch cushion in a single, fluid motion. She continued to hold the ceramic mug that held her hot chocolate without spilling a drop. Everything she did appeared so flawless and effortless. If I had attempted the same maneuver, especially with one injured wrist, I would have spilled down the front of my stupid Christmas sweater.

"What's wrong, Cassidy?"

"It's dumb," I said. I suddenly felt a combination of embarrassment and shame.

"Nothing you could do would ever be 'dumb,' darling."

I took a breath. "I'm having some kind of holiday crisis," I revealed. "I never thought about Christmas or holiday traditions when I was enlisted. It was just another day on the calendar, with maybe a special meal or something. But now that I'm back, now that I'm just a regular person, I kind of want it to mean something."

"Like your dating To Do list," Julia observed. "Like you're making up for lost time."

I nodded. "Uh huh."

Saying the words aloud had made me feel vulnerable; I was grateful for her patience and understanding. Another, lesser, person might have thought I was making a big deal out of nothing, but Julia knew my idiosyncrasies almost as well as I did.

"What did you have in mind?" she asked. "What traditions would you like to re-create?"

"That's the thing," I frowned. "I'm sure we had traditions growing up, but there's nothing specific that I'm really itching to re-create. Is there something you want to do?"

"I had thought about spending Christmas Day with my mother," she admitted, "but I wouldn't want to put you out."

Julia's singular goal since her father's acquittal had been to regain custody of her mother, both physically and legally. With her father's death, the only obstacle remaining had been paperwork and finding a new assisted living space. Legal custody was only a formality. Getting Julia to settle on a home for her mom had proven to be far more challenging. In the end, Julia had decided on a facility in the nearby suburbs. The St. Paul and Minneapolis buildings we'd toured had been too noisy, too crowded, and too urban for Julia's tastes. If her mother was to be removed from Embarrass, she hadn't wanted to upset her more with a totally foreign experience.

I'd offered to come with Julia when she picked up her

mom from Embarrass to transport her to the new facility. It hadn't exactly been a full throated offer, but I didn't want Julia to feel like she was on her own. We were a team, even if old people and hospitals made me uncomfortable. Julia had gently refused my help. I'd tried to school my features and not look too relieved, but I was sure Julia knew the task wasn't exactly a favorable one.

I didn't want to vocalize that spending Christmas Day at an assisted living facility sounded like a terrible idea; I didn't want to be selfish. Having her mother re-homed in the Twin Cities meant sharing Julia's time, especially on holidays.

"Do you want to go to St. Cloud?" she asked.

"Shipping me off already?" I laughed.

"No, I meant the both of us."

"You ..." I blinked several times. "You want to spend Christmas with my parents?"

"It's not necessarily about *wanting*," she clarified. "I *want* to be alone with you in the condo, but the holidays should be bigger than us."

"I'm okay with us being selfish," I readily insisted.

"Not worried about getting on Santa's naughty list?" Julia mused. "I'm sure your mother would love to see you."

"So would yours," I pointed out.

"What if we did both?" she suggested. "Do you want to spend your birthday in St. Cloud?"

My response was immediate. "*Hell*, no."

Julia smiled at my emphatic reaction. "Then let's do Christmas Eve and Day in the city. I'll even throw you a birthday party. After I spend some time with my mom, we can go to St. Cloud for a few days."

I chewed on my lower lip as I contemplated her suggestion. "How long were you thinking?"

"Not long. I can work remotely, but I should really be back in the office. I'm sure you have to be back for work, too. Speaking of work," she seemed to sigh, "I'll be home late on Friday. My office is having a holiday party. I abhor these kinds of things, but I should probably make an effort since I'm so new at the firm."

"The last time you were at a holiday office party, didn't you make out with Melissa Ferdet?"

I tried to keep my tone light, but I couldn't help how my stomach twisted every time I thought about the two of them working together.

"Technically the last holiday office party I attended was in Embarrass," Julia corrected, "but yes, I know to what you're referring." She arched an elegant eyebrow. "Worried about a repeat performance, dear?"

"No," I huffed.

I wanted to admit all of my insecurities to her. It was more than just our age difference that made me feel out of my league; it was the whole package. Class, education level, lived experience—I could have droned on and on about all of the ways I didn't quite measure up or deserve to be her partner. A partnership suggested equality. Through no fault of Julia's, I still felt undeserving. She had never deliberately made me feel less than; those were my own misgivings and inadequacies that I needed to overcome.

"Would you want to come?" she posed.

The invitation took me by surprise. "I don't know. Sure? I mean, I guess that's what you do when you're dating someone, right?" I chewed on my lower lip. "Do you *want* me to come?"

"This is new territory for me too, darling. I've never had a significant other to bring along to these kinds of things."

"We'll play it by ear," I suggested. Julia's noncommittal answer had me playing it neutral, too. "This case has me in Prior Lake every other day, so who knows if I'll even be around."

"Come if you're able," she approved. "Just ..." She hesitated. "Don't wear that."

"Oh, don't worry," I told her with a smirk. "I have every intention of burning this sweater after tonight."

Chapter Fourteen

Melody Sternbridge showed up with an oversized box of donuts. I'd only recently arrived to the basement office that morning, barely having had time to take off my jacket, but at least she hadn't been awaiting my arrival this time. She dumped the pink cardboard box onto my desk and flipped off its lid to reveal a baker's dozen of variously frosted treats. The sugary perfume battled with the persistent scent of burnt coffee that always seemed to linger in the police department.

"I hope you're not allergic to gluten," she grunted.

I stood with her entrance. "What's the occasion?"

"Peace offering." She took off her winter gloves and flopped down in the same chair she'd occupied only days before. I hadn't bothered moving it back to its original location. "I realized I've been pretty pushy and rude. You're doing the best you can with limited resources."

My fingers wiggled over the open box as I took stock of the glistening treats. "I've dealt with worse," I allowed. "It kind of comes with the territory."

"Why'd you become a cop anyway?" she asked.

"I was in the military before this. It was a pretty natural transition."

Melody's features took on a new look as if I'd suddenly become interesting to her again. I instantly regretted sharing anything about my background, no matter how broad or vague. I'd once been front-page news in a small town newspaper. I wanted to avoid that from happening ever again.

"How'd you get into podcasting?" I asked, desperate to detour attention away from me.

"I went to college for journalism, but I wasn't able to get a job in my field after graduation. It started off as a hobby," she said, "telling other kinds of stories. Once I made the transition to True Crime, things took off so I stuck with it. The money is obviously a factor," she admitted with a small shrug, "but I feel like I'm making a difference doing this. I'm helping people," she asserted.

"And entertaining bored suburban moms," I couldn't help adding.

Melody flashed an annoyed look in my direction. "I'm taking back my donuts."

A new voice entered the office: "I had an idea."

My attention shifted from Melody's face and moved in the direction of the third voice. Stanley walked through the entrance of the Cold Case office. He stopped abruptly, his snow boots squeaking on the cheap flooring, when he realized I wasn't alone. "Oh. Sorry. I can come back."

I ushered him closer. "Come on in, Stanley. This is Melody Sternbridge," I introduced. "She's that podcaster who was looking into the Danika Laroque case. Melody, meet Stanley Harris. He works for the Cold Case division, too."

Melody removed her knit cap and fluffed at her long red locks. "Charmed," she greeted. She batted her eyelashes a few times. "Has anyone ever told you that you have a voice for radio, Stanley?"

Stanley looked unsteady on his feet. "Oh, uh. N-no."

I looked between the weirdly flirtatious podcaster woman and my work friend. Stanley had a habit of getting tongue-tied around pretty women. *Any* women, actually.

I cleared my throat. "Stanley. You had an idea?"

He blinked once. "Right," he said, seeming to get back on track. "I was piecing together our crime scene, or at least the gas station where Danika worked from old photographs when I thought about it. We were lamenting not having video surveillance, but then I thought about the other technological infrastructure that would have been around at the time."

He paused as if expecting me to finish his thought.

"And?" I pressed.

"Pay phones," he said. "I don't have any images that prove there would have been a pay phone around the gas station, but it makes sense."

"You think Danika might have made a phone call?" I guessed.

"It's not much; it's a maybe. I'd like to look into calls to and from a potential pay phone around the time she got off of work. Maybe we could identify the last person to talk to her. Maybe they were the last person to see her, too."

I considered Stanley's idea. It seemed tenuous, but I was mindful of something Julia had said about these cases. Even the smallest thread or anomaly might lead to something bigger. "Do phone companies hold on to call records for thirty years?"

"I'm not sure," he admitted. "But it's worth looking into, don't you think?"

"It's the boyfriend. It's always the boyfriend," Melody chimed in.

Stanley turned to the seated woman. "What's your evidence?"

"Nothing concrete," she conceded, "but that doesn't mean he didn't do it."

Stanley seemed to scowl. "Wild conjectures and conspiracies might fly on internet discussion boards, but out here in the real world, we need proof. Scientific, irrevocable proof."

He'd only raised his voice a little, but I'd never seen Stanley so worked up. He typically possessed a mild, almost robotic demeanor.

Melody rolled her eyes in an exaggerated manner. She grabbed her gloves and her hat and stood up. "Detective Miller," she sniffed, "I'll be in touch."

I thought she might confiscate her gift of donuts, but she stalked out the office door without them. Her melting, snowy exit left boot-shaped puddles on the tile floor.

"She bugs you, eh?" I innocently remarked.

Stanley frowned. "But not you?"

"Oh, she's annoying," I admitted. "But, hey. Free donuts?"

I clenched and unclenched my fingers around a stress ball that resembled a rotund Santa Claus. Each time I squeezed the little red sphere that mimicked his body, the figure's black and white cartoonish eyes bulged out. I had forced myself to stop snacking on the bribery donuts Melody

Sternbridge had left to avoid looking like Santa Claus myself.

"When exactly did Danika Laroque go missing?" I posed aloud.

Stanley delicately picked at a jelly donut. He ate the pastry with a plastic knife and fork to presumably avoid getting frosting or raspberry jam stuck in his beard.

"1984."

"But when in 1984?" I questioned. "Like, what month?"

Stanley licked sugar off his right fingertips before pressing a few keys on his computer's keyboard. "February," he announced.

I chewed on the inside of my lip as I pondered the intelligence. *February.* The month of love. I wondered if Julia would want to celebrate Valentine's Day or if she considered it a fake holiday invented by the candy and greeting card companies.

I'd always been stressed out around Valentine's Day. As a kid, I'd panicked about which pre-printed message I should give to which of my classmates. "Will You Be My Valentine?" *Hell, no.* I didn't want anyone to get any funny ideas that I might have a crush on them. When I got older, Valentine's Day had morphed into a way for the popular kids to shame everyone else. I wasn't exactly popular in high school, but I hadn't been an outcast either, largely because I'd been on the swim team. But I also had never been on the receiving end of any secret red roses you could send your crush as a school fundraiser. I'd been too chicken shit to send any either, so I'd mostly made fun of the holiday.

I remembered one of the guys on the swim team being totally baffled by the single red roses that got delivered during the school day. He couldn't figure out where the flowers had come from. You couldn't grow roses in Minnesota in February.

February.

"She's not buried." I murmured the words to myself. I sat up straighter in my office chair. "Stanley," I announced. "She's not buried."

My colleague looked away from his illuminated computer screen. "Huh?"

"The ground would have been frozen solid in February. If someone wanted to get rid of the body, she's not getting buried. Not in the earth, at least."

"Where is she then?" he posed.

"Where is she. Where is she. Where is she." I chanted the mantra to myself.

My eyes fell to a poorly framed map of the state that clung precariously to the concrete walls of the Cold Case office with the assistance of blue tacky material. The state's motto was printed at the top of the map: *Minnesota. Land of 10,000 Lakes.*

"She's not underground. She's under *water.*" My heart lodged in my throat. "You cut a fucking hole in the fucking ice. Drop the body in there. No one's finding that."

I heard Stanley exhale. "I think you might be right."

I swore the hair on my arms was standing up. "No one's going to think twice if they see a vehicle out on the ice. No one's going to give a second look to someone cutting a hole in the ice, not even at night." I could feel my confidence grow. "They'd think you were fishing, not making a body disappear."

Stanley abandoned his donut and sprang into action. He

clicked his fingers over his keyboard and pulled up aerial shots of the Prior Lake region. "It would need to be a body of water big enough that people would go ice fishing on it," he said, thinking aloud. "Probably not the most popular one if you want to avoid anyone actually seeing you dumping a body."

I picked up my office phone and dialed the number for Officer Azure. I assumed if anyone could help us narrow down area lakes, it would be him.

"Prior Lake Police." I recognized his voice on the other end of the call. "Azure here."

"Azure, this is Cassidy Miller, Minneapolis Cold Case."

"Oh, hey, Miller," he greeted. "What can I do for you?"

"This might be a weird question," I began, "but how many lakes are in Prior Lake?"

"At least fifteen. Why?"

"Do people go ice fishing on them?"

"Shit, yeah," he confirmed. "Prior Lake itself is really popular. The ice gets at least a foot and a half thick in winter."

"How about on trust land?" I posed. I doubted someone would venture too far off the reservation to dispose of Danika's body. They wouldn't want to take that added risk.

Azure made a thoughtful sound. "There's a couple. Mystic Lake, which is right by the casino. That's a pretty popular spot. There's also Arctic Lake." He paused. "But now that I think about it, the SMSC aerates that water to reduce fish die-off in winter."

"So it doesn't freeze over completely?" I questioned. I could feel my throat tighten at the admission.

"Not completely, no."

"Thanks, Azure. You've been a great help."

My palms felt clammy once I ended the call. Stanley regarded me, waiting for the answer.

"Arctic Lake," I said with grim satisfaction. "That's where we'll find her."

※

"Jesus, it's colder than a witch's tit today." Officer Brendon Azure breathed warm air into his cupped hands. He glanced sideways, as if suddenly remembering his company, before mumbling a sheepish apology.

I was used to crude and coarse language. I, in fact, was often an active participant in that kind of behavior. But that didn't stop other male cops, especially those who didn't know me very well, from apologizing for their word choice in front of me.

"Colder than penguin snot," I briskly concurred.

The wind was still that morning, but even without the wind chill, the outside temperature was well below freezing. I hugged my torso and silently cursed that I hadn't worn a warmer jacket. My signature leather jacket and the Harley Sportster went hand-in-hand; they were both impractical for Minnesota's winters, but vanity and stubbornness continued to win over the realization that I needed to evolve.

Officer Azure had met up with me at Arctic Lake earlier that morning, along with a small team of the county's police divers. Because we suspected the body was under water, the cadaver dogs hadn't been brought in despite being skilled enough to detect human remains that were hundreds, if not thousands of years old.

I'd driven to the city of Prior Lake by myself; Sarah and Stanley had remained at the office. Searching Arctic Lake might take several days, and there was no guarantee Danika Laroque's remains would even be under the pond's motionless water. Cooler water temperatures delayed decomposition, but thirty years had passed. If anything remained of Danika Laroque, I suspected there would be nothing left but skeletal remains. Arctic Lake had no discernible current, but aquatic animals would accelerate the breakdown of flesh. But even bones could provide clues about her disappearance. And the discovery of her whereabouts might provide some closure for her family.

Unlike the town's namesake body of water—Prior Lake—at twenty-five acres, Arctic Lake was much smaller. Its center reached a respectable thirty-one feet deep, but overall the body of water only averaged depths of nine and a half feet. It also wasn't as popular as nearby Prior Lake. In recent years the SMSC had partnered with the Spring Lake Watershed District to improve its water quality and eliminate the invasive carp.

Driving up to the modest-sized lake had solidified my hunch that Danika's body had been dumped at that location. Not only did the water never freeze over completely because of the tribe's aeration system, it was also relatively private. No houses or cabins dotted the shoreline. Few docks provided lake access, and yet a narrow, unpaved road ran parallel to the water's edge. A vehicle could drive close enough to the lake and a single driver could easily dispose of the body without anyone observing their activities.

Azure and I watched the diving team from a short wooden pier. They'd only been able to load a fifteen-foot inflatable boat with an outboard motor into the lake. Anything heavier would have sunk the boat trailer's wheels into the marshy shoreline. Two divers took turns exploring the lake bed, sifting through mud, sand, and decomposed organisms in search of something that didn't belong there. They wore wet suits, but I could only imagine how cold the water was, especially at the lake's deepest levels.

An involuntary shiver passed over my body. Azure glanced in my direction. "You don't have to be here, you know. I can call if they find anything."

His words were without malice or judgment; I really didn't need to be there. But I'd become too invested in this hunch panning out to sit and wait by the phone.

"No, I'm good," I resisted. I jerked my thumb in the direction of my parked Crown Vic. "I'm just going to warm up in the car for a little bit."

I hustled back to my police car. It looked more exhausted than usual next to the brand new SUV Azure had driven. I slid behind the steering wheel, but didn't start the engine. Just being inside the car was several degrees warmer than it had been by the lake.

Beyond the rapidly fogging windshield, Officer Azure looked somber. I considered inviting him to sit in the car with me, but he had a vehicle of his own. Plus, he'd dressed more appropriately for the weather than me. His leather jacket was police issued—significantly warmer than mine with a popped up faux fur-lined collar. It was times like this that I lamented no longer wearing the light blue patroler's uniform. I outranked Azure, but the combination of my gender and my lack of uniform sometimes resulted in imposter syndrome.

In the absence of something to do, I called my friend

Rich's phone. It had been a while since we'd last talked, and I had a request about which I'd been procrastinating.

"Hey," I greeted when he answered his phone. "You got a minute?"

"I always have time for you, Mama Cass," came his easy response.

"Do you like your job?"

Rich didn't have an immediate response, but I doubted he'd anticipated the question. It wasn't that long ago that I was sitting in his cubical in the First Precinct, practically begging him to find me a new job. Things hadn't gone as planned in Embarrass—namely the night terrors hadn't dissipated. I wondered if he thought I was spiraling out again.

"It's a job," he stated neutrally. "It pays the bills."

"Yeah, but do you like working in IA?"

Rich wasn't a beat cop like the rest of my police friends. He had a few years on all of us and had transferred to working for Internal Affairs. When I'd proactively taken myself off of active duty, back when my PTSD had first flared up, Rich had been a big help in my transition to desk duty. Ultimately I'd become dissatisfied with sitting behind a desk all day and had sought out the opportunity up north in Embarrass.

"Why?" he asked.

I hadn't expected Rich to be so evasive, but perhaps that was all the answer I needed.

"Julia got a new job at a big law firm in the city. She'll be doing *pro bono* work and focusing on unlawful convictions. She's in the process of hiring a team, which includes a private investigator." I paused to let Rich take in the information. "Think you might be interested?"

Instead of answering my question, he posed one of his own: "Why aren't you?"

Now it was my turn to hesitate. "Ahh ..."

"Don't shit where you eat, right?"

"Eloquent as always, dude," I snorted.

"Let me think on it," he said. "I *am* kind of itching for something new, but I'm not sure what that might be."

"Fair enough," I allowed. "I can have Julia send you the details."

"How *is* Julia?" he asked.

"She's good," I confirmed. "She's making me have a birthday party."

"How cruel," Rich chuckled.

"Do you want to come or not?" I huffed in annoyance. "It's Christmas Eve, so I understand if you're busy or whatever."

"I wouldn't miss it, Rookie. I'll let Gracie know, assuming she's invited, too."

"Let me know what?" I heard a muffled but familiar voice in the background.

"Are you with Grace right now?" I asked.

"Yeah. I took the day off," he revealed. "I'm up north at your old stomping grounds."

"I should feel lucky you answered the phone at all," I teased my friend.

I heard some rustling as if the phone was exchanging hands.

"Cassidy?" I recognized Grave Kelly Donovan's high register.

"Hey, Grace," I greeted.

"Hi!" she chirped. "How are you?"

"No complaints," I said in truth.

"I miss you," she said, not bothering to mask the whine in her tone. "Let's get together soon."

"I miss you, too," I returned. "I don't know when I'll be in Embarrass next."

I'd used up most of my PTO for Julia's father's funeral. We'd only intended on staying in Embarrass for a few days, but ultimately settled his affairs and clearing Julia of any wrong doing had taken some time.

"I'll be in Minneapolis next weekend," she said. "Rich and I are trying to alternate weekends. Do you and Julia want to hang out? Maybe get dinner with us on Friday night?"

"Julia has a work party on Friday. How about Saturday instead?"

"Oooh. Work party," Grace cooed. "That sounds serious. What are you going to wear?"

"Oh. I don't know if I'm even going to go," I deflected. I hadn't made up my mind. Julia hadn't appeared overly eager for me to go, which had me dragging my feet.

"Of course you are! Don't you want to be the impressive trophy wife that Julia gets to show off?"

"Trophy wife?" I echoed with a laugh. "That's fresh. More like consolation prize."

"Cassidy Miller." Grace's voice had taken on a serious tone. "You are going to buy a new dress, I am going to do your makeup and hair, and you are going to make all of those other lawyers absolutely green with envy that Julia gets to go home with you."

"Why do I feel like I've just stumbled into a scene from a rom-com movie?" I grumbled.

Grace practically squealed in my ear. "Makeover!"

"This sounds like I don't have a choice," I lamented.

My attention strayed from the phone call when I noticed new action near the lake's perimeter. Officer Azure had left the small wooden pier to get closer to the shoreline. The diving team had returned to their boat and seemed to be motoring in his direction.

"Grace, I've got to go," I said in a distracted rush. I hustled her off the phone call with a promise to talk soon.

It was cold beyond the comfortable confines of the squad car. The wind had picked up since I'd retreated inside. I jogged from the parked vehicle to join Officer Azure. My boots sank into the cold, marshy embankment.

Azure and I helped drag the front of the police boat onto dry land.

"What's up?" Azure asked. "Are you taking a break?"

One of the divers pulled back the cap of his wetsuit. He was older than I'd originally assumed with a head full of silver hair. "We found something. *Someone*."

I couldn't breathe.

The diver turned his body away from us. He collected something from the blue tarp that had been laid across the boat's floor. When he turned back, I noticed he now held something in his hands.

A skull. A human skull. The bones had been picked clean. No flesh, no hair remained. It looked like it belonged in the corner of a high school science classroom, not at the bottom of a lake.

Azure spoke before I could find my words: "Shit."

Chapter Fifteen

Afghanistan, 2012

We travel at night. The terrain is more challenging to navigate with only the moon and stars to light our way, but it's gotten too hard and too dangerous to move when the sun is at its highest point.

Pensacola thinks he's going to die; he's told me as much.

"Leave me," has become a kind of mantra.

He'd never been optimistic about his chances, but now he's downright depressing. I respond with various refusals to his pleas.

"No."

"Shut up, dude."

"Fuck no."

"Not a chance."

"Make me."

But it's hard to pretend for so long. I'm not even sure *I'll* survive this ordeal.

What do you think of this one?

The texts and accompanying hyperlinks had been happening nearly every day since I'd agreed to let Grace help me get ready for Julia's work party. While I could have feigned annoyance, it was actually kind of nice to have a girl friend who could help me out with this kind of stuff. I did want to look nice for Julia's office party—maybe not the trophy wife part—but I wanted her to be proud to be seen with me in front of her new, fancy colleagues.

I could hold my own during any of our other pre-planned dates, but this was different. Everyone with whom she worked had multiple degrees while I'd only ever graduated from high school. They all made six-figure salaries and presumably dressed the part. I made a decent living, and my pension would keep me comfortable long after I hung up my badge, but I didn't drive a luxury sedan, and the only labels in my clothes closet were from Target.

"Detective?"

"Sorry." I hastily put my phone in my back pocket. The device continued to vibrate as Grace Kelly sent more dress ideas.

It was probably wildly inappropriate to be thinking about dresses when I was supposed to be paying attention to the medical examiner, but the date of Julia's work party was rapidly approaching.

I hadn't been sure a medical examiner would be able to determine the cause of death for a body—now little more than a scattered collection of bones—that had been submerged in water for close to thirty years. But science was close to magic these days. The coroner's records had listed Danika's death as *homicidal violence,* a phrase often used when a death is surrounded by mysterious circumstances but authorities lack enough solid evidence to pinpoint the exact cause.

Stanley and I had set up an appointment with the medical examiner's office at their earliest convenience to see the remains ourselves. Our connection to the coroner's office was a man named Gary. He and Stanley knew each other from college, back when Stanley had wanted to become a medical examiner himself.

The garish fluorescent lights of the sterile space glared down on dull grey bones. The skeleton hadn't been complete when we'd removed it from Arctic Lake. After discovering the human skull, the ribcage and two arms had come next. Further investigation of the sandy lake floor had produced a pelvic bone and parts of her legs. The coroner had laid out Danika's remains on the examination table to resemble a person as best as he could for the autopsy.

I'd seen plenty of dead bodies between my time in the military and with Minneapolis police, but they'd always been new; they'd still looked like themselves. Mostly. It was a different sensation to see an aged skeleton, worn down by exposure to the elements, and to consider that the bone had once been wrapped in warm, living flesh. That a young woman had once embodied this space. I still couldn't rectify why Danika's bicycle had been found buried on someone else's property, but perhaps the killer believed the yellow bike would be more easily found in the water than a weighted-down body.

"If I was a betting man," Gary pronounced, "I'd say death

by strangulation."

I turned to the man. "You can tell that, even from a skeleton?"

Gary grabbed a metal tool from a nearby wheeled cart. The thin metal rod had been nestled among other gadgets that better resembled torture tools. He stepped closer to the lower half of the incomplete skeleton.

"We found some strange indentations in both femurs." He used the metal tool to point toward the upper leg bones. "But that wouldn't have caused a fatality." He flicked his wrist like the metal rod was a magic wand and landed next near the upper spine. "Her hyoid was fractured. It's this u-shaped bone in the neck," he explained. "You typically find that broken in homicides by strangulation."

"Strangulation." I chewed on my lower lip. "Seems pretty intimate." I looked to my Cold Case partner. "The boyfriend's alibi checked out?"

Stanley nodded. "Uh huh. Police cleared him from being a person of interest nearly immediately."

I returned my gaze to what little remained of Danika Laroque. "Let's double-check it."

∽

It was a cold and sunny morning during my fifth trip to Prior Lake. Officer Azure had been the one to tell the Laroque family about uncovering Danika's remains, but I had a new set of questions for the family in the wake of that discovery. The chances of finding foreign DNA or fibers on the skeletal remains was slim to none, but it was well within our rights to thoroughly process the bones before returning them to the

Laroque family for a proper burial. The lab was backed up more than usual because of the upcoming holidays, but Danika's family had waited thirty years to find her. I hoped they'd have the patience to wait a little longer for us to process her remains.

Sarah had wanted to take the trip with me. I didn't mind her company, plus as a representative of the Victim's Advocate office, she was trained in softening my rough edges. She knew how to get information without re-traumatizing the victim's family.

We met Jenny Laroque at her Prior Lake home. She offered the customary tea or coffee, which Sarah and I both refused, before she ushered us into the dining room as before. But unlike our initial visit, this time Jenny wasn't alone. An older woman was already sitting at the dining room table when we arrived.

"This is my mother," Jenny explained. "She wanted to be here for this."

I nodded in greeting at the older Laroque woman. She was small, like elderly women tend to be, but she looked fierce rather than frail. Her grey-white hair was styled in short, tight curls like she'd recently been to the salon. Bronzed, weathered hands folded over each other. Dark, intense eyes scrutinized Sarah and myself as we took our seats at the table.

"Híŋhaŋni láȟčiŋ," Sarah greeted.

"Mom doesn't—." Jenny cut in. She looked once in her mother's direction. "We don't speak Dakota."

I frowned. So much for relying on Sarah's insider charms.

Mrs. Laroque pursed her lips. "My mother would have taught me and my siblings and then I would have taught my children if it hadn't been forbidden in the white school she attended."

"Mrs. Laroque," I began, not wanting our visit to get derailed before it had even started, "we're very sorry for your loss."

She didn't use words. But I heard it in the sound she made. Thirty years of buried emotions flooded to the surface, one complicated emotion after the next.

"It's ... bittersweet. All these years, I wanted to believe she left for a better life, but now I know that she was never really gone. We finally know what happened. We can finally bring her home."

"How did you—how were you able to identify her?" Jenny asked.

"We were able to extract DNA from one of her molars," I revealed. "I don't want to bother you or waste anymore of your time, but I do have a few questions."

Mrs. Laroque inclined her head, allowing me to continue.

I looked down at the pocket-sized notebook I'd been scribbling thoughts into ever since we'd started searching for Danika's body in Arctic Lake. "Would there be a reasonable explanation why Danika would have been out on Arctic Lake the night of her disappearance? Did she go ice fishing or might she be visiting friends out there?"

The coroner's report suggested a violent ending to her life, but there was always the possibility that those injuries had been sustained post-mortem.

Mrs. Laroque shook her head. She hugged at her narrow torso over the snowflake-covered sweater she wore. "It was dark and cold and snowing. I can't imagine anyone being out on any lake that night."

"You're sure it was snowing?" I asked.

She nodded. Her milky gaze left my face to stare out one of the dining room windows. "I think about that from time to time. I should have picked her up after work. It was snowing, and she only had her bike. Maybe if I'd gone out that night, she'd still be here."

In my line of work, I heard a lot of wistfulness. A lot of *if onlys* and *if I had to do it all over again*. It wasn't my job to make people feel better about the choices they'd made, but I did feel sorry for this woman and for her loss. No parent should have to outlive their child.

"What about her boyfriend, Jim Knutson?" I asked. "Didn't he normally give her a ride home from work?"

Mrs. Laroque's eyes came back into focus. "Jim? No. No. They'd broken up."

I sat a little straighter in my chair. "They were broken up?"

That was a detail that hadn't made it into the 1984 police report. It also hadn't made it into Melody Sternbridge's recent interview with the man.

Mrs. Laroque rested her hands on the table top. "I'm not sure of the specifics, but they hadn't been together for a while. They must have broken up just before Christmas. I remember because he still gave her a present, even though she'd been the one to end things."

I looked in the direction of my Cold Case colleague. Sarah silently nodded as if to say Mrs. Laroque's information was notable. A visit to the ex-boyfriend's house would be next on our list. He'd given police in 1984 a story; how much of that story was true was yet to be seen.

I had expected another massive house with a garage larger than the home in which I'd grown up. But when Sarah and I pulled up to Jim Knutson's house that afternoon, not long after leaving Jenny Laroque's French Provincial mansion, we discovered a simple, single-family home with an attached one-car garage.

A red Ford F150 was parked in the long paved driveway that led up to the house. The garage—too small for the extended cab vehicle—had its door open. I spied a vintage muscle car inside. The hood was lifted and a man was bent over, tinkering with the mechanical parts inside.

I dragged the bottoms of my boots on the pavement to avoid startling the man. My right hand hovered above the empty space where my service gun would have been if I was still a beat cop with a utility belt. I still had a police-issued weapon, but it was in a lockbox in a desk drawer in the Cold Case office. I wasn't really worried about confronting Jim Knutson, but he'd quickly become our prime suspect.

Sarah walked up the driveway a few feet behind me. I wondered at her level of comfort to be interviewing a key suspect. Whenever she'd tagged along with me, we typically visited with victims' families and friends. She was trained in conversations, not combat. I doubted anything would happen, but even routine traffic stops could go sideways.

I stepped a few feet from the open garage door. "Mr. Knutson?"

"Who's asking?" The man slowly disentangled himself from the old car's engine block.

Jim Knutson was an average man. Average build. Not

necessarily handsome or ugly. He had a full head of light brown hair that he wore in a nondescript style. His nose was crooked like it had been broken several times. Despite it being mid-December, he wore only a stained t-shirt and blue jeans. His exposed skin was red from high blood pressure or exposure to the winter elements.

"I've already found Jesus."

I blinked one. "Pardon?"

The man grabbed an old rag and used it to wipe at his grease-covered hands. "Aren't you one of those Mormons?"

I heard Sarah's snicker.

"No, sir. I'm Detective Cassidy Miller, Minneapolis Cold Case Division. This is my colleague, Dr. Sarah Conrad."

Sarah loved it when I used her official title.

"Oh. Sorry," the man said haltingly. "I saw the clothes and just assumed."

I looked at down at my outfit. I wore my typical work uniform of dark dress pants and a dark button-up shirt. Did people who attended the Church of Latter Day Saints wear motorcycle leather jackets?

"We're investigating the 1984 disappearance of Danika Laroque," I told him. "I believe you used to date."

Jim Knutson nodded. "Uh huh."

"Do you recall where you were the night she went missing?"

His grey-blue eyes shifted in his skull. "Do I need a lawyer or something?"

"We're just following up on a few anomalies from your initial statement to police," I clarified.

"Anomalies?" he repeated.

"You didn't mention to police that Danika had broken up

with you. And you didn't tell that to Melody Sternbridge either," Sarah remarked.

"Does that matter?" Jim leveled his eyes on Sarah. "Danika and I were always breaking up and getting back together."

"In a murder investigation," Sarah returned, "yes, it matters."

"Murder?" The man's voice lilted up.

"We have reason to believe her death wasn't accidental," I told him.

There was no reason to divulge every detail from the coroner's report to a person of interest, but observing their reactions could sometimes be revealing.

"Death." Jim Knutson's forehead wrinkled with a new emotion. "You found her."

"Yes, sir," I confirmed.

The man audibly exhaled. He seemed to brace himself on the edge of the antique vehicle. For a second I worried he might faint or have a stroke.

I let the information sit with him for a long moment.

"I was at a bar that night." He repeated what we already knew. "You can check with Sam Carson and Bill Blodget. They were there that night, too."

"We will," Sarah promised.

The conversation had grown tense. I didn't want this man to lawyer up. We had enough challenges with a thirty-year-old case without our chief suspect clamming up.

I nodded in the direction of the vintage vehicle. "Is that a '69 Camaro?"

The man's features momentarily brightened. "Good eye."

"I had a Hot Wheels car that looked just like it when I was little."

Jim ran his hand over the flawless chassis. "Just winterizing the old girl. It was my first major purchase when I graduated high school."

I did some quick mental math. I'd known Jim Knutson had been older than Danika when they'd dated, but I hadn't realized the age difference had been so great.

"It's a beauty," I admired.

"It's a money pit," he laughed, "but I can't bring myself to sell it. Too many memories."

His features took on a funny look, almost like he might cry. I became uncomfortable on his behalf.

Jim Knutson swallowed with some difficulty. He coughed once and ran his fingers through his short hair. "What, uh, what else do you want to know?"

"I think we have enough for the moment," I decided. "We'll be in touch though."

Sarah spoke up the moment we were back in the unmarked police car. I started up the vehicle and sat in the driveway to let the older car warm up again.

"I can't believe you didn't arrest him."

"He's a person of interest," I observed, "but we don't have anything concrete that connects him to Danika's death. It's not illegal to be someone's ex-boyfriend."

"Not that," she corrected with a snort. "He said you dressed like a Christian missionary."

I rolled my eyes as I shifted the police vehicle into reverse.

Chapter Sixteen

Jim Knutson had told police that he'd been at a bar just beyond the reservation's borders on the night of Danika Laroque's disappearance. Attempts to corroborate his whereabouts were complicated by the fact that none of the men who'd vouched for him back in 1984 still lived in the area. We'd eventually find them, but it would take some time to track down their contact information.

More problematic were the chances that, thirty years later, any of them would be able to remember anything about that night. Memories change over time. They fade, they become distorted and confused. And some things a person might remember may not have even happened in the first place. The bar didn't even exist anymore. It had been sold in the early 2000s and demolished; it only existed in old photographs and in people's flawed remembrances.

I would have been consumed with the details of the case if not for Julia's office party. DNA testing on Danika's recovered bicycle had yet to come through. Danika's remains had similarly been sent to the lab, but it would probably be weeks until anything came back. In some ways it was useful that I had Julia's party to fret over rather than obsessively check my work email for updates.

My cellphone rang with an incoming call. It was Julia, not the office with an update.

"Are you on your way?" she asked when I answered the call.

"Almost. Work went a little long today." I recited my practiced lie. "Don't worry though. I'll be there soon."

"I can just come home," she said. "I don't really need to be here."

I could anticipate Julia's annoyance at my delay. She hadn't wanted to go to the work party in the first place. If there was one thing my girlfriend despised, it was small-talk with inane people.

"I'll be there soon," I said with feeling.

I hung up with Julia and turned my attention back to the full-length mirror in Julia's bedroom. I pushed large, soft curls away from my face and released a single breath. "Not too shabby," I told my mirrored reflection.

Grace Kelly used a lint roller on the delicate fabric of my new dress. I hadn't been convinced about the dress until she'd also done my makeup and hair. "Julia's eyes are going to fall out when she sees you in this dress," she approved. "It's almost a shame I won't get to witness it myself."

I smoothed down the fabric of the ruby red fitted dress. There wasn't much to smooth down, however. The dress clung so tightly to my slight curves that you could practically see the slight indentation of my bellybutton beneath the material.

"I don't look like a hooker, do I?" I suddenly worried.

"I believe the phrase you're looking for is *sex worker*," Grace Kelly gently corrected. "And no—not that I know what that would even look like. You've got a figure to die for, Cassidy. Might as well remind Julia about it."

I continued to regard my reflection. Grace's encouraging words were helpful, but my nerves would only be quieted after Julia's appraisal.

"Am I allowed to look yet?" came an exasperated male voice from elsewhere in the condo.

"Come see!" Grace called back.

Rich appeared in the doorway of the bedroom. Grace had banished him to the living room while she transformed me.

I heard his low whistle. "Damn, Cass. You look like a girl."

I shook my closed fist threateningly. "Watch it, buddy."

Rich held up his hands like a shield. "No offense. I only meant to say that you look nice."

"She looks better than *nice*," Grace Kelly chirped. "She looks *hot*. Sex on legs."

Rich looked back and forth between his girlfriend and me. "I don't know if I'm supposed to be turned on or threatened," he deadpanned.

Grace ducked her head in embarrassment. "Oh, whatever. Girls can compliment each other without it being weird."

"Oh, I'm not complaining, babe," Rich said with a wolfish grin.

His reaction earned him a slug in the arm. "Hey!" he protested. He rubbed his palm over the area I'd punched. "I bruise easily."

"Uh huh. Delicate little flower you are," I said, rolling my eyes. I tugged at the bottom hem of my dress. "I can't believe you guys talked me into this."

Rich chuckled pleasantly. "Take it from me, Rookie—there's no reasoning with Gracie once she's set her mind to something."

∾

I nervously checked and re-checked my reflection in the mirrored walls of the elevator. Grace Kelly had reassured me that I looked fine—that I wasn't going to get arrested for indecent exposure—but I still felt naked. I wanted to wow Julia, but between the high heels and exposed upper thighs, I couldn't help but pine for pajamas and that six pack of beer in the back of Julia's refrigerator. My heart leapt into my throat when the elevator stopped and the doors silently opened.

After a final tug on the lower hemline of my dress, I stepped out of the elevator. I quickly scanned the open office floor plan to gain my bearings. The elevator opened to a reception desk, but just beyond that, short-walled cubicles filled up most of the open floor space. Glass walled private offices and several conference rooms with closed doors lined the perimeter walls.

No one sat at the reception desk—everyone was participating in the holiday party—so I walked beyond the gate-keeping station and tried to look like I belonged. It was an ill-fated challenge; everywhere I looked I saw white men in tailored suits. I was used to being the only female in the room, first as a Marine and then later as a police officer, but at least those men had had the decency to look me in the eye. It felt like every man I walked by couldn't get their eyes to lift higher than my thighs.

I walked on shaky legs and equally wobbly ankles in search of Julia. My instinct was to find the open bar I was sure this party had and to ply myself with alcohol until I forgot my nerves, but I needed to find my girlfriend first. The longer I scanned the room with no familiar faces in sight, the more my anxiety had me second-guessing my plan. One stranger after another populated the law firm's office space—hell, I would have been happy to have even seen that terrible Melissa woman.

I reached for the pocket that held my cellphone until I remembered that I'd left my leather jacket, and with it my wallet and cellphone, downstairs with security and the coat check station. I couldn't even text or call Julia to find out where she was. I'd just about given up hope of finding Julia on my own when I spotted her familiar silhouette leaving one of the glass walled offices. I resisted the urge to sprint in her direction. I instead lingered in the background to observe her interactions with her new co-workers.

Like I'd wanted to do myself, Julia picked her way through the sparse crowds to where a bar had been set up on the office floor. I watched her order a glass of red wine before tucking several crisp green bills into the hired bartender's tip jar. She leaned back against the bar and flicked absently at her hair to keep it out of her eyes. She drank slowly from the long-stemmed wine glass and flashed brief smiles at the various people who approached. No one lingered in her vicinity longer than picking up their next drink, however.

As I observed her, Julia retrieved her cellphone and began typing on the touchscreen keyboard. I wondered if she was playing on her phone to distract herself from her still-foreign surroundings. I wondered, perhaps, if she was texting me, demanding to know why I was so late or if I was ever going to show up.

"Hey, are you new?"

An incoming voice—a man's—interrupted my Julia gazing.

I turned toward the unsolicited question. "Oh, I don't work here," I said.

The man standing beside me was tall—well over six feet tall. His jet black hair, tightly cropped at the sides but longer on top was youthful and trendy and probably annoyed his more conservative bosses. Despite the haircut, he looked the part of a fancy lawyer, or at least his three-piece suit did.

He shoved a hand into his pants pocket. The other hand held a short plastic glass filled with some kind of alcohol. "A party crasher," he grinned conspiratorially. "I like your style."

"No, no," I denied. "Nothing like that. I'm here ..." I clamped down on my tongue. I'd nearly said I was here with my *girlfriend*, but I'd always avoided outing Julia, first with the people of her hometown, and later with those with whom she worked.

"I'm sorry," I unnecessarily apologized. "I've got to go."

I didn't linger longer to explain myself. I did what I should have done from the beginning; I strode in the direction of the dark-haired woman, still staring at her phone.

Julia still didn't look up from her phone as I approached. Her resting features were stern and unapproachable, but I thought it was one of the most beautiful faces I'd ever seen.

I tugged again at the bottom hem of my cocktail dress

before clearing my throat. Julia's caramel-colored eyes flicked up at the sound.

I awkwardly raised my right hand in greeting. "Hi. I'm here."

She didn't return my greeting. Instead, I watched her slowly wet her lips as she drank in my appearance, from the stiletto heels I'd borrowed from her closet up to my styled hair and careful makeup. I felt ready to shrink under her wordless inspection—to run away or laugh it off as a big joke.

But then she finally spoke: "Follow me."

She didn't wait for me to respond or give me the opportunity to ask questions. She set her barely-touched wine glass on the bar and turned away to walk in a new direction. I looked to see if anyone had observed our interaction. No one seemed interested in us, however, caught up in their respective holiday celebrations.

I didn't know the layout of Julia's office floor, having never visited her work until this point. I assume she might show me to her office, but she walked past the closed door from where I'd seen her exit earlier. Her name was engraved on a placard that hung on the outside of the door. I couldn't explain why, but my heart swelled with pride and other endearing emotions. Julia had been a lawyer for much longer than I'd known her, and in that time she'd held some pretty impressive titles like City Attorney. To have her name on the outside of an office door again felt like a massive accomplishment. With the exception of a miniature vanity license plate I'd bought in my teens while vacationing with my parents, I'd never had a sign with my name on it.

Julia continued to walk briskly to an unknown destination. She didn't look back to see if I continued to follow her. It really wasn't a question or up for debate, however. I'd follow her anywhere.

I focused on the slight sway of her pert backside, hidden beneath dark dress pants. I marveled at how her no-nonsense power suits could be mutually severe, yet feminine. But maybe that was only because I knew the flimsy lace underthings she habitually wore underneath the business layers or the soft, supple, feminine form they covered. I clenched my thighs and grimaced as I trailed behind her. She'd yet again managed to get me wet without so much as a touch or a glance.

Julia still didn't look back even when she pushed open the door for the gender neutral bathroom. I followed her inside with my heart hammering inside of my chest. Julia was a fiercely private person. I could only conclude that she'd wanted to separate us from the rest of the party so no one would witness or overhear whatever she had to say to me. She didn't shy from confrontation, but she would want to avoid making a scene in front of her new co-workers.

The apology was out of my mouth before the bathroom door had even closed. "I can go home and change," I blurted out. "Or I could just go home."

Confusion troubled Julia's beautiful features. "Go home?"

I looked down at the fitted dress that still had me doubting myself. "I didn't want to embarrass you in front of your fancy lawyer colleagues."

Julia shook her head, still not understanding what I was trying to say.

I tugged on the lower hem of my dress for what felt like

the millionth time. "The dress," I stated plainly, "do you not like it?"

Julia stepped closer and grabbed my hand. Before my brain could register the jerky movement, she had shoved my hand down the front of her pants. The pants had some give; my fingers slid beneath a lacy barrier and traveled across trim, coarse hair. My middle finger bisected her sex to discover warm, silky arousal that coated the tip of my finger.

"Does it *feel* like I don't like your dress?"

I pushed my hand deeper into her pants. My unoccupied hand unbuttoned the front of her pants to provide more room to maneuver.

Julia's own hand came to rest on top of mine. Her fingers wrapped around my wrist. "Lock the door."

I nodded my understanding. Unwilling to remove my hand from her pants, I walked her backwards towards the closed but unlocked bathroom door. I reached beyond her to twist the latch that deadbolted the door and shut us off from the holiday party happening just on the other side.

"Good girl," she murmured approvingly. "Now fuck me."

My lips curved up at the edges. "Yes, ma'am."

With my right hand still lodged between her thighs, I used my left hand to tug down her work pants, just below her narrow hips. I pulled hard on the slightly elastic material until I was satisfied I had enough room to do what I wanted to her. This wouldn't be a drawn-out lovemaking sessions beside an open, crackling fire. No soft, adoring touches. There would be no romantic candlelight to flicker attractively against her olive toned skin.

I withdrew my hand from the front of her underwear, but

only so I could push the gusset out of the way and penetrate her from a new angle. I pressed a single finger against her pouting entrance. I pushed forward, but not enough that I actually penetrated her. I brushed at her swollen clit with the pad of my thumb. I could feel the delicious heat and tightness of her waiting sex, but I resisted pushing against her any harder. I heard her breathy sigh when my single finger finally pushed beyond her outer lips and entered her liquid heat. I remained motionless and just enjoyed the feeling of being enveloped by her.

Having sex in a semi-public space wasn't new for us, but an office building bathroom, no matter how visibly clean it looked, was a bit of a shock. Julia must have *really* liked the dress.

I eased my finger out of her sex, and replaced the single digit with two. She was tight but ready for me. I kissed her mouth to swallow down her initial moans and sighs. I had no idea if the door that separated us from Julia's co-workers—the door her back was currently pressed against—possessed any sound muting properties.

I slid solidly into her. Every time I bottomed out, I heard her breath hitch in her throat. I would have been happy to tease her, not quite giving in so easily to her earlier demand that I fuck her, until I had her wriggling with impatience and verbally berating me for more. But everything had a time and place; and this time called for brutal efficiency.

The bathroom door rattled, but it had nothing to do with our activities. The rattle was followed by brisk knocking on the door. The sound startled me. I would have jerked my hand out of Julia's pants if not for her clamping the fingers of her uninjured wrist around my own.

Her dark eyes flashed under the unflattering bathroom lights. "Give it to me, Cassidy," came her throaty command.

I thrust into her harder until she practically stood on her tiptoes from the force of it. The knocking at the bathroom door continued, but this time I didn't stop.

"What part of a locked door do you not comprehend?" Julia snapped at the unwanted interruption.

"Sorry!" came a muffled apology.

I renewed my efforts, fucking her with my fingers until my bicep ached and burned. Julia's moans and sighs had similarly escalated, and she bit her right hand to keep from screaming. I couldn't do much to manipulate her clit with her underwear still in place, but I imagined how the material might brush against the slightly protruding nub each time I slammed into her.

"Close," she gasped. "I'm close."

I curled my fingers at the bottom of each thrust. I pressed the ends of my fingers hard against the spongy upper wall until she was clawing at my bicep. Her pussy clenched around my arousal-coated fingers. It felt like she was swallowing me again and again. Devouring me. A hungry mouth that was greedy for more.

I wanted her to scream, to announce her orgasm, but she only bit harder on her own hand.

"Cumming." Her voice was a hoarse whisper.

I slowed, but didn't stop the movement of my fingers.

A simple tap to my shoulder indicated her completion. I eased my fingers out of her panties and proceeded to tug her dress pants back their original position. Julia silently observed my actions as I took on the responsibility of reorganizing her bottom half.

"You lied," she accused. Her voice was quiet. "You weren't late because of work."

"No," I disassembled. "I needed a little extra time to get ready."

"Indeed." She touched her fingers to one of the soft, bouncy curls that framed my face. "You look exquisite."

Grace Kelly had helped me maximize the curl in my naturally wavy hair. I'd been worried it was too Beauty Pageant Contestant, but now I was thankful Grace had insisted we go all out.

I kissed her fingertips, one at a time. I couldn't hide my proud, cocky grin; the indentations of Julia's perfect teeth were branded on the top of her hand, like a bite taken out of an apple. "Do you want to go home?"

"Yes. Desperately," she revealed. "But I need to show my face a little longer at this party."

"Am I still invited to stick around?" I ventured.

"Do you want to stay?" she posed.

"Well, I got all dolled up," I said in lieu of a direct answer.

A small smile played at the corners of her painted lips. "Half an hour more, and then we'll go."

I washed my hands before we left the bathroom, mindful that I might have to shake someone's hand if Julia introduced me to her new co-workers. As much as it thrilled me to have Julia's cum on my fingers, it probably wouldn't have been a good first impression.

Julia led us back to the office party. "Where did that outfit even come from?" she asked. "It certainly hasn't been hanging in your closet all this time."

"I got the dress online," I said. "But the shoes are yours."

Julia's step faltered only slightly. "Red bottoms?"

I gave her a sheepish look. "I hope you don't mind."

"I'll only mind if you don't wear them more often," she declared. "They're not called *Fuck Me Pumps* for nothing."

I didn't bother biting back the telling groan. I wanted to ditch the party for her condo in the worst way.

"I didn't want to embarrass you in front of your new co-workers," I explained myself. I cleared my throat. "I also maybe wanted to show up that Melissa woman."

"You know you have nothing to worry about with her."

"And *you* know I'm always going to worry," I countered. "You two have a lot in common. A lot more than we do, at least."

"I have no interest in dating myself," Julia sniffed.

I gave her a coy smile. "You're not so bad."

"Let's go find Melissa right now," Julia decided.

My eyes widened. "O-oh. Really?"

Julia took firm purchase of my right hand—the hand that had only recently been between her thighs. She tugged me down the hallway and past empty cubicles. I stumbled to keep up, a combination of her quickened pace and my inexperience in high heels.

"Julia!" A female voice rang out. "There you are. I was worried you'd ducked out early before the real fun had started."

Melissa Ferdet was a tall, statuesque woman. Even without her high heels she was a few inches taller than either myself or Julia. Like Julia, Melissa wore a slim, fitted suit. Long, straight, auburn hair fell past her shoulders. Her bright green eyes were an unusual color, which had me wondering if they were the product of color-altering contacts or if they occurred naturally.

"Oh, I was just showing Cassidy around the office," Julia smoothly explained. "Melissa, this is my *fiancée*, Cassidy Miller."

I might have been the only one stunned by the descriptive label. Melissa, like Julia herself, had a well-practiced poker face. I supposed the ability to control one's emotions came in handy in the court room. "It's very nice to meet you, Cassidy. What is it that you do?"

"I-I'm police," I stuttered, still too stunned by Julia's introduction to articulate more.

"Police?" Melissa echoed. "I don't think I've ever seen a police officer in a dress like that." She laughed at her own joke. "Maybe I should hang out at police stations more often."

"Cassidy is lead detective for Minneapolis' Cold Case division," Julia expanded.

"Cold Case, eh? Impressive pair, both of you," Melissa approved. Her attention seemed to move to another part of the room. "I should go say hi to the Partners," she said in a distracted voice. "Cassidy, it was a pleasure to meet you."

I could barely manage a garbled goodbye before the woman was rushing off to another part of the room.

"That went better than I anticipated," Julia remarked. "Melissa was actually a little human."

"*Fiancée?*" I hissed. "What was that about?"

"I put a lot of thought into how I might introduce you to my colleagues," Julia said smoothly. "*Girlfriend* is too infantile. And it a room full of lawyers, *partner* would be confusing."

"So it's just for this party then? Tomorrow we go back to being Cassidy and Julia?"

"What do you mean?"

"Are we engaged?"

My question came out sharper than I'd intended. I didn't know how to feel about her party-specific label for me. I was touched she'd wanted her co-workers to know the seriousness and depth of our relationship, but I was also a little annoyed. Why did she get to decide we were engaged, if only for the night? Why hadn't she asked for my approval to use the word first?

I'd once proposed to her—moved by a particularly pedestrian moment, but also the realization that I wanted to spend the rest of my life with this woman. She'd dismissed the impromptu proposal with the promise that we had time—that neither of us was going anywhere.

"No. We're not engaged. Neither of us has a ring," she said pragmatically.

"Do you *want* to be engaged?"

"This really isn't the place for this conversation, dear."

I knew she was right, so I gave her a pass for the moment. But I hoped to convey in a single look that this discussion wasn't over.

Chapter Seventeen

Afghanistan, 2012

I could leave him. Not to die, of course. But I could travel more quickly without him. The scenario plays over and over in my head. I could hide him on the side of the road. I could find help and come back to get him. But I'm not even sure where we are; I could wander for days without running into anyone while Pensacola slowly dies.

"Leave me," he says again. His voice sounds weak.

My feet stop moving, but only long enough for me to turn and berate him. "Get it through that thick skull of yours." My volume is elevated. "I'm not fucking leaving you."

A car's engine revs in the distance. My instinct is to duck and hide. There's no way my frustrated shouting is going to get us caught. Not like this. Not after all we've been through.

I drag Pensacola on his sled farther from the side of the road. A low-lying ditch provides enough cover that the high beams of the vehicle's headlights shouldn't be able to see us.

I huddle beside Pense, trying to make my body smaller and undetectable.

"I'm a married man," Pensacola wheezes. "Stop trying to cop a feel."

"You wish, buddy," I shoot back.

The vehicle's engine is loud. I shut my eyes as if it will make me invisible. The vehicle sounds big. Diesel engine, not a regular car or pickup truck. I hear it downshift, and that's when I make my move.

If Pense yells at me, his voice is drowned out by the roar of the engine and the beating of my heart, echoing in my ears.

* * *

"Hey, Miller. What did you get your girlfriend for Christmas?"

"Say that again?"

Sarah Conrad peered at me from over her computer monitor in the Cold Case office. "Christmas?" she repeated. "Lesbians do celebrate that, right?"

My heart lodged in my throat. "Shit."

I heard Sarah's audible gasp. "Miller, are you telling me you forgot to get your girlfriend a Christmas present?"

"I haven't had to buy anyone anything in like a decade!" I squeaked out my excuse.

It wasn't an exaggeration. It wasn't like I went Christmas shopping in Afghanistan and sent presents home to my parents. They were just happy to video conference with me on the day of the holiday. I'd never had a significant significant other either. I'd basically missed Julia's birthday, too, but that was only because she hadn't told me when it was. In fact, I wouldn't have even known the exact year of her birth except, morbidly, I'd seen her birth date etched on a tombstone in the Embarrass cemetery at her family's burial plot.

"I'm dead," I announced. "Julia is going to kill me."

"Oh, it can't be all that bad," Sarah dismissed. "Get her some smelly candles and bath salt. Girls love that shit."

"I'm not dating a *girl*," I protested. My heart began to race as if I'd consumed way too much caffeine. "I'm dating a very particular, discerning woman who can afford whatever she wants. What the hell do you buy a woman like that?"

"You don't," Sarah said simply. "You either spend your entire paycheck on a fancy-ass piece of jewelry, or you get her something money can't buy. Are you crafty?"

I raised an eyebrow. "What do you think?"

Sarah raised her hands. "Hey, I don't know. Maybe you're secretly a scrapbooker or you're really good at knitting. I don't judge people and their hobbies. Our boss is an amateur taxidermist for God's sake."

I rubbed at my face. "Shit. Shit. Shit."

"There's still time," Sarah tried to encourage. "We do happen to have, like, a ridiculously large mall in the area. Maybe you'll find inspiration there."

"*The mall?*" My voice had become even more incredulous than before. "I think I'd have better luck making her a birdhouse out of popsicle sticks."

"You could always stick with her birthday theme. Maybe do a little toy shopping together?"

It took me a second too long to remember that I'd told Sarah about my arrangement with Julia on her previous birthday. A strap-on and nylon harness had been waiting for me in a shoe box on the breakfast table the morning of her birthday. I'd had to wait until the following night to actually *give* Julia her present, however, because of work obligations.

"Oh, uh, maybe," I said noncommittally.

"There's so many options," Sarah mused. "You could have her presents figured out for years to come." She laughed at her own suggestion. "Years to *come*. Get it?"

"Yeah, I caught that the first time," I said weakly.

"There's nipple clamps and vibrators, clit stimulators and pussy pumps." She hummed in thought. "Does Julia like to be tied up? You already have the handcuffs."

I could feel my face flush. "Okay, new topic."

"What?" Sarah pouted. "There's nothing wrong with being sex positive."

"Maybe I'm a little old fashioned," I admitted, "but I don't think we need all those bells and whistles."

"You mean ball gags and riding crops," she seemed to correct.

I coughed. "*Anyway*. I'm sure I'll come up with something. I appreciate the help though."

"Anytime!" Sarah said brightly. "After all, what girl doesn't want her *stocking stuffed* around this time of year?"

∽

I grabbed one of Julia's slender legs and positioned it over my shoulder. Her thighs fell open, affording me better access to her weeping sex. I slid two digits deep into her pussy. Julia's sex gripped tightly onto my persistent fingers and her bare heel drummed against my back. When I dipped my head to lash my tongue against her clit, she grabbed the back of my head and held me in place. With her left wrist still heavily bandaged and largely immobile in a splint, she couldn't do much else.

I kept my fingers motionless and fluttered the flat of my tongue against her swollen clit. Her eyes closed while I flicked her clit and her outer lips with just the tip of my tongue. The shaved skin was silk beneath my tongue and mouth. I kept my touch light, not necessarily because I worried she might re-injure her wrist, but rather to keep her from orgasming too quickly. I wanted to be greedy with her body and her time.

"Mmm, that's nice, darling," Julia approved.

"You're lucky your wrist is still hurt."

Julia opened one eye and raised her eyebrow. "And why is that?"

"Because I'd have you on all fours on the mattress and use your birthday present on you."

Julia's long eyelashes fluttered, and for a moment, she looked flustered. I bit back a triumphant grin; it was a rare occasion when she let me top her, not only physically but also verbally. I'd once believed that Julia Desjardin was a pillow princess. I'd been more than happy to discover my early assumptions about her had been dead wrong.

I nibbled on her inner thighs, but continued to fill her with my motionless fingers. Her top row of teeth sought out her lower lip. I could tell she was having a hard time not lifting her hips off the mattress which might force me to finally move the two fingers inside of her.

I took my time swiping my tongue over the hood of her clit. I rolled the sensitive bud back and forth. Back and forth. With two fingers still deep inside her, I pulled her lips apart ever so slightly, and flicked the tip of my tongue against her clit.

"Cassidy," she breathed. "Fuck."

I flexed my digits and curled up. She made another sound —a low moan—and her own fingers tightened in my hair.

"Jesus," she gasped. "Whatever you're doing, don't stop."

I flexed my fingers again and fluttered my tongue against her clit. I wanted her to feel simultaneously full and stretched while not having enough contact against her clit to get off. The quiet grunts coming from the head of the bed told me she was bordering on frustration. But Julia Desjardin did not beg.

I tightly gripped her upper thigh with my free hand. I flattened my tongue and licked hard against her clit. Julia made a garbled noise and lifted her backside off the bed. Her back arched and she thrust her pelvic bone against my open mouth. The movement forced my fingers to penetrate her deeper. Her sex gripped my first and middle fingers.

"Again," she commanded.

I licked her hard again.

"Again, Cassidy." Her voice sounded rough.

I licked her a third time. I curled my fingers and pressed up against her inner walls.

"Fuuuuuck." She drew out the uncharacteristic curse word as I imagined the intensity of her orgasm.

I remained on my stomach between Julia's parted legs. I withdrew my fingers from her pulsing sex to trace invisible figures on her inner thighs, painting the skin with her arousal. Her fingers, those on her uninjured right hand, toyed with the hair that curled near my temples.

"That was lovely, darling," she breathed. "Thank you."

I kissed the inside of each of her still-quivering thighs. "Just making sure I'm not replaced by a shower faucet," I quipped.

"You're in no danger of that happening," she assured me.

She sighed. The exhalation sounded tired rather than content.

"Are you okay?" I asked. "How was work?"

"It was fine. Always a little better than the day before. But I'm regretting introducing you as my *fiancée* to Melissa."

I frowned at her words. But I wasn't brave enough to ask her why.

"She's like a dog with a bone," Julia complained, "persistently nagging me about not having a ring."

I frowned more deeply. "What do you say in response?"

"That we're evolved; that we don't need antiquated signs of commitment. That engagement rings were invented by the diamond industry." Julia sighed again. "Plus, she wants to know everything about you and how we met."

I lifted my head in interest. "Oh yeah? What do you tell her?"

Julia shrugged. "The truth."

"How I cruised into your hometown and swept you off your feet? How you tried to resist my charms, but I was just too enchanting?"

Julia rolled her eyes, but a ghost of a smile played on her lips. "How you wouldn't take no for an answer until I finally took pity on you?" she countered.

"I prefer my version of history," I scoffed.

Julia hummed. She resumed brushing her fingers through my hair, pushing some of the more unruly curls away from my face. Her touch was light and gentle. I wanted to keep talking, but the rhythmic motion of her fingers, compounded with long work days, threatened to lull me to sleep.

"Why do you think she's suddenly so interested in your private life?" I asked. Another thought—this one much darker—pushed its way to the front of my anxieties. "Is she going to try to steal you away from me?"

"More like the other way around, I'm afraid," Julia said, a sour look on her face. "Melissa is a competitive beast. She might be partner at the firm while I'm brand new, but that won't stop her from trying to take everything I have."

"This doesn't sound very healthy," I remarked.

"I'm a big girl," Julia dismissed. She twisted a blonde lock around her second finger. "I can handle Melissa."

I had my own anxieties and opinions about this person from Julia's past, but I also trusted her. If Julia wasn't worried, there was no reason for me to be either.

"Have you gotten your first case yet?" I asked.

"No. The Partners are still letting me ease into things. I probably won't take on a case until after the new year."

"Isn't that when you're having your eggs frozen?" I prompted.

The fingers that had been lightly playing with my hair froze as well. "I can multitask."

I felt the energy in the room shift. "I just mean, if you're too busy," I verbally scrambled, "we don't have to do my birthday party."

The fingers in my hair resumed their tender ministrations. "I'm throwing you a party, Cassidy."

"You don't think it's childish?" I openly worried. "A twenty-nine year old having a birthday party?"

"Twenty-nine," Julia sighed wistfully. "Do I even remember what I was doing back then?"

"Building fires in caves?" I quipped. I knew I was metaphorically playing with fire myself.

Julia's caramel-colored eyes perceptively narrowed. "I'm not so sure you're getting any presents. You're definitely on Santa's naughty list this year."

The mentioning of the big man in the red suit had me frowning. What the hell was I going to get Julia for Christmas? Sarah's suggestions—outside of the sex toys—had actually been pretty helpful, but that didn't alleviate the heavy pit of dread that had settled in my stomach.

Time was ticking down with only a week and a half until Christmas. I'd always been a bit of a procrastinator, but this wasn't something I could keep delaying. I'd been blindsided by Julia's birthday because of her weird hang up about our age difference, but there was no acceptable reason for me to be blindsided by Christmas. It happened every year on the same date.

"I'm not expecting any presents," I insisted. "For either my birthday or for Christmas."

"No presents?" Julia echoed. "Don't you know your girlfriend is a high-profile lawyer now? You really should start filling out your Wish List, darling."

Julia was being playful, but my mind was occupied elsewhere. I continually returned to Sarah's suggestion that I get Julia something that money couldn't buy. But what did Julia Desjardin want? Babies came to mind, but I didn't have the right body parts to make that happen. The ubiquitous puppy or kitten didn't feel right; pets would only mess up the nice things in her condo.

There were non-monetary things I'm sure she desired—world peace and all that. Her mother was suitably resettled in her assisted living facility. Julia might have wanted her mom living under the same roof as us, but that wasn't very realistic. She hadn't been able to do that even in Embarrass when she'd been the small town's city prosecutor. I could have proposed to her for a second time, this time with an actual diamond ring, but her refusal the first time around had made me a little gun shy.

"You look like you're thinking pretty hard over there."

Julia stroked her fingers through my unruly curls. My hair felt as jumbled as my thoughts.

I made a humming noise in the affirmative. "I have an idea of what I want to get you for Christmas. But it's not very traditional."

"You say that like it's a bad thing," she censured. "We've never been very traditional, you and I. What did you have in mind?"

"When we visit my parents," I started, taking a breath. "I think I want to tell them about us."

"Us?" she questioned.

"Being together," I clarified. "Me being gay."

Julia blinked. "You're going to Come Out to your family on Christmas? Are you sure?"

"Yes."

"That's a terribly sweet gesture, darling," she affirmed. "I would understand, however, if you need more time or if you think Christmas isn't an opportune moment."

"If you're there, they can't make a big deal about it," I reasoned. "My mom would rather die than cause a scene when company's over."

"Even if said company is your live-in girlfriend?" Julia wondered.

"They should know. I owe it to them," I decided. "But I owe it to you more."

Julia's words were gentle. "You don't owe me anything, Cassidy. I'm not keeping score."

"Speaking of keeping score ..." I shifted on the mattress to prop myself up on my elbows. "You owe me an orgasm. A couple of them."

Her lips ticked up in an amused smile. "Is that so?"

An easy smile fell to my own lips. "Don't worry. You can pay me back when your wrist is better."

I watched her slowly drag her tongue across her lips. The exaggerated movement had me shivering.

"What are you thinking?" My voice had become tight.

"I think I've figured out what I'm getting you for Christmas."

Chapter Eighteen

The results from testing Danika Laroque's remains arrived late in the afternoon. The off-site lab had sent their findings to our colleagues at the Minneapolis Crime Lab Unit instead of directly faxing them to the Cold Case office. If the crime had occurred in the Twin Cities, our own lab techs would have processed the evidence. We also would have had a faster turn around on the forensic analysis.

Celeste Rivers, the icy blonde lab tech who was our contact in the Crime Lab Unit, read me the bad news. "No DNA. No unexpected fibers."

I'd already anticipated as much. Danika's body had been submerged in a freshwater lake for three decades. The likelihood of a stray hair or wool sweater lint sticking to her skeleton hadn't kept me up at night.

"The integrity of the bones were extremely compromised," she seemed to apologize.

"So they found nothing," I guessed.

"Not nothing," she corrected. "I'm not sure if this means

anything to you, but they did find trace amounts of thermoplastic acrylic lacquer stuck to her shin bones. The small indentations the coroner discovered in her leg bones retained the material."

"Should I know what that is?" I asked.

"It's paint?" Celeste noted, her voice lilting up. "Specifically, car paint."

I knit my eyebrows together. "There was car paint on her bones?"

"Not exactly. It's the finish that protects the paint from scratching," Celeste clarified. "Today, car makers use a polyurethane-based enamel. But back in the day, it was thermoplastic acrylics."

"How far back in the day are we talking?"

"I had to look it up," Celeste admitted, "but it looks like anytime between 1950 and 1970. Your victim went missing in the 1980s though, right?"

My pulse quickened. I knew Celeste had probably been racking her brain as to how old car paint sealant had gotten on the bones of someone who went missing in 1984. But she didn't know what I did.

∼

I didn't turn on the lights and sirens when I drove to Jim Knutson's home in Prior Lake. Officer Azure followed closely behind in his own squad car, although I doubted I'd need the backup. We parked the police vehicles side-by-side in the wide blacktop driveway.

The front door of the single-family home opened and the screen door slammed behind him as Jim Knutson stepped outside to meet our arrival. His flannel shirt was open in the front. The aged t-shirt underneath was from the last time the Vikings had been in the Super Bowl. He hadn't bothered to put on a jacket or shoes.

I reached for the metal handcuffs stored on my duty belt. I normally left the belt in the office, but had brought it out of retirement for this very purpose. "Mr. Knutson, you're under arrest for the 1984 murder of Danika Laroque."

The man's head fell forward until his chin touched the top of his chest. His next words were quiet, but clear: "Oh, thank God."

I'd never before arrested someone who was relieved to have been caught. In my experience, people fought back the moment they saw the handcuffs or the zip ties. Jim Knutson, however, had only held out his wrists as if to make my job easier.

Once we brought him back to the Prior Lake police station, no specialized interrogation methods had needed to be employed. I didn't need to gain his trust with fast food and a pack of cigarettes. Officer Azure and I hadn't even needed to role play Good Cop/Bad Cop. Jim Knutson freely admitted to being responsible for Danika Laroque's death.

I was loathe to admit it, but Melody Sternbridge had been right all along. The most obvious scenario—that Danika had been picked up by a seemingly Good Samaritan who had then attacked her—hadn't been the correct one. It had been the boyfriend all along—or, in our case, the ex-boyfriend.

Danika had broken up with Jim sometime before Christmas of 1983. She'd wanted to leave the reservation again with no entanglements, which meant ending things with her on-and-off-again boyfriend. Jim claimed it had been an amicable split; he'd even continued to give her rides home from work. But on that night, February 28th, 1984, he'd been drinking at a bar with his friends. He'd left the bar to pick up Danika from the gas station, but she'd refused the ride home, not wanting to get into a vehicle with an impaired driver.

Jim said he'd followed behind her in his car—his 1969 Camaro—while she'd walked along the gravel roadway with her bicycle. He'd called out to her to get in the car, but she'd refused him again and again. Finally, rejected and dejected, he'd stomped on the gas pedal in hopes of a dramatic exit. But he'd had too much to drink that night and the roads were slippery from a recent snowstorm. The vintage muscle car had never handled very well in the winter anyway. Jim lost control of the car and struck Danika.

Getting rid of the body had been easy. With the bad weather there were less cars on the road than what was typical at that hour. Arctic Lake was a quick, isolated drive. Danika's body had sunk beneath the dark water before—Jim claimed—he could even really process what had happened. When he brought his car to the auto shop to have the front damage repaired, he'd told the staff that he'd hit a deer. The yellow banana seat bike had remained in the trunk of his car until the ground had thawed and was soft enough to dig into.

After making his confession, Jim Knutson sat in the sterile interrogation room of the Prior Lake police department with his head in his hands. I didn't know how to feel about the man. He'd never married, had never left the area. His guilt over what had occurred that night had made it impossible for him to move on. He had expected to be caught every other day; he'd believed it was only a matter of time, but months had turned to year, which had turned into decades.

There was no statute of limitations for an action resulting in the death of another person. Vehicular manslaughter had a statute of limitations in other states, but not in Minnesota. Criminal vehicular manslaughter, even the accidental killing of someone, was punishable by up to ten years in prison. No doubt a judge would tack on extra years for the disposal of Danika's body and interference with the original missing person's case, but barring any health complications, Knutson would be out of prison within his lifetime.

I didn't know how to feel. Was this a victory for the Good Guys? Had justice actually prevailed? Or would Jim Knutson's festering guilt have been punishment enough? Was he actually going to *feel better* about himself once in prison, finally absolved of his sins? In my limited time working for Cold Case, I'd come to the realization that none of this was black and white. There were no tidy, satisfying endings. I tried not to think too hard on the matter. I wasn't a particularly religious person, but I did believe in karma. Everything, in theory, would work out in the end.

∽

"We made an arrest."

Melody Sternbridge's eyes went wide at my arrival and announcement. "Come in," she urged. "Do you want something to drink?"

I stepped inside the overly warm house, but only to get out of the winter winds that had picked up since returning to Minneapolis. My stop to the podcaster's home had been an impromptu detour on my way back to the Fourth Precinct.

"No. I can't stay long," I said. I could have called instead of making the house call, but a part of me felt indebted to the admittedly annoying woman.

"Who was it?" she needed to know.

"Jim Knutson."

Melody thrust her closed fist in the air. "I knew it!"

"He confessed, too," I added. "There won't be a trial except for his sentencing. Case closed."

Despite Jim Knutson's detailed confession, I couldn't stop thinking about Danika's fractured hyoid bone. The autopsy report identified that it had been broken through strangulation, which didn't match up with Knutson's story. The neck bone could have been fractured postmortem, and there were fractures in her leg bones that indicated she'd been struck by a vehicle.

We could have challenged the details of Knutson's confession—maybe being struck by a car had only injured Danika and Knutson had finished the job with his bare hands —but the DA's office would want an iron-clad case, and Knutson was ready to plead guilty to involuntary vehicular manslaughter. I would have to be satisfied with that.

Melody sat down on her couch as though hit with a heavy realization. "Wow. Just like that. It's over."

"Knutson was your anonymous online tipster, too," I revealed.

This time, her face contorted in surprise. "What?"

"Guilty conscious, I guess." I shrugged. "To be honest, he looked kind of relieved when we showed up to arrest him."

"Why didn't he just turn himself in?" she demanded. "Why make police go through all of that? Why make *Danika's family* go through all of that?"

They were the exact questions I had asked him myself.

I shook my head. "Cowardice and fear. He told me if he was supposed to be caught—supposed to face punishment for his actions—he wanted to be sure it was meant to be. He gave just enough information to get police involved again, but not enough to actually solve the crime."

Melody scowled. "What an asshole."

I barked out a short laugh. "Yeah. My thoughts exactly. Anyway," I motioned with my head in the direction of the front door. "I should get going. I just wanted to give you the update."

Melody rose from the couch and walked with me toward the front door. "I appreciate the visit."

"No problem. You're a pain in my ass, and I still can't stomach anyone getting internet famous off of unsolved crimes," I qualified, "but without you putting our feet to the fire, we probably wouldn't have fast-tracked Danika's case. So for that, thank you."

"You know how you can properly thank me, Detective?" The look she gave me was sly.

I grimaced at her question. "An interview for your podcast?"

Melody Sternbridge batted her long eyelashes. "It's like you can read my mind."

⁓

Julia watched from the living room couch as I typed out the number. I had it programmed into my cellphone, but it was the only phone number I knew by heart. I didn't even have Julia's number memorized. The phone rang several times. My parents were one of the only people I knew who still had a landline. I imagined my mom in the unfinished basement doing laundry or elbow deep in soapy dish water.

She sounded predictably breathless when she finally answered the phone. "Hello?"

"Hey, Mom."

"Cassidy! Sweetie! How are you? What's new? How's work? Big plans for your birthday? How about Christmas?"

I bit back a soft laugh at her rapid-fire questions. "That's kind of why I'm calling. Think I could come home over Christmas weekend?"

"Of course!" she approved. Her voice pitched up in obvious excitement. "Your room is always here for you. You never have to ask."

I rubbed at the back of my neck. "I didn't know if you'd already made plans or were going somewhere."

"Where would we go?" my mom seemed to laugh. "I'd have to use a crowbar to get your dad out of his La-Z-Boy."

"Do you ..." I flicked my eyes in my girlfriend's direction. "Do you mind if Julia comes along?"

I bit my lower lip. Would my mom even remember the name? Julia Desjardin was a force of nature, but that might not mean much to a former piano teacher in St. Cloud.

"She won't be spending Christmas with her family?" my mom asked.

"She's spending Christmas Day with her mom," I said. "But it's just the two of them these days."

If my mom had additional questions, she smartly didn't follow up with them. "Of course," she approved. "The more the merrier."

Her statement about 'more' had me balking. "Only you

and dad, you promise? I don't need a Miller family reunion overwhelming us."

I was preparing myself to Come Out to my mom and maybe my dad. I didn't need all the aunts, uncles, and cousins there, too.

"It's just your dad and me," she vowed. "I'm getting too old to play hostess to all those people."

"Don't overdo it, okay?" I prompted. "It's just me and Julia. You don't have to go all out or make a big deal."

"Oh, where's the fun in that?"

My tone was a warning. "Mom."

"Okay, okay," she backed down. "It'll be a boring weekend at home with your parents. Happy?"

"Very."

I hung up with my mom after making her promise again that she wouldn't invite half the town over. I put my phone on the coffee table and flopped down next to Julia on the couch. I rested my head on her shoulder and she shifted her position on the couch to help me get more comfortable.

With anyone else, I might have complained about how exhausting my mom was or what a Debbie Downer my dad was these days. But Julia had just lost her father and her mom would eventually forget who she was. I was mindful of both of those facts and wisely kept any parental complaints to myself.

Julia grabbed the television remote from the coffee table and, without me having to ask, turned on the Timberwolves game. They were losing to Milwaukee. I snuggled tighter against her on the couch, and silently enjoyed my reward.

Chapter Nineteen

Afghanistan, 2012

My boots hit sand and then the tightly-packed gravel of the roadway. My sight is blurry. I still can't make out the shape of the vehicle behind its blinding headlights. I stop in the center of the road and wave my arms above my head.

I've made my choice. We're not going to die out here. I'm not going to let Claire become a widow. We're going home.

And depending on the vehicle's driver, it'll either be in First Class on a commercial airplane or stowed underneath with the rest of the plane's cargo in a pine box.

∽

I arrived by myself to my birthday party, which was taking place at the taproom of a local craft brewery. Julia had been the one to pick out the location. She'd taken care of all of the other details as well. The only instructions she'd given me was to show up on time.

It was just after the dinner hour and the brewery was unexpectedly busy for being the night before Christmas. Traditionally, the night before Thanksgiving was the busiest bar day of the year. Young people returning to their hometowns for the holiday might meet up with old childhood friends or simply need to get away from overbearing parents. I supposed the same could be true for Christmas Eve, hence that night's bar crowd.

If Julia and I had been in St. Cloud for my birthday, I might have been tempted to escape my childhood home for at least a few hours. We were planning on making the drive up to my hometown the next day after Julia spent some time with her mom. It was to be a short trip, so I doubted my mom would let us leave the house during the visit without a major guilt trip.

I couldn't decide if I was looking forward to bringing Julia to my hometown and staying under the same roof as my parents. I'd almost wanted Julia to suggest we get a hotel for the duration of the visit, but instead she'd been insistent on us spending as much time as possible with my mom and dad.

I'd promised her I would Come Out to my parents for Christmas. I hadn't yet decided how or when that was going to happen. I knew that regardless of any pre-planning on my part, it was going to be uncomfortable for everyone involved. But it was something that needed to be done. I loved Julia. And to truly love her, to love her the way she deserved to be loved, my family needed to know who she was to me.

"There's the birthday girl!"

My friend Brent, a.k.a. Viking, sauntered up the me. He

threw his beef arms around me and practically severed my spinal cord with how tightly he hugged me.

"Easy on the goods, man!" I light-heartedly complained. "I'd like to make it to my thirtieth birthday."

Brent dropped me to the floor. My rubber-soled boots struck the taproom floor, and I felt its reverberations up through my knees.

I winced and rubbed at my kneecaps. "Geez, dude. I'm gonna report you for senior abuse."

My friend Angie walked up to us. "Senior?" she chuckled. "You've got that baby face, girl. I bet you still get carded."

She wasn't wrong.

Angie handed Brent a pint of dark beer. "Nothing but IPAs for days," she seemed to complain, "so I got you the milk stout."

"Thanks, Ang," Brent said. "You know I like my beer like I like my women."

The two shared a laugh and clinked their glasses together.

I looked back and forth between my two friends. I never knew what to think of their vibe, especially as of late. With Rich paired up with Grace and our other friend Adan basically wifed up with his girlfriend, Brent and Angie were the last ones from our friend group without significant others. It was like a game of musical chairs and they were the last two standing.

A new voice joined the fray. "Cassidy Miller!"

Thin arms grabbed me around the midsection like a safety baring down on a quarterback. Grace Kelly Donovan swung around me like a human hula hoop.

"Happy birthday!"

I tried not to visibly wince at the volume and high pitch of her voice. "Hey, Grace. I'm glad you could make it."

"Us seeing each other is starting to become a regular thing," she said, smiling. "I like it."

"Yeah. Thanks for the makeover the other day," I acknowledged. "It was a big hit."

"I *bet* it was," Grace said knowingly.

I coughed at her suggestion. "Where, uh, where's Rich?"

"Oh, he's in the bathroom," Grace said, flipping a dismissive hand. "I swear, that man has the tiniest bladder."

I was excited to see so many familiar faces, especially considering it was Christmas Eve, but I hadn't yet spotted the most important one.

"Has anyone seen Julia?" I asked.

All of my friends shook his or her head and murmured apologies of having just shown up. Julia's tardiness wasn't worrying, but I was curious as to why she might have been delayed. Unlike my own surprise lateness at her work party, Julia wouldn't have had a reason for a dramatic makeover. It was hard to improve on perfection.

My cellphone vibrated in my jacket pocket with an incoming message. I expected it would be Julia explaining her absence, but her text had me frowning instead. *Go see the bartender*, her message read. *He has your present.*

I looked up from my phone and across the room to where I knew the bearded bartender was stationed behind the long bar. I mumbled an excuse to my friends, although I doubted anyone was paying that close of attention, and walked across the brewery floor.

I had to wait a few moments while the lone bartender finished fulfilling a number of drink orders before I finally gained his attention. I cleared my throat, unsure of what I was supposed to say.

"Hi. I'm Cassidy. Uh, I think you have something for me?"

With anyone else, like one of my cop friends, I would have expected the whole 'this-stranger-has-something-for-you' line to have been a setup. I highly doubted Julia would be so juvenile as to pull that kind of prank on me, especially on my birthday. But I was still unsure about asking.

Recognition lit up the young man's features. He signaled for me to wait while he ducked beneath the bar to retrieve something. He returned to his full height moments later and set a key connected to a keychain with the brewery's logo in front of me.

I stared at the key—my present?—for a few seconds. "Uh, thank you?"

He grinned a little wider. "It opens that door," he said. He pointed in the direction of a double set of doors, both closed. The words *Employees Only Beyond this Point* warned patrons from wandering too far from the brewery floor.

I plucked the key from the countertop, fairly confident I knew what, or *who*, I would find behind those locked doors. That the brewery's staff might also know should have had me blushing, but I didn't. It was my birthday, and if Julia wanted to surprise me with not-so-sneaky brewery sex, I wasn't going to suddenly get shy.

I nodded my thanks to the man before striding confidently towards the presumably locked double doors. It would have been polite to tell my friends that I'd be back soon, but realistically I had no idea how long I would be. Again, I reminded myself that it was my birthday; I was allowed to be a little selfish.

Beyond the double doors I discovered the production side of the brewery. It was significantly larger than the tap room that the public got to see. Giant steel fermentation tanks dominated the space along with numerous pallets filled with metal kegs. The pungent scent of proofing bread, which I knew to be from one of beer's essential ingredients—yeast—perfumed the air.

The room was silent, the bottling station quiet for the night. My shoes sounded hollow against the concrete floor. Only the muffled sounds of music and conversation in the next room filtered into the production space.

I walked along the silent brewing equipment with my ears and eyes focused on finding my girlfriend. I was so zeroed in on finding where Julia might be hiding that the vibration of my cellphone in my leather jacket pocket nearly startled me.

A second text of the night illuminated the phone's screen: *You're getting warmer, Detective.*

A small smile tickled my lips. I looked up from the phone, but still couldn't see her, although she apparently could see me.

I walked a few more steps in the same direction. My phone buzzed again in my hand: *Warmer.*

Text messages typically lacked emotion, but even without the use of emojis, I could practically hear her warm, amused tone in the one-worded message.

A few more steps produced another text: *You're burning up.*

I lifted my eyes from the phone's screen and again

scanned my surroundings without success. Despite her text messages, I was starting to doubt she was even in the same room.

When I turned a corner, still empty with the exception of more beer-making equipment, another text filled my phone's screen: *Colder.*

The directional text was followed by another message, this one from Rich: *Where did you go?*

I'll be back, I wrote him. It didn't exactly answer his question, but at least he could relay to everyone that I hadn't entirely disappeared.

"Julia?" I called out. I didn't mind the sentiment behind Julia's game, but I also didn't want to be on a wild goose chase all night.

A delicate cough, like someone clearing their throat, drew my attention to an elevated catwalk that I hadn't noticed before. I spied high-heeled shoes and the hint of a delicate ankle first. The leather stilettos were impractical and out of place in the industrial space. With a light touch to the banister, Julia descended the metal staircase. Her high-waisted pencil skirt and heels made the maneuvering more challenging, but Julia had never let her surroundings dictate her fashion choices.

I waited at the bottom of the steps with my phone in my hand and my heart in my throat. My gaze scanned up the femininely muscled calves, encased in dark grey nylons, as she closed the distance between us. Her fitted wool skirt was a few shades darker than her stockings. A sheer, black blouse completed the outfit. The long-sleeved shirt was open at the top; a double strand of iridescent pearls hung just below the hollow of her throat.

When she reached the bottom step, she placed her hand on my cheek. I hadn't seen her since she'd left the condo earlier that morning. It might as well have been a lifetime though.

"Hi." I finally regained enough air to greet her.

Her ruby red lips lifted on one side. "Hello."

"What's all this?" I questioned. "A secret brewery rendezvous? Do you know the bartender or something?"

"Or something." She curled her finger, beckoning me to follow.

I walked a few steps behind her, always appreciative of the view. She stopped suddenly and turned to face me. I stayed still as she approached.

The touch of Julia's tongue against my lower lip coaxed a low sound from the back of my throat.

"Hands up, Detective." The words were murmured into my ear.

I did as she told me. I raised my arms high in the sky. As I followed her instructions, my fingers brushed against a metal horizontal pole that had no visible beginning or end.

Julia stood behind me. I shuddered when I felt the press of her body against my back. She trailed her fingertips up my elevated arms until her hands met mine. Wordlessly, she guided my hands and curled my fingers over the metal pole. I was putty to her guiding touch, eager to do or be wherever she wanted me.

"Hold onto this," she instructed. "And if you know what's good for you ..." She let the final three words fall slowly from her painted mouth: "Don't. Let. Go."

I tightened my fingers around the elevated pole and gave it an experimental tug to test its stability. I didn't know if the metal rod served some purpose in the beer-making process, but I figured it would have been made from stainless steel or copper if that had been the case. Plus, I trusted Julia would never do something that might damage someone else's property.

Julia stroked her fingers down the center of my back. I could feel the bite of her short, manicured nails even through the material of my flannel shirt. "Do you know what I'm going to do to you?"

I shook my head even though I had a pretty good idea.

"I'm going to fuck you while all of your friends wait on you, wondering why on earth you'd be missing your own birthday party."

Her response caused my breath to hitch in my throat. I'd once asked her not to take it easy on me, and she'd stayed faithful to that promise.

She started with the top buttons of my buffalo-checked shirt and worked her way down. She moved methodically and efficiently. She didn't tease me—yet. It was obvious she had an agenda, and my shirt played little to no part in her plan. With my arms still elevated and my hands curled around the metal bar, she couldn't completely remove either my shirt or my bra. She seemed satisfied to let my shirt hang open in the front. I could no longer see the doorway through which I'd entered moments earlier. As much as I hated being exposed and vulnerable, I knew Julia wouldn't have gone to all of this trouble only for us to be interrupted or walked in on.

Julia stood in front of me. I felt her cool, nearly disinterested gaze on my exposed flesh. Her feminine fingers trailed up my abdomen, between my breasts, and up my breast plate.

Those same fingers gently settled around my neck, lightly squeezing, but not enough to truly obstruct my breathing. Just her proximity and the knowledge of what might come next—namely, *me*—was enough to have me gasping.

"Ask me nicely," she quietly commanded.

I swallowed beneath her fingers. "Julia. Please."

The fingers around my neck subtly squeezed. "You're going to have to do better than that, Birthday Girl."

"Please, Julia. Fuck me."

Julia released my neck. Her fingers moved next to my mouth where they tapped against slightly parted lips, demanding entrance. "Get me ready for you."

I opened wider and she slipped her first and middle finger into my mouth. Her fingers slid along my flattened tongue. She stuck them deep in my mouth, not to the point where I was gagging, but enough to make me blush. I closed my lips around her thick fingers and worked my tongue along the underside of her digits.

"Good girl," she murmured.

If I hadn't been holding on to that metal bar, my knees would have buckled and failed me.

While I sucked on the fingers on her right hand, her left hand was busy with the top button and zipper of my jeans. She'd recently been cleared by her doctor to forgo the splints and wraps; her wrist was fully healed, but it would take some physical therapy for her to regain full flexibility and strength. I was only so happy to be doing my part for her PT. She needed both hands to wiggle my fitted jeans past my hips and to pull down my underwear as well. With my jeans bunched around my ankles, the gusset of my underwear revealed evidence of my early excitement.

Julia removed her fingers from my mouth and I found myself gasping. She stalked behind me, and I held my breath in anticipation. I shifted my palms on the metal pole, but was careful not to let go. My triceps were beginning to ache from their elevated position, but I would never complain to Julia about that.

Her hot mouth pressed between my shoulders through the material of my flannel shirt. She wrapped her arm around my midsection, and her fingertips sliced through the front of my shaved pussy. She spread my wetness from my slit to my clit, a combination of my saliva and arousal. I was always wet for her. My eyes snapped open when I felt a slippery finger slide past my pussy to toy with the second opening farther back.

"Maybe another time," she mused.

I could only whimper with need.

Her fingers returned to the opening of my sex. She pressed her fingertips against me, but not hard enough that she might slip in. With her standing behind me but touching me from the front, the sensation was almost akin to masturbating—only this was better. Much better.

I tried to widen my stance for her, but those damn jeans around my ankles only allowed for so much movement. I wouldn't be able to get rid of them entirely without first taking off my leather boots. The longer she toyed with me, the more acutely aware I became that I was missing my birthday party. In truth, the only person I wanted to see that day was the woman currently licking the outer shell of my ear and slowly manipulating my clit in small circles, but I stupidly didn't want to be rude to my friends. It was

Christmas Eve, and they'd chosen to share the holiday with me.

"Julia ... baby," I breathed.

"I know, darling," she appeased.

Her fingers left my clit, and I felt her dexterous touch elsewhere. Her first and ring finger settled on my pussy lips and gently spread me apart. Her middle finger pressed against my dampness. I released a long breath when she finally penetrated me.

I felt full from only the single finger. She'd worked me up to the point that my inner muscles had already tightened.

"Don't let go," she murmured.

As if I could forget.

Julia pressed the length of her body against the back of my own. I could feel the softness of her breasts pressing into my upper back. I wanted to touch her. To manipulate her nipples. To pinch and pull at the hardened buds until she cried out. But instead, I gripped the metal bar above my head tighter.

Julia masturbated me with both hands. She rubbed at my clit with increased urgency while a single finger in my sex became two. The muscles in my abdomen clenched, and my breathing became more labored.

"Fuck that's good," I encouraged her. "Just like that, baby."

Julia maintained her speed and pressure and command. My upper thighs began to quiver, and I struggled to remain standing. I could feel my body turning to liquid from her deft touch. Aided by upper body and core strength, I somehow managed to stay on my feet.

The tightness in my abdomen radiated outward. Each affected muscle began to twitch and seize.

"Oh fuck," I groaned. "I'm gonna cum."

The fingers between my thighs and the fingers pressed against my clit never paused, never faltered. I closed my eyes and gave myself over to the intense wave of my orgasm.

Shit. If this was twenty-nine, I couldn't wait to turn thirty.

My heart hammered in my throat as I bent down to grab my jeans and underwear. Both were still bunched at my ankles. My fingers and arms tingled from being elevated for so long.

"Don't pull those up yet," Julia instructed. "I've got one more present for you."

"One knee-wobbling orgasm wasn't enough?"

I'd barely had enough time to recuperate from what I'd thought had been my birthday surprise.

Julia retrieved a small, flat box from where it had unobtrusively sat on a nearby beer keg. Her face was neutral as she passed me the wrapped box. "I know you hate when your birthday and Christmas presents are rolled into one gift," she explained. "Besides, everyone should have something to unwrap."

The only thing I wanted to unwrap was her, but I accepted the gift-wrapped box without comment.

I held the small box in my hands. It was light, almost like it contained nothing at all.

"You really didn't have to," I began my protest.

Money and things that could be purchased with money had always made me uncomfortable. Julia had always had a more sizable salary than me, even when she'd been a public defender. We hadn't talked about it, but I imagined her new job with Grisham & Stein had come with a sizable jump in pay.

"I know," she concurred. "But think of it as a present for me, too."

I continued to stare down at the elegantly decorated box. "Okay," I said, still uncomfortable with the gesture.

I took my time with the ribbon, bow, and wrapping paper, keenly aware of Julia's eyes on me. I abhorred being the center of attention, even if it was only the two of us. I was eager to see what was inside of the box, but I carefully unwrapped the small package rather than tear into it like an eight-year-old kid on Christmas morning.

I separated the top from the bottom of the box and peered inside. Delicate black lace peeked out from beneath festive holiday crepe paper.

I fished the garment out of the box. "You got me underwear?"

The material looked expensive—far nicer and much more expensive than what I typically wore.

"Not just any kind of underwear," Julia mused.

She reached into her jacket pocket and pulled out a slim, black device that looked similar to a small remote. She pressed her thumb against the mechanism, and the lace in my hands began to buzz.

"Oh shit." I swore without meaning to.

Julia's smile was nearly maniacal. "Are you ready for your birthday party, darling?"

. . .

I walked with an uncertain gait from the brewing room to the tap room where my friends were waiting for me. Julia walked beside me with her hand in the small of my back. It was a role reversal of sorts. I typically was the one to open doors or guide her while we walked. It wasn't entirely unpleasant, but it was a little unnerving.

"What's your safe word?" Julia's question was quiet; I almost hadn't heard it.

I turned to her before we reached my friends. "You think I'll need one?"

"Better safe than sorry," she reasoned. She leaned a little closer and dropped her volume even lower. "Unless you want to yell out 'Dear God, Julia, stop destroying my clit' in front of your nearest and dearest friends?"

If her words were intended to make me back down, I was too stubborn to heed her warning. "Mistletoe," I decided. I raised a defiant chin. "But I'm not going to need it."

"We'll see." Her smile was so sweet it was saccharine.

"There's the birthday girl!" Rich greeted as we approached my group of friends. "And her better half," he said with a deferential nod to my girlfriend.

In my absence, more of my friends had shown up to the informal gathering. Rich and Grace Kelly, Brent, and Angie were joined by my other closest police friend, Adan, and his girlfriend, Isabelle.

Rich gave the two of us a particularly smug and mischievous smile. "Julia, I hope you weren't too hard on dear Cassidy with all of those birthday spankings."

"Rich!" Grace squeaked. She swatted at her boyfriend's arm.

"Oh, she can handle it," Rich dismissed.

I stole a glance in Julia's direction. She'd abandoned us for the bar area, presumably to get something to drink. I watched the crowds literally part as she approached the busy bartender. They could have simply been being kind, but more than likely Julia had flashed a fierce look that had people scattering out of her way. Some people might desire a partner who was generous with their kindness. I, however, thoroughly enjoyed Julia's idiosyncrasies and icy tendencies. It made the quiet moments spent with her and the niceties that she lavished on me even more special.

Grace's voice pulled my attention back to my assembled friends. "Big plans for tomorrow or just a quiet, cozy Christmas at home?"

"We're, uh, we're actually headed to St. Cloud tomorrow," I revealed. "Going to spend a few days with my parents."

Grace Kelly's eyes went wide. "Ooh! Is Julia meeting your parents for the first time?"

I nearly said yes, until I remembered that she'd already met my parents at a jungle-themed restaurant in the Mall of America. I hadn't exactly introduced Julia, however. I hadn't told my parents that she was much more than a roommate. I'd felt guilty about my cowardice ever since, which made our upcoming trip to St. Cloud even more important. I was nervous—anyone in my position would be. But I was actually looking forward to the trip and the opportunity to make things right. It was time that I Came Out to my parents, and I couldn't have been more proud to reintroduce Julia to them as my significant other.

But Grace Kelly didn't need all of those details.

"Uh huh," I settled for.

Julia rejoined our group not long after. She pressed a cold pint of beer into my hands. "For the birthday girl," she murmured.

I looked at the beer as if expecting something to jump out of it. "Thanks, babe. Nothing for you?" I asked, noticing her empty right hand.

"No," she dismissed. "I want to stay sharp. But you have fun," she encouraged. "It's your special day, after all."

Her right hand disappeared into the pocket of her suit jacket. Almost immediately, the hidden device in my new birthday underwear began to purr. The vibrations were small, but the contraption fit snug against my clit.

Julia smiled innocently. "How are you doing? Need anything else?"

Her hand remained in her pocket, where I assumed she kept the underwear's remote control. The vibrations noticeably intensified with her question.

"Nope," I gulped. "I'm great."

My eyes searched the smiling faces of my friends. Had they noticed any change? We were gathered in a close circle, but as long as I kept my cool, there was no reason for them to suspect anything was happening inside of my pants.

Julia leaned a little closer. A particularly pleased smile curled at the edges of her ruby red mouth. "Should I open up the throttle, dear?"

She purposefully enunciated each word as if my brain might be too rattled to understand the reference.

I smiled at her between grit teeth. *Oh, it was going to be like that, huh?* "Do your worst."

Julia's hand returned to her pocket. The vibrations

against my sex seemed to double in speed. It was like someone was playing a drum solo on my clit.

"Jesus!" I tried to hide my exclamation behind an exaggerated cough.

"You okay, Cass?" Angie questioned.

I smiled weakly in my friend's direction when she gave me a strange look. "Just peachy," I wheezed. "Beer went down the wrong tube." I struck my closed fist against my chest for effect.

An intense heat rushed from my center down to my extremities when the vibrations continued without reprieve. I clutched my pint glass so hard, I worried it might shatter in my hand. I could only hope that the festive music streaming over the PA system was loud enough to drown out the obvious buzzing sound coming from my pants.

I somehow managed to set my beer on a nearby wooden barrel that doubled as a cocktail table. I no longer trusted my hands to hold the heavy glass, and there was no way I was going to be able to casually sip at my drink without choking on its contents. I focused on my breathing and tried to pay attention to the conversations happening around me.

Rich and Grace were spending the holiday in the Twin Cities. It was her first Christmas outside of Embarrass, which she felt guilty about, but her two sisters and their respective families—I'd nearly forgotten she was a triplet—would more than compensate for her absence. Both Brent and Angie were scheduled to work the next day. Neither had significant others or family close by, so they tended to volunteer to work the Christmas holiday. Plus, they would make time and a half for the holiday hours. Adan was ... I tried to focus on my friend's face. What was Adan saying? His lips moved, but I couldn't make out the words.

I shut my eyes when another intense wave washed over me. Someone was speaking, but I could no longer distinguish individual voices. My knees buckled, and I braced myself against the wooden barrel. I was getting lit up like a Christmas tree. I couldn't orgasm in a crowded beer bar —could I?

"Seriously, Cass," I heard Angie's concern. "You're looking a little rough."

I shut my eyes and grimaced. "Just ... a little heartburn," I lied.

"I'll go get you some water," she offered.

"Okay, thanks," I choked out.

My lower body was on fire, but no water would be able to extinguish that kind of burn. There was no place I could go, no way to adjust myself to provide some relief. I couldn't tell if the damp heat between my thighs was from sweat or from arousal, but it was probably a mixture of both. Was my birthday underwear waterproof, or rather cumproof? I was leaking like a busted faucet; I genuinely worried the accumulating liquids might cause the whole mechanism to short out.

I cast my eyes back to my friends. Brent was on his phone and Grace and Rich were preoccupied with their own conversation. Adan and Isabella had their heads bents together. No one was looking at me.

"J-Julia!" I couldn't help the volume of my voice. "Did you s-see the m-mistletoe over there?"

My girlfriend looked far too casual, and for a brief moment I worried she'd forgotten the safe word. "No? I must have missed it."

The buzzing between my legs seemed to intensify like the damn underwear was revving its engine. My abdomen tensed. *No, no, no, no.* I clutched the edge of the beer barrel table like it was a life raft on the ocean. My knuckles turned white from the death grip. The rough, unfinished edges dug into my palms.

My vision blurred, and I offered up a one-worded prayer. "Mistletoe!"

The vibrations immediately stopped and Julia swooped beside me to wrap her good arm around my midsection. To an outsider, it probably looked like an affectionate gesture rather than a necessity. Her sturdy arm might have been the only reason I remained on my feet, however.

"Jesus," I quietly hissed. "What happened to the safe word?"

She nuzzled her nose into my hair. "I knew my girl could take just a little bit more. Are we even now?"

"Even?" I echoed the word.

"Orgasms, dear," Julia clarified. "Are we finally caught up? I hate being in debt to anyone."

"That's what this was about?"

Julia shrugged but didn't let go of me. "I may have been thinking about doing something like this for a while."

"Is this one of those aforementioned fantasies?"

The arm around my middle tightened. "Having my partner give up total control to me? Having the power to unleash your orgasm with the push of a button?" Julia's tone dropped to a delicious burn. "Watching you come undone in a public space, in a room full of your closest friends, with none of them being the wiser to what's happening below your waist? Seeing you squirm and sweat and try to mask your pleasure when all you want to do is lose control and scream?" She batted her long eyelashes. "Is that to what you're referring, dear?"

I swallowed thickly, miraculously turned on all over again. If she kept this up, I'd never make it to my thirtieth birthday. "Yeah. That'd be it."

Julia smiled serenely before helping herself to a sip of my beer. "Maybe."

Chapter Twenty

Julia stood before her open closet door. "Why did you let me procrastinate on packing?"

Christmas morning had been a quiet affair with Julia spending the better part of the day at the assisted living facility where she'd recently re-homed her mom. I had been invited to tag along, but I'd politely declined the offer. Julia didn't pressure me to come with her, which suggested that this was something she'd wanted to do on her own.

I watched my panicked girlfriend from the bed. "We'll only be gone a few days," I reminded her. "Just throw some things in a bag and we can go."

Julia turned on her heel. "Throw some things in a bag?" she repeated in an incredulous tone. "Don't you want your parents to like me?"

"Fancy clothes will have absolutely no impact on them," I promised. "In fact, they might like you even better all dressed down."

Julia's shoulders slumped forward. "I think I liked it better when they thought we were roommates."

I hopped up from the bed. "Babe, you have absolutely nothing to worry about. I'm the one Coming Out, remember?"

"I know, which is why I want to look my best for you."

"When's the last time someone introduced you to their parents as their girlfriend?" I asked.

She bit her lower lip. "Never. You?"

"Same," I admitted.

"God, we're quite the pair," Julia ruefully chuckled.

"It's going to be fine," I tried to appease.

I felt Julia's pointed stare. "When are you going to do it? When are you going to tell them?"

"I ... I hadn't thought that far ahead."

Julia's voice was censuring: "Cassidy."

I held up my hands in front of me like a protective shield. "I don't want to ambush them, you know? I can't just spring it on them the moment they open the door."

Julia folded her arms across her chest. "I don't see why not," she protested. "'Mom, Dad, you remember my girlfriend, Julia.'"

"They're going to hear *friend* who is a *girl*."

"Partner, then," she amended.

"They'll think we've gone into business together," I countered.

I heard her displeased noise. "You're being ridiculous."

"I could always introduce you as my *fiancée*," I grinned. "They'd definitely hear that."

"And give your poor mother a heart attack?" Julia huffed. "I'd rather not."

The energy in the room had palpably shifted. Rather than being nervous about the trip to St. Cloud, Julia now sounded annoyed. She noisily rattled through the hangers in her closet in search of the perfect outfit.

I watched her from my position near the end of the bed. "I'm going to do it this weekend," I vowed in earnest. "But let me do it my way."

∽

St. Cloud was little more than an hour north and west of the Twin Cities, but holiday traffic and early winter sunsets had made the relatively reasonable drive a little longer than usual. The lack of sunlight didn't matter though; I could have found my parents' house while blindfolded.

Julia turned into the short driveway in front of my parents' house. My parents didn't go all out with Christmas decorations, but they weren't Scrooges either. A single, sensible strand of multi-colored lights outlined the dimensions of the modest ranch-style house. An illuminated plastic Santa Claus peered down from his perch on the slanted roof. I'd never been self-conscious about my roots or how I'd grown up, but I was wildly aware that several copies of my parents' home could fit into the footprint of Julia's mansion in Embarrass.

I hopped out of the passenger seat and headed to the trunk of the Mercedes. Julia didn't put up a fight when I hefted both of our bags out of the trunk and proceeded to walk up the concrete walkway that led to my parents' front door. Snow covered the yard but the driveway and sidewalk leading to the front door had recently been cleared. Rock salt covered the walkway, crunching beneath my winter boots.

"That's very chivalrous of you," I heard Julia's voice behind me, "*roommate*."

I froze in place with our bags in either hand. "Your ... your wrist," I excused. "It's still not one hundred percent."

Julia caught up to me. She stroked her fingers along my jawline as she passed me by. "There's only one way to really test out that theory," she mused. "It's too bad roommates don't do those kinds of things to each other."

I swallowed hard. The evening air was chilled, but Julia's suggestion had me overheating. "You're going to torture me all weekend."

It wasn't a question. I knew too well how she might torment me under my parents' roof—and not in an enjoyable way, either.

Julia smiled mildly. "Just helping you keep up the façade, darling."

"I'm going to do it!" I proclaimed.

My voice came out a little too loud. The front door swung open at that moment and my mom stood in the doorway.

"Going to do what, sweetie?" my mom asked.

"Oh, uh, nothing. Just a work thing," I lied. "Nothing to worry about."

Luckily, my mom was too excited by our arrival to press me for more details.

She threw her arms around me and enveloped me in an overly exuberant hug. With my hands already occupied with luggage, I had no choice but to stand and endure my mom's affection.

"Hey, Mom."

"Oh, it's so good to see you!" my mom enthused. She took her time with every vowel. Perhaps I'd been living in the cities for too long; her accent was hard on my ears.

Julia stood back a few feet from the awkward reunion, but she didn't go unnoticed for long. My mom abruptly ended our hug and rushed toward Julia like a defensive back on his way to the quarterback. My girlfriend soon found herself on the receiving end of a Nancy Miller bear hug. I watched Julia's features morph from surprise to discomfort to acceptance in the span of a few seconds. Her entire body seemed to relax into the prolonged embrace.

I cleared my throat after becoming inexplicably choked up by the show of emotion. My mom was a big hugger—I was used to that. She got excited over small, seemingly trivial things. But would the open show of affection continue, I wondered, when I finally revealed to my mom who Julia was to me? Would she still so freely give out those hugs after I Came Out?

I still had no idea how I was going to tell my parents. I'd thought about nothing else during the relatively quiet drive from St. Paul to my hometown. I'd tried to picture myself in various rooms of my parents' house and what opportunities they might afford. Drying the dishes from dinner while my mom washed? Shoveling the driveway with my dad? Watching late night television? Nothing felt right. Nothing made sense. I hoped that the universe would present me with the right moment, but I knew that was too much to expect. It was going to be awkward. It was going to be uncomfortable regardless of what I might try to plan or visualize. No amount of *manifesting* would make this any easier on anybody.

"I'm so happy you could make the trip, too, Julia!" My mom finally released her from the crushing hug. "I've been cooking all day, so I hope you brought your appetite."

"I hope I'm not putting you out, Mrs. Miller," Julia said.

My mom waved her hands. "It's absolutely no trouble. The more the merrier, especially around the holidays. And remember," she corrected, "it's Nancy, not Mrs. Miller. You're not one of my old piano students."

"Well in that case, Nancy," Julia graciously returned, "thank you for opening your home."

"Can we go inside?" I stamped my feet, dislodging loose snow from the bottom of my boots. "I'm built for sand these days, not snow."

"Come in, come in!" my mom said, ushering us inside.

Heat pouring from the pellet stove warmed the front of my parents' house. I removed my leather jacket and waited for Julia to slide out of her wool peacoat.

"Bruce!" my mom called out the moment we stepped inside. "The girls are here!"

I couldn't immediately see my dad—he hadn't been waiting at the front door like my mom had—but I imagined he was probably in his La-Z-Boy easy chair in front of the TV in the living room.

"Bruce!" my mom called again. She left Julia and me in the front foyer in search of my dad.

Julia bent down to take off her boots. "Am I meant to leave these here?"

Her question barely registered with me. I hadn't been nervous before, but my heart had taken residency in my throat the moment we stepped inside.

"Cassidy—do we leave our boots here?"

I blinked several times. "Yeah. That's fine."

Julia squeezed my right bicep and looked me over. Her dark eyes filled with concern. "Are you okay?"

I swallowed. The gravity of what I intended to do had hit me like an IED. "I'm-I'm a little nervous," I admitted.

"If it happens, it happens," she allowed. "If you're worried it will spoil the visit, it can wait."

I shook my head with vigor. "No. It's going to happen. Right now."

I cleared my throat, fully prepared to shout my sexuality from the entryway.

Julia laid a hand on my forearm. "Why don't we have dinner first," she gently recommended. "Your mother has been cooking all day, and no one should have to Out themselves on an empty stomach."

We left our bags in the front foyer and washed up in the half-bathroom off the kitchen before sitting down at the dining room table. My mom was busy setting various serving dishes and casserole containers out on the table.

"Bruce!" she yelled out. The volume of her voice had me flinching. "Dinner's on the table! Dig in girls," she directed to us. "Don't let it get cold."

I took in the various ceramic containers and serving dishes spread out across the table. My mom had even put the leaf in the table to make it longer. "Dang, Mom. I'm a good eater, but not *that* good."

"I didn't know what you might like, so I made a little of everything," she explained.

There was no pattern or obvious theme to the meal. It wasn't quite a Thanksgiving or Christmas spread. The main protein was fried chicken. Everything else could be classified as a casserole or salad, although in the upper Midwest, we were pretty liberal with our use of the word 'salad.'

"Everything looks wonderful, Nancy." Julia had always been better at the graciousness thing than me. I should have been more appreciative of the obvious effort my mom had put into the meal.

I'd nearly finished filling up my plate with fragrant, bubbling hot food by the time my dad made his way to the dining room. My mom didn't say anything about his tardiness, but I was offended on her behalf. He silently spooned hot dish onto his plate and claimed a coveted chicken leg for himself. He didn't say hello to either Julia or myself. My dad's lack of decorum made me aware of my own tendencies to be less than refined at the dining table. I made a mental note to be more mindful of table manners for Julia in the future. Sometimes it was useful to have models you *didn't* want to emulate as much as role models whom you admired.

"How were the roads?" my dad grunted out.

I sat at attention. This wasn't idle small-talk; it was how Midwesterners—uncomfortable with emotion—showed we cared.

"Clear the whole way here," I said. "I was worried about black ice, but it was just warm enough. Didn't see any deer either."

My dad didn't look in my direction as I spoke. He kept his focus on his plate, which he periodically added more food to, as if he worried me might run out before he'd had his fill.

My mom spoke next: "So, what's new?"

It was an innocuous question, like when someone asks how you're doing. Did they really want to know, or were they simply being polite? But my mom had opened dinner conversation with the same question for as long as I could remember. I'd rarely been forthcoming about what I'd learned in school that day or what the new drama was with my small group of swim team friends, but she still asked whenever we were at the dining room table.

"We closed another Cold Case," I said.

"Oh?" My mom's voice sounded interested.

"Yeah. A girl went missing thirty years ago. We found her and we arrested the person responsible." I purposely refrained from using words like *murder*, *death*, and *skeletal remains* in front of my family.

"Cassidy is really doing well," Julia chimed in. "She's already helped close three cases since joining the department. I think it might be a record."

"Whatever," I deflected. "*You're* the accomplished one. Julia just got hired by one of the biggest law firms in the cities to do their *pro bono* cases."

Julia hid a smile behind her glass of two-percent milk. "Not bad for two small-town girls."

"Where did you grow up, Julia?" my mom wanted to know.

"Embarrass."

My dad hadn't been paying much attention to our conversation until Julia's admission. Something akin to recognition flashed across his features. "Embarrass? You're that lawyer?"

Shit.

Everything in my body tensed. The last time I'd sat at my parents' dining room table, I'd recently left Embarrass. My dad had heard all about Julia's legal defense of her dad from his childhood best friend—Larry Hart, Embarrass' Chief of

Police. It hadn't been a very flattering portrayal of Julia, and I'd promptly left the table and the house.

My fingers clenched around my utensils, although I didn't know why; it wasn't like I was going to stab him with my fork. "Dad."

My dad cleared his throat. "Larry told me about your dad. I'm sorry for your loss."

Julia included her head toward my dad. "I appreciate the kind words, Mr. Miller. I'm not sure I deserve them though. I betrayed a lot of people's trust back then, including your daughter's."

If I'd thought Coming Out to my parents was going to be an uncomfortable conversation, it couldn't have been much worse than this.

My mom and I spoke at the same time.

"All in the past!" I squeaked.

"Who wants dessert?" she bellowed.

I wanted to follow my mom's speedy retreat to the kitchen, but I didn't want to leave Julia alone with my dad.

My mom returned quickly, perhaps not wanting to leave us alone with my dad either. When I saw her dessert selection, I covered my face with my hands. She strode into the room carrying a multi-tiered grocery store cake ... with a baby Jesus cake topper.

My mom set the monstrosity in front of me and produced a lighter. When her thumb rolled over the mechanism to create a small flame, I realized the baby Jesus cake topper doubled as a candle.

"We're going to hell," I muttered.

"Oh hush," my mom censured. "It's just a little fun."

I winced as she began the opening notes: "*Haaaaaaappy Birthday to youuuuuuu.*"

I had no choice but to sit through an awkward rendition of the Birthday Song. My mom had perfect pitch from years as a piano teacher. Julia quietly sang along while my dad's mouth moved without producing any sound.

I watched it all through the cracks between my fingers. The baby Jesus's head started to melt before I could blow out the flame.

We'd gotten to my parents' house late that night, and once dinner had been eaten and dishes had been washed and put away, it was basically time for bed. My parents' house was small, with only one level for living. They didn't have a finished basement to escape to, so conversations and television watching ended whenever my parents went to bed. My dad was an early riser even though he'd been retired for several years. My mom would unwind in bed with a romance novel and a cup of decaffeinated tea.

The hide-a-bed in the living room shrieked and whined when I pulled the collapsible mattress out of the couch. It probably hadn't been used since I was in high school unless my mom banished my dad to the couch after a fight. My mom had made the decision for us that I would be sleeping on the ancient torture device while Julia would spend the night in my childhood bedroom. She claimed she didn't want us to have to share the small bed, and short of Coming Out to her at that moment, I had no good reason to insist that we didn't mind the squeeze.

I laid awake in the darkened living room. A persistent

blue-green glow from the DVD player kept me company while in the next room, the refrigerator periodically turned on and interrupted the silent night with its low hum. I twisted this way and that on the ancient mattress. No matter how I positioned myself, a hard metal rod seemed to poke me in the middle of my back. I missed the memory foam mattress from Julia's condo, but I missed the woman who slept beside me even more.

I tried to be stealthy rolling out of bed, but the hide-a-bed gave me away. I stood motionless in the living room and waited to see if my movement had woken up my parents. When no one appeared, I left the living room and quietly crept down the hallway.

I stopped in front of my closed bedroom door. A gap between the floor and the bottom of the door was illuminated from a light on in the room. I lifted my hand and quietly drummed my fingers against the door.

"Yes?" I heard Julia's voice.

I leaned a little closer to the shut door. "It's me," I whispered.

I heard the rustling of sheets and the squeak of feet on floorboards before the door opened a few inches. Julia appeared in the doorway. She'd already changed into her pajamas—thin cotton joggers and a v-neck t-shirt.

"Hey," I greeted, keeping my voice low. "How's it going in here?"

Julia's manicured fingers curled around the edge of the door. "Good. I've got freshly laundered sheets, an eye mask, and a bottled water. Your mother is quite the hostess."

I peered beyond Julia to the interior of my old bedroom. It looked the same as it had in high school. The same ugly carpet. The same posters on the walls. Swimming medals and trophies lined the bookshelves and dresser drawer. The Navy Cross I'd been awarded for saving my buddy Terrance Pensacola still sat in the sock drawer.

"Want some company?"

Julia's lips quirked. "Nancy seems to think we shouldn't share."

I ignored her response. "So here's the plan. I'll wait until I'm sure they're sleeping, and then I'll come back."

"And you'll, what? Set an alarm to go back to the couch before they wake up?" Julia shook her head. "If you would just *tell them*, we wouldn't have to sneak around."

"Tomorrow," I promised.

"Then tomorrow, maybe I'll share a bed with you." Julia smiled as she slowly closed the bedroom door in my face. "Sweet dreams, *roomie*."

Chapter Twenty One

The next morning, I was in the kitchen having coffee before the rest of the house was up. The curtains in the living room hadn't offered much protection from sunrise. It was hard enough sleeping on the pullout couch in the first place without early morning sun blasting me.

I took my time to enjoy the quiet of the house. As soon as my mom woke up, that peace would be erased. Today was the day. Today was the day I was going to Come Out to her.

I still didn't know how or when to do it. I hadn't taken the time to write down a big speech either. It wasn't that I found comfort flying by the seat of my pants, but I was no wordsmith. I was no great brain. Even if I sat down with a pen and paper and plotted out what I wanted to say to my mom, I would still get tongue-tied when the moment arrived. I might as well fumble through that conversation as my most authentic, organic self.

I heard the creak of footsteps on the laminate floor. Julia, not my mom, entered the kitchen in running tights and an old sweatshirt that I recognized as belonging to me. Her bed head made me smile. If I had been the one staying with my significant other's parents, I would have hidden out in the guest bedroom or at least showered and fixed my hair.

She greeted me with a soft kiss to the top of my head.

"Good morning," I murmured. "I made coffee."

Julia nodded, still looking sleepy. I'd left an extra coffee cup on the kitchen counter so she wouldn't have to hunt for her own. She poured herself a cup of coffee and joined me at the small kitchen table where I'd eaten innumerable bowls of cereal in my youth.

Julia's hands cupped the ceramic mug. She dipped her nose inside and inhaled. I heard her pleasant hum echo inside the coffee cup.

"How'd you sleep?" I asked.

"Good." She brushed at her unruly hair. "It was a little surreal to be surrounded by all of your things, like a time capsule from years ago." A small smile played at the corners of her lipstick-free mouth. "I had no idea you were such a Britney Spears fan."

I made a face. "I can't believe my mom hasn't taken down those posters."

"Oh hush. It's charming," she insisted. "A whole new side to you I didn't know existed."

"Yeah," I snorted. "A super embarrassing part of me."

"Good morning!"

I turned away from Julia in the direction of the cheerful greeting. My mom stood in the archway that separated the kitchen from the dining room. She looked a little more put-together than either Julia and myself, but she was still in her pajamas.

Julia and I returned our mumbled good mornings.

My mom remained in the entryway. "Do you girls need breakfast?"

I glanced in Julia's direction. She shook her head.

"No thanks, Mom," I said. "I think we're both still full from dinner."

"What are your plans for today?" my mom asked.

I looked again to Julia. She shrugged beneath the ancient sweatshirt. God, I loved it when she wore my clothes.

"I don't think we have any," I admitted. "What do you want to do?"

It was obvious my mom was trying to mask her excitement. "Feel free to say no, but there's something I'd like to do."

She motioned for us to follow her.

It took some effort on my part—my lower back ached from spending the night on the uncomfortable mattress—but I stood from the small kitchen table and trailed after my mom's retreat. Julia followed a few steps behind me.

I blinked a few times at the chaos spread across the dining room table. Several silver cookie sheets were filled with flat planks of gingerbread. A variety of ceramic bowls containing sugary candies and fluffy white frosting joined the slabs of gingerbread. None of it had been on the table when I'd first woken up.

"What's all this?" I asked.

My mom swayed where she stood. "Your father isn't interested in these kinds of things, so it's usually just me now that you're out of the house."

She hadn't actually vocalized her request, but it was obvious what she was asking us to do.

Julia was the one to speak next: "We'd love to build gingerbread houses with you, Nancy."

"Oh good!" my mom enthused.

I was apparently outnumbered.

I sat down at the dining room table and claimed one of the cookie sheets for myself. I'd never actually assembled a gingerbread house before. It wasn't a Miller family tradition, but I assumed I'd figure it out. I wondered at the sheer amount and variety of supplies my mom had assembled. How long after my phone call, alerting her that we were coming for a visit, had she waited before rushing to the store to buy the gingerbread house materials?

In addition to the slabs of gingerbread—pre-cut pieces that would make the roof and four walls—she'd laid out bowls of multicolored frosting and piles of candy with which to decorate our respective homes. Gumdrops, candy canes, red vines, peppermint disks, and other various candies covered the dining room table.

Julia required no prompting or instructions. She commandeered one of the frosting piping devices and began to glue together the walls of her candy home.

I started with the four walls of the house. Not knowing what I was doing, I layered on thick smears of frosting at the joints and pressed the pieces together until I was satisfied that the frosting had set.

"Is this a Miller family tradition?" Julia asked.

The base of her house was already complete—no surprise there.

"No. We never did this kind of stuff," I replied.

"Oh, you make it sound like we were a bunch of Grinches when you were growing up," my mom chastised. "I always made sugar cookies for you to decorate to leave out for Santa. And when you were much younger, you and your dad would leave a bale of hay outside for the reindeer. You'd get so excited on Christmas morning to go outside and see the hoof prints in the snow."

"Yeah. Encouraging the urban deer population," I snorted.

"Oh hush," my mom censured. "Julia, does your family have any special holiday traditions?"

I tried to give my mom a look that said *don't*, but she wasn't looking in my direction. It felt almost on purpose.

"A few," Julia confirmed. "Nothing as hands on as this, though. My father would drive us around the neighborhood to look at the holiday lights. My mom stayed behind. She used the excuse that she needed to finish making dinner, but as I got older, I realized it was so Santa could make his visit. We'd finish driving around the neighborhood and when we got home, there were presents under the tree and candy in our stockings. Then on Christmas Day we'd load into the car and drive out to my grandparents' house."

"That sounds lovely," my mom approved. "And it's so nice that you can appreciate your mom's role in making those memories happen. The hidden labor of mothers is often lost on our children."

I sucked in a sharp breath. Having these two women at the same crafting table might have been a mistake.

Julia's gaze was intensely trained on her half-constructed gingerbread house. She carefully arranged gumdrop candies on the roof. "The grand irony is that my mother might not even remember those moments anymore."

I heard my mom's soft gasp. "Oh no. Is it ..."

Julia sat up a little straighter in her chair and audibly sniffed. "Dementia," she confirmed. "She's been living with it for several years now. I'm grateful that she hasn't forgotten me yet, but I know it's only a matter of time."

My hand tensed beneath the dining room table. I wanted to grab onto Julia's hand and at the very least give her a reassuring squeeze. But without having Come Out yet, I found myself embarrassingly paralyzed. Luckily, my mom wasn't frozen. She *did* grab Julia's hand. The fine bones and tendons on the top of her hand flexed with maternal affection. The two women shared a sympathetic smile while I dumbly sat apart and disconnected from the moment.

I scowled when one of my roofing slabs slid off the base of its house.

"Too much frosting," my mom clucked.

"You could always make it a midcentury modern house," Julia chimed in.

"Thanks for the feedback," I grumbled.

"Cassidy did a wonderful job of decorating the Christmas tree in the apartment," Julia remarked. It felt like she was going out of her way to defend me in front of my mom. "She took the task very seriously, making sure each ornament was perfectly placed."

"That doesn't surprise me," my mom said. "She always was such a detail-oriented child. Very ..." My mom paused as if searching for the right word. "Mission driven. Almost to the point of obsession. I'd give her the grocery list and she'd come back with everything checked off and give me back every single cent in change. Nothing unaccounted for. Nothing I hadn't requested."

Julia cocked her head thoughtfully. "That's surprising. I

don't know why, but I guess I thought she was a bit of a wild child in her youth. Kind of cavalier and carefree?"

"Cassidy? Carefree?" My mom chuckled. "Goodness, no. She was such a worrier. I was sure she'd give herself an ulcer before high school."

"I'm loving this trip down memory lane," I deadpanned.

"When Cassidy joined the Marines, I wasn't surprised," my mom offered up. "I worried about her—what mom wouldn't—but I knew she'd excel in that environment. I only wish she hadn't been sent so far away for so long."

I'd long ago lost interest in my gingerbread house. My mom was revealing things she'd never told me before. I had never known how she'd felt about my enlistment or my time spent in Afghanistan. I only knew that neither of my parents knew how to talk about it with me—not that I was very forthcoming myself.

"Did you know, Julia, that Cassidy won the Navy Cross? It's a very prestigious award in the military. She saved a man's life over there."

"I *did* know that," Julia confirmed. "In fact, I've met Terrance and his wife. Did you also know they recently had a baby boy and they named him Miller?"

My mom's breath sounded like a squeak. "Oh my goodness. Cassidy! Why didn't you tell me?"

"I don't know," I grumbled. At the time, it had felt like an odd thing to brag about, including to one's parents.

"Your daughter is very humble," Julia remarked. "She's not one to shine a light on herself even when she deserves the recognition."

"She doesn't tell me anything," my mom openly

complained. "Julia, you'll have to be my eyes and ears for me. Or at least encourage my daughter to call more often."

Julia gently smiled. "I'll do my best, Nancy."

This time I *did* reach for her—underneath the table. I held Julia's hand in mine and traced hearts into her palm with the pad of my thumb.

We continued work on our respective gingerbread houses over the next half an hour or so. Julia and my mom continued to swap stories while my ears burned to be the center of attention for such a prolonged time. They gabbed like long-lost friends while I focused my attention on my mess of a gingerbread house.

Eventually, Julia stood from the table. Both my mom's and my eyes raised along with her elegant motion.

"I need a shower," she announced.

She bent slightly at the waist in my direction. Her movement stalled short of where I sat, and instead of kissing my cheek as was her custom, she patted the top of my shoulder like an awkward game of *Duck, Duck, Grey Duck*. The pause, the flinch, didn't escape my notice. I knew the almost instinctive movement to swoop down low and kiss my cheek. I hated that my Closet was the reason she had to alter her behavior.

I worried my lower lip as Julia disappeared down the hallway in the direction of the bathroom.

"This was fun," my mom happily observed. "I know the holidays are almost over, but you should take your houses home with you. Your dad will eat all of this candy otherwise, and he certainly doesn't need all that sugar."

"Mom."

She carried on as if she hadn't heard me. "One of the days

you'll have to invite me over. I'd like to see where you're living these days. Maybe help with the decorating."

"Mom," I tried again.

"Mmhmm?" she hummed.

I took a breath. "Julia and I aren't roommates." I swallowed hard. "We're together."

My mom didn't look away from her candy cane sidewalk. She'd broken down the peppermint pieces and was using them as pavers. "I know."

I leaned forward in my chair. "No, I mean we're, like, *together*-together."

"Cassidy." My mom finally set down her sugary construction materials. She leveled her gaze on me. "Do you think I was born yesterday?"

I gulped. "You ... you knew?"

"Mothers know these kinds of things."

"But how?"

"You never really had any boyfriends in high school," she explained with a small shrug. "Nothing serious, at least. Besides, I see the way you look at her."

"The way I look at her?" I squeaked.

God, had my mom caught me undressing Julia with my eyes or something?

"Like you're in love," she answered. Her tone was very matter-of-fact. "If you were trying to keep it a secret, you didn't do a very good job."

I stared down at my lap. "Does ... does Dad know?"

"If he does, he hasn't said anything to me about it."

Coming Out to my mom had been an important first step, but I hadn't really been worried about her reaction. I was more nervous about my dad. He'd been polite to Julia when we'd had burgers at a jungle-themed restaurant in the Mall of America, but his first introduction to Julia had occurred months earlier when his childhood best friend, Chief Larry Hart of Embarrass, had told him about my abrupt departure from the small town's police department. In my experience, older men could be just as gossipy and cruel as the fairer sex. Chief Hart had not painted a flattering picture of the woman who had eventually become my live-in girlfriend.

"When are you going to tell him?" my mom asked.

"Uh, never?"

"Cassidy Anne Miller," she scolded. "You don't keep something like this a secret from your family."

I picked up a candy cane and used it to stab at a pile of white frosting that was doubling as a snow drift. "He's not the easiest person to talk to."

"You need to do it," she emphasized.

I knew she was right, of course.

"I'm proud of you for finally telling me," my mom congratulated. "But you're still sleeping on the couch tonight. Call me old fashioned, but until you're married, it's separate beds for the two of you."

"Mom!"

After I helped my mom clear off the dining room table and package up all of the leftover candy, I made my way to my childhood bedroom. The door was closed, so I assumed Julia resided on the other side.

I quietly knocked on the door. "Everybody decent?"

"You can come in," I heard her allow.

I opened the door and stepped inside. Julia sat on the

unmade bed in the same clothes she'd been in earlier. Her hair, wet from the shower, was wrapped in a bath towel.

"I left you some hot water if you'd like to go next," she announced. She leaned forward and untangled the towel from her hair. "I'd almost forgotten what it's like to live in a house where you have to worry about things like that." She briskly rubbed at the damp raven strands until they stood out as though electrified.

I closed the door behind me and leaned against it. "I did it. I told her."

Julia's head snapped up. Her towel-dried hair stuck out this way and that. "You did?"

I nodded. "She said she already knew."

A number of emotions flickered across her features. Finally, Julia hummed. "Your mother is a crafty one. And I'm not just talking about the gingerbread houses."

I sat beside my girlfriend on my childhood bed. I grabbed her hand in mine and intertwined our fingers.

"How do you feel?" she asked.

I shrugged a little. "Not sure. Should I feel different?"

"I suppose we're no longer teenagers sneaking away to cop a feel beneath the bleachers," Julia remarked.

I dropped a single kiss to the top of her shoulder. She smelled good. Clean from the shower. The lingering perfume of her fabric softener mingled with her own natural scent. I pressed my lips to her shoulder again, but moved closer to her exposed neck.

"What are you doing?" Julia's voice was a low murmur.

I paused long enough to respond: "Celebrating me Coming Out to my mom?"

Julia rose from the bed. "I am not going to betray Nancy's trust by letting you have your way with me in here."

I stared up at her. "I can be quiet! She'd never know."

Julia flashed a sardonic smile. "No offense, darling, but you're not as sneaky as you think."

∽

After we'd humored her with the gingerbread houses, my mom seemed determined to cram every Christmas activity invented into the long weekend. We made cut-out sugar cookies and decorated them with miniature sprinkles and homemade frosting. We had a movie marathon of my mom's favorite classic Christmas films like *White Christmas* and *Holiday Inn*. We played Christmas trivia at the dining room table and nibbled at the leftovers from her initial welcome dinner *smorgasbord*. She stopped just short of us cramming around the piano and singing Christmas carols.

I could have complained or put up a fight or even rolled my eyes, but deep down, I found myself enjoying every moment. My dad had spent most of the time in front of the TV or outside in his work shed, so I felt confident swiping a frosting-covered finger across Julia's nose while we decorated cookies or holding hands when we cuddled on the couch to watch one of my mom's Christmas movies.

It felt good—*really* good—not having to hide my affection for Julia. I'd thought myself content to be closeted around my parents since I rarely spent much time with them. I hadn't realized how liberating it would feel to be my full, authentic self around my mom.

When we'd been in St. Paul, I'd told Julia I hadn't

wanted to spend an extended amount of time at my parents' house. In reality, I was nearly disappointed that the weekend had passed so quickly. But Julia and I had to get back to work and to our lives. Plus, I was looking forward to sleeping in the same bed as her again.

Our bags were packed and in the trunk of Julia's black Mercedes. Early morning sunshine reflected like precious gems against the fresh snow in the front yard. Neither of my parents wore jackets as they stood in the driveway to see us off.

My mom handed me a tin container that I knew would be filled with sugar cookies. She hugged me tight. "Oh, it was so good to see you!" she enthused. "Don't stay away for so long next time, okay?"

I nodded, surprised that I meant it.

My mom beckoned to Julia and trapped her in a three-person hug. "You two take care of each other."

I could feel Julia's arms tighten around my mom and me like a silent promise.

In contrast to my mom, my dad wasn't a hugger. He lingered at the outer edge of the group hug.

"Thanks for clearing off Julia's car," I said in lieu of a proper goodbye. Several inches of snow had fallen overnight.

He grunted before handing me something small, flat, and paper. I knew what it was without having to look. My dad always gave me money—usually a fifty dollar bill—whenever I left the house after an extended visit. He'd been doing it ever since I'd enlisted. Whenever I tried to refuse him, he insisted, telling me it was for gas. After a while, I'd stopped trying to reject the kindness.

The gift of money wasn't a surprise, but his next words

were: "She's a good girl, Cass," he said in his usual gruff tone. "You did good."

A lump formed in my throat. I couldn't find any words. I could only be an observer as my parents walked back inside the house.

I heard the doors of the Mercedes unlock, followed by Julia's gentle timbre. "Come on, Marine," she coaxed. "Let's go home."

Epilogue

The live band interrupted its set to make note of the time. "We're only a few seconds from midnight!" the lead singer gleefully announced into his microphone. "Make sure your glass is filled and you've got a cutie by your side!"

The woman at my side leaned her figure into mine. "I've never needed an excuse to kiss you," she said, nuzzling her nose against my ear, "but I could get used to this."

With my hand at Julia's waist, I held her just a little closer.

I'd nearly suggested we spend the evening at home. I was starting to feel a little holiday fatigue, but Julia had insisted that we go out. Minneapolis no longer shot off fireworks to ring in the new year, so I'd been able to enjoy my evening with her without stressing about the possibility of a waking flashback. It felt good being able to celebrate with Julia with no reservations or hesitation. And we had plenty to celebrate —her new job at Gresham & Stein was going well, and the

Cold Case team had been able to bring closure to another case.

Julia had gotten tickets through her law firm to some high-end swanky soirée with a live jazz band. Uniformed waitstaff swooped around the dance floor with unlimited trays of champagne and tiny chestnuts wrapped in prosciutto. My first choice would always be a Juicy Lucy at the 5-8 Club or any artery-clogging gloriousness from Mickey's Diner, but at least I'd found an excuse to wear the dress from Julia's office party a second time.

Fashion-wise, I doubted this was the start of me wearing more skirts or dresses or even revealing clothes, but I couldn't deny how much I enjoyed the way Julia looked at me in the outfit. I wasn't so modest as to deny that I was typically easy on the eyes, but when I stepped out in that figure-hugging red cocktail dress, Julia made me feel utterly craveable. She'd specifically asked for an encore appearance of the dress, and I was only so happy to oblige. If I was lucky, maybe we'd also have a repeat performance of what had happened in the locked bathroom of her office building.

The anticipation had been building all night. Someone passed around funny paper hats, Mardi Gras beads, noise makers, and plastic glasses that identified the new year. I normally didn't go for all that over-the-top corniness, but even I couldn't help chanting along with the crowd as the clock ticked closer to midnight.

The group counted down in unison: "Ten, nine, eight, seven, six, five, four, three, two, one! Happy New Year!"

I flinched at the chaotic sound of kazoos mixing with confetti poppers. They sounded like gun shots. Julia's hand lightly ghosted across my lower back. The reassuring touch kept me tethered without fear of mentally teleporting to an Afghanistan desert.

"Happy New Year, darling." Happiness shone in her caramel-colored eyes. I imagined I'd find the same look reflected in mine.

"Happy New Year," I returned with a broad smile.

I pressed a firm hand in the small of Julia's back and dipped her backwards. I heard her quiet sound of surprise before I covered the noise with a dramatic kiss. When I finally pulled her upright, her features looked mildly flushed. It made me wonder where the closest bathroom stall might be.

"Are you hungry?" Julia spoke into my ear to be heard over the band's opening notes of "Auld Lang Syne."

"Starved," I admitted with an enthusiast nod. The hors d'oeuvres at the elegant party hadn't been nearly enough to fill me up. "I'm not sure what would be open at this hour though."

"Mickey's is nearby, isn't it?" Julia proposed, naming my favorite 24-hour diner.

"Yeah," I confirmed. "But I didn't think you'd want all that grease and carbs."

Julia reached for my hand and intertwined her fingers with mine. "I suppose I can make an exception just this once."

∽

I felt positively giddy as we hustled from the fancy party to a location that was more my speed. In high heels, the snow-dusted sidewalks were nearly unnavigable, but we somehow managed to pick our way the few blocks from the New Year's Eve celebration to Mickey's iconic diner car without slipping. Julia held my hand tight like I was a balloon she didn't want to float away.

I stamped my feet and blew warm air into my cupped hands when we entered the diner. Because of the late-night holiday, nearly every table was occupied, but through some miracle, a small booth by a window—the perfect table for two—was unoccupied. A frazzled waitress, a half-filled coffee pot in one hand, pointed to us and then to the empty booth. We took that as our cue that we should take a seat.

Julia slid into one side of the empty booth while I took over the opposite padded bench. I grabbed the laminated menus I found perched between the bottles of ketchup and mustard and passed one across the table to Julia.

I rubbed my hands together as I scanned down the deep fried options. I flicked my eyes up to meet Julia's. "Will you judge me if I get a milkshake with my burger and fries?"

Julia smiled indulgently. "Ask for two straws."

"You're fucking perfect."

Julia didn't have the opportunity to comment on my praise or profanity before the hurried waitress arrived at our table. She'd continued to hold onto the coffeepot like it was her lifeline. She held two red plastic water glasses pinched between the fingers of her freehand like a Skill-Crane machine at the arcade. It was decidedly unsanitary, but I was there for the burgers, not the beverages.

"I'll be right back for your order." The waitress's voice sounded distracted and disinterested.

When she set the glasses down, the bottoms of the plastic cups hit the table at a funny angle. Instead of nailing the landing, the cups wobbled and then tipped over. The former contents of the water glasses flooded across the table's surface and promptly poured over its edge, all in the direction of Julia's lap.

I heard the tell-tale surprised hiss that let me know it had been a direct hit.

"Oh my gosh," our waitress gasped in horror. "I'm so sorry."

I scrambled to my feet as quickly as I could in heels. I grabbed handfuls of flimsy, cheap napkins from the dispenser on the table and did my best to contain the puddle of ice water before more could waterfall onto Julia's lap.

Julia appeared frozen in her seat, having been stunned into immobility by the icy water. Her outstretched arms hung in the air like she was being robbed, and her painted mouth formed a perfect O of surprise.

The waitress snagged a suspicious-looking rag—one that was probably used to wipe down dirty tables—and dropped it in front of Julia. "I'm so sorry," she apologized again. "This day has been crazy." She began to haphazardly wipe at the liquid mess, causing ice cubes to ricochet in every direction.

"It's fine, dear," Julia said between grit teeth. "Accidents happen."

"Stay there. I'll-I'll be right back," the waitress promised before hustling away and out of sight.

With our waitress's hasty departure, I continued to mop up spilled water. "If this doesn't bring me back ..."

I tried to joke in an attempt to keep the evening from souring. I couldn't help but feel partially responsible. I hadn't been the one to knock over the drinks, but Julia never would have suggested we go to Mickey's if not for me.

Julia picked at the pile of saturated paper napkins crumpled on the table. A disgusted look crossed her features. "Why is it always me who gets drinks spilled on them?"

"I'd offer to be tribute on your behalf," I said in earnest, "but you seem to be a magnet."

"At least it was only water this time," she mused.

"You did a nice job not tearing off our waitress's head," I noted, jerking my thumb in the direction of wherever she'd disappeared to. I thought Julia's good behavior deserved some kind of recognition.

"Like I said—it was an accident," she allowed. "And I'm sure she's had a long night of dealing with drunk assholes."

I hummed in approval. "Look at you being so reasonable and level-headed."

Julia sighed, almost like she was disappointed with herself. "I blame this kinder, gentler version of myself on you, you know. All your bad influence."

I reached across the table and over the soggy mountain of napkins to grab her hand. I smiled and squeezed her hand in mine.

Our waitress reappeared in that moment, swooping in like a storm. She swept her hand across the table top and dumped the empty plastic water glasses and wilted napkins into a large grey bin reserved for bussing tables.

"Again, my apologies," she said in a rush. Two skinny champagne flutes, each filled to the brim with pale, fizzing liquid, were set on the table in front of us. "Compliments from management," she explained before she whisked away again.

I stared with curiosity at the new addition to our table.

"Mickey's has champagne? I didn't think they had a liquor license."

"I have no idea," Julia shrugged. "Maybe they do for special occasions."

I leaned forward in my seat and squinted at the bubbling beverages before us. Something was off about my glass. Something seemed to be lodged at the bottom of my drink.

"What is that?" I wondered aloud. Was our waitress so klutzy that she'd inadvertently dropped something into my glass?

I slowly blinked as the mysterious object at the bottom of my glass began to take shape. Tiny champagne bubbles clung to the sides of a disk—no, a circle. An open circle. Tiny bubbles clung to the sides of a ring.

"You can't." The words tumbled out. "That-that's not fair."

"I most certainly *can*. And I most certainly *did*." Julia looked pleased with herself.

I'd never been a chatterbox, but I was also rarely at a loss for words—except when it came to this woman. I continued to stare at the ring, eyes wide open, as if shutting my eyes for even a millisecond might disrupt the moment.

"Did you get tired of lying to your coworkers about us being engaged?"

Julia frowned. "I hope you're joking. Because I'm dead serious about this. Cassidy Miller, I want to marry you."

My throat tightened with emotion. *Okay*. No more self-deprecating jokes.

The planning that had gone into the evening suddenly revealed itself to me. "Leaving the New Year's Eve party early. Only one open table at Mickey's." I licked lips that had gone dry. "You did this—you let a stranger spill water on you just to propose."

"A small price to pay in exchange for the look on your face."

"How do I—how do I get the ring out?" Rom-coms never showed what happened after the engagement ring showed up at the bottom of the glass. It felt clumsy and inelegant to stick my fingers in the champagne flute to fish out the ring.

Julia lifted her own glass to her parted lips. "Please don't knock it over. I've had enough champagne baths for a lifetime."

I still wasn't entirely sure how to retrieve the ring. I picked up my glass and tipped it back. I drank the stemware's contents in one prolonged sip.

Julia's voice pitched in alarm. "Cassidy!"

I opened my mouth. I'd swallowed the champagne, but the heavy engagement ring sat on my tongue.

"Oh good Lord," she muttered.

I maneuvered the ring down to the tip of my tongue. I balanced it on my lower lip before firmly taking purchase of the ring between my thumb and forefinger. "Still want to marry me?" I posed, only half kidding.

The ring was a marvel. I had never considered what my wedding day might be like or the design of my ideal engagement ring. But somehow Julia had chosen the exact ring I never knew I even wanted.

She leaned forward in her chair. "Do you like it? Your mom helped me pick it out."

My head snapped up at the admission. "She did?"

Julia nodded. "How did we do?"

The ring was heavy—too heavy to be made of silver. Platinum if I'd had to guess. It wasn't a traditional, feminine engagement ring with the giant, protruding diamond that would get caught on my bulletproof vest. Julia's selection was simple, understated, and elegant—a single band with six or seven smaller diamonds embedded into the solitary band.

"I—It's perfect." My praise wasn't hyperbole. It was exactly my style when I didn't even realize I had a style.

Julia looked from the ring up to my face. "So?"

My heart was too full, but at the same time, I discovered myself ... disappointed? After Julia had told Melissa Ferdet that we were engaged, the real thing almost felt anti-climactic. Was I being an idiot? Was I making too big a deal out of all of this? It wasn't that I didn't want to marry Julia—I was desperate for us to be engaged. But another part of me had wanted to surprise her with the proposal instead.

"Can I ... I need a minute."

Julia's gaze followed me as I rose from the table. "Oh," she said. I could hear the disappointment in the single uttered syllable.

I felt terrible for the interruption, but I needed air; the busy diner had become too crowded, too chaotic. I strode away from the table with a tightness in my chest. I pushed past the diner's exit and out into the frigid St. Paul night.

The brisk night air shocked my senses. I'd rushed away without much thought and had left my winter jacket behind. I rubbed uselessly at my bare arms. The red cocktail dress I'd been so eager to wear a second time offered no shelter from the elements.

I didn't wander far; I hovered close to the diner's main entrance. Mickey's resembled an old railroad dining car. Its oversized windows offered little in the way of privacy. From my spot out front I had an unobstructed view of the restaurant's diverse clientele, with most folks engaged in some level of New Year's Eve revelry. It was like a moving picture, separate vignettes of life represented in each window frame.

I could still see Julia through one of the diner's large, plate-glass windows. She'd remained seated in our booth. The waitress with her half-filled coffee pot stopped by the table. I watched her mouth move, but I couldn't make out the words.

Julia wasn't looking out the window. She'd retrieved the engagement ring from the table, although I hadn't deliberately left it behind. Her attention was focused on the glittering band as she flipped it back and forth between pinched fingers.

I felt like punching the air. *What the hell was I doing?* Why was I determined to mess things up for myself? The woman of my dreams had proposed to me in the most humbling way, and I'd walked away—pouting and throwing a fit because she'd actually bought a ring and had premeditated her proposal.

"Fuck."

I needed to make this right. I hoped it wasn't too late.

I re-entered the busy diner. My steps were quick and light as I made my way back to our table. I cleared my throat when I returned to my seat.

Julia looked up at me. Worry and regret haunted her regal features. "I messed this up, didn't I?"

"Not possible." I grabbed her fidgeting hands across the table. "I'm the one who made things weird. I'm sorry."

"I know we haven't been together for very long," she said,

"but I can't imagine my life without you. You've dismantled every wall."

"I love you, Julia. I don't ever want to be without you."

"I'm still waiting on your answer. Cassidy Miller." She tried to sound stern, but her voice wobbled with uncertainty. "Are you going to make me get down on one knee?"

"No. But just remember who asked whom first," I said with a cheeky grin.

Julia finally smiled as well. "Whatever you say, darling. As long as you're saying yes."

"One million times yes."

I held out my left hand so Julia could slide the ring down the knuckles of my fourth finger.

It was a perfect fit.

About the Author

Eliza Lentzski is the author of lesbian fiction, romance, and erotica including the best-selling *Winter Jacket* and *Don't Call Me Hero* series. She publishes urban fantasy and paranormal romance under the penname E.L. Blaisdell. Although a historian by day, Eliza is passionate about fiction. She was born and raised in the upper Midwest, which is often the setting for her novels. She lives in Boston with her wife and their cat, Charley.

Follow her on Twitter and Instagram, @ElizaLentzski, and Like her on Facebook (http://www.facebook.com/elizalentzski) for updates and exclusive previews of future original releases.

Made in United States
Troutdale, OR
10/20/2025